John Somerset was born in Melbourne, Australia and spent his childhood on the Surf Coast of Victoria. This was the time of the birth of modern-day surfing, with the introduction of the Okanui surf board. His early experiences on the Surf Coast of Victoria culminated in a poorly-funded trip to the North Shore of Hawaii, long before it became the surfing mecca of today.

He was educated at Geelong Grammar, which had just begun its Mt Timbertop campus in which boys of fifteen spent one school year in the Victorian Alps. This, plus an agricultural science course at Melbourne University imparted a lifetime love of the bush. And a fascination with gold.

In between a working life in advertising and marketing, John has travelled Australia's outback by 4WD; including Lasseter Country.

He lives and writes at Anglesea, Victoria with his wife and one-eyed kelpie.

To,
Michael Collins Persse MVO OAM, my English teacher.

John Somerset

LASSETER'S TRUTH

A Novel

AUSTIN MACAULEY PUBLISHERS™

LONDON ∗ CAMBRIDGE ∗ NEW YORK ∗ SHARJAH

A CIP catalogue record for this title is available from the British Library.

ISBN 9781528994187 (Paperback)
ISBN 9781528994194 (Hardback)
ISBN 9781528994217 (ePub e-book)
ISBN 9781528994200 (Audiobook)

www.austinmacauley.com

First Published 2022
Austin Macauley Publishers Ltd®
1 Canada Square
Canary Wharf
London
E14 5AA

My wife, Marion, for your faith, help and encouragement.

Graeme Weber, friend and real-life geologist still prospecting for gold in Lasseter Country, for your valuable technical advice. Here's wishing you luck with the diamond drill.

Bruce Postle, for the cover picture and author's portrait, your skill is worth far more than the bottle of Chardonnay, even though you failed miserably to make me look young.

Ian Russell and Ron McDonald, for luring me out from behind my desk and up through the Kimberley to the top end, for your invaluable advice on forgotten skills like how to spike tyre punctures, clean out sand-clogged carbies, rescue impossibly-bogged vehicles, replace axle bearings, swim with crocodiles and race crabs.

Foreword

The Legend of Lasseter's Reef

In 1929 and again in 1930 Harold Bell Lasseter (1880-1931) made different, and possibly conflicting, claims that either in 1911 or in 1897, he had discovered an enormous gold deposit. On 14 October 1929 he wrote a letter to Kalgoorlie federal member, Albert Green, claiming to have discovered 'a vast gold bearing reef in Central Australia' 18 years earlier and that it was located at the western edge of the MacDonnell Ranges. He made a similar claim to other officials and was interviewed by a commissioner and a geologist, however the government took no action to investigate the claim.

In March 1930 he provided a different story to John Bailey of the Australian Workers' Union. In this claim Lasseter details that as a young man of the age of 17, he rode on horse from Queensland to the West Australian gold fields, during which he stumbled across a huge gold reef somewhere near the border between the Northern Territory and Western Australia.

He told of a 5-mile quartz reef, within a day's walk of a water hole. Landscape markers included 'three mountains shaped like three ladies in bonnets having a conversation, and another about 35 miles to the south, shaped like a Quaker's hat with the top cut off.'

However, Lasseter had been sentenced to reform school at that time, which detracted somewhat from his credibility. According to the story told to Bailey, Lasseter's Reef was about 700 miles (1,100 km) west of Alice Springs in a line towards Kalgoorlie. He claimed that subsequent to this discovery he got into difficulties and was fortuitously rescued by a passing Afghan camel driver who took him to the camp of a surveyor, Joseph Harding. Harding and Lasseter were said to have later returned to the reef in the attempt to fix its location, but failed because their watches were inaccurate.

According to Lasseter, he spent the next three decades trying to raise sufficient interest to fund an expedition into the interior. But at the time the fortunes being made from the gold rush at Kalgoorlie in Western Australia meant that no-one was prepared to risk trekking into the uncharted desert wilderness of Central Australia, even if the supposed discovery was as rich as Lasseter claimed.

By 1930, with Australia in the grip of the Great Depression, the attractions of desert gold were much greater, and Lasseter succeeded in securing approximately £50,000 in private funding towards an expedition to relocate the reef under the auspices of Central Australian Gold Exploration Company (CAGE). Unusual for the time, this expedition included motorised vehicular transport comprising a massive 6-wheeled Thornicroft truck and a Gypsy Moth DH60 aircraft, renamed the 'Golden Quest'. Accompanying Lasseter were experienced bushmen Fred Blakeley (leader) and Frank Colson as well as George Sutherland (prospector), Phil Taylor (engineer & driver), Blakeston-Houston (governor-general's aide, 'explorer') and Errol Coote (pilot).

On 21 July, 1930 the group left Alice Springs, reporting that Lasseter was a sullen companion and a vague guide. They headed for Ilbilba (aka Ilbpilla Soak) – an aerodrome created earlier that year for Donald George Mackay's expedition, near Lake Mackay. The group endured logistical difficulties and physical hardships (including the loss of the plane). On reaching Mount Marjorie (now Mount Leisler), Lasseter declared that they were 150 miles (240 km) too far north of the search zone. Exasperated, Blakeley declared Lasseter a charlatan, and decided to end the expedition. They parted with Lasseter at Ilbilba.

Lasseter insisted on continuing the trek, accompanied by a dingo-shooter, Paul Johns and his team of camels. Lasseter, whose behaviour was increasingly erratic, set off towards The Olgas. One afternoon, Lasseter returned to camp with some concealed rock samples and announced that he had relocated his gold reef. He refused to reveal its location. Johns, who by now doubted Lasseter's sanity, accused him of being a liar. A fight ensued, and Johns left Lasseter to his own devices, returning to 'civilization'. Lasseter himself disappeared into the desert sands with two camels.

In 1931, a search for Lasseter was conducted by a bushman, Bob Buck. Buck eventually found Lasseter's emaciated body at Winter's Glen and his personal effects in a cave at Hull's Creek. From Lasseter's diary it was learned that after Johns had left, Lasseter's camels bolted, leaving him alone in the desert without any means of sustaining himself or returning. He encountered a group of nomadic Aboriginal people, who rendered assistance with food and shelter; but a weakened and blinded Lasseter eventually died of malnutrition and exhaustion, having made a belated attempt to walk from the Hull's Creek cave to Uluru or the Kata Tjuta.

Australian adventure-story author Ion Idris in his book *Lasseter's Last Ride,* gives a detailed description of Lasseter's time with the Aborigines leading up to his death. Lasseter's diary notes were later discovered hidden from the Aborigines under camp fires. The tribe had apparently shunned Lasseter after their Kurdaitcha man 'pointed the bone at him' – he was condemned to be ignored and no longer cared for, eventually succumbing to starvation.

Various statements by Paul Johns reveal the areas where he and Lasseter travelled and searched while together: the Peterman and Rawlinson Ranges, then south-west to the Warburton Range, then a zigzag course evidently following the ranges eastward to the Western Australian border ending at the Petadi rock hole at the eastern end of the Mann Range in South Australia. Almost out of supplies, they then returned to Ilbilba where they parted.

Geologists have made various statements as to whether or not there are gold bearing areas in Lasseter Country. In 1931, geologists T. Blatchford and H.W.B. Talbot accompanying Bob Buck pronounced the region as unpromising, but they only inspected the Peterman Range and the eastern end of the Rawlinson Range, travelling no farther west than Sladen Waters. In 2014, geologists W.D. Maier, H.M. Howard and R.H. Smithies likened the southern part of Lasseter's search area to the Bushveld Complex in South Africa, where gold deposits do occur and said the region has high potential, quoting a 2002 report of copper-gold vein style material found north of the Cavanagh Range.

No maps showing the location of Lasseter's fabled gold reef were ever found, and over subsequent decades the tale of the reef and its discoverer has assumed mythic proportions – it is perhaps the most famous lost mine legend in Australia, and remains the 'holy grail' among Australian prospectors.

Which begs the question:

Was Lasseter a con man or did he tell the truth?

HISTORICAL & GEOGRAPHIC REFERENCES:

https://lasseteria.com

https://en.wikipedia.org>wiki>Lasseter's_Reef

Bonzle.com Digital Atlas of Australia/Peterman Ranges

Lasseter's Last Ride by Ion Idris: Published by Angus & Robertson, 1931

Prologue

A perfect day to die. The sun was high in the cloudless sky of the Great Australian Desert, and nothing moved except the heat shimmer and an occasional sand devil, spiralling in the light northerly wind. Every bird, animal, and insect had sought their chosen shade, and Jack Johnson was no exception. Even lying on his camp bed in the shade of the cave entrance, it was still hot. Jack closed his eyes and focussed his mind on his 'cool thoughts' mantra.

He started with his favourite 'cool' vision. Jack never tired of it. Cool, cool water, and that one day in the winter of '66, before Bells was discovered by the crowds. Alone out the back sitting on his Gordon Woods longboard, a dolphin popping out of the distant swell his only company. When it came, the wave was not exceptionally large, but it was perfect, and Jack had paddled into the connection sought by every soul surfer but found only by few. He didn't consciously surf it; Jack and the wave somehow merged as an almost spiritual experience and lying with his eyes shut forty years later and thousands of miles from the ocean, that oneness with that one wave came back as if it were yesterday. A Star Wars tragic; Jack smiled at the memory of his very own connection with the Force, then lay back to revisit his life.

There was plenty of time before they came.

Chapter 1
Jack

Thoughts of the beach naturally ran to thoughts of Julie, Jack's first love, and although he didn't know it at the time, the only true soul mate he ever knew. Julie came back in his mind's eye; starting with the all-important first kiss on the back beach; wrestling her stubborn bra hook in the back seat at the drive-in; the 'first time' beside the dying bonfire after everyone had left. Jules at seventeen. Great memories, but like a guilty shadow, that line of thinking ended with a too-sharp recall of her tears when Jack told her he had met Ariel in Melbourne, and it was all over. Jules got her own back three years later when she became engaged to Jack's best mate Dave and was forever out of reach. Jack wondered what they were doing at this moment and, with a deep sigh, wished them well.

He opened his eyes and looked down at his helicopter staked out on the flat below the cave, which jolted his memory back to the lottery marble that sent him to Vietnam, the Iroquois chopper, and the mission that nearly killed him at Long Tan, fighting a politician's war that was not only lost from the outset, but ruined the lives of many of the men he had rescued from both the jungle of the Triangle and the opium dens of Saigon. The Distinguished Service Order was no compensation for his irreparably smashed ankle plus loss of faith, but it did signal the start of one hell of a ride back home. The desert silence gave Jack the luxury to think deeply about many things, including the Vietnam War and its impact on himself, his friends, and even his country.

Jack came from a military family, with his father and both uncles veterans of World War 2. He was particularly proud of his dad, a fighter pilot who came home from New Guinea with a shard of metal in his leg and a DFC on his chest. A number of Australian pilots had been decorated flying Spitfires and Hurricanes in the Battle of Britain and over Europe, but Jack reckoned his dad was better than those much-revered RAF aces in that flying his RAAF Wirraway at the battle of Buna-Gona, he managed to shoot down not only one of the Japanese Aichi dive bombers, but a Zero fighter. The Wirraway was a vastly inferior fighter which on paper had no chance at all against the much faster and more manoeuvrable Zero, and which his dad explained was a pig of a plane that was of more danger to its pilot than the enemy! A second Zero got him, "Because the bloody Wirraway had a worse turning circle than the Queen Mary, and was even slower!" Repatriated to the Royal Melbourne Hospital, the doctors finally fished the shrapnel out of his leg, but Johnny Johnson walked with a limp for the rest of his life, for which he blamed the government, "For not spending a bit of money on some Spitfires for us. It's a wonder the bloody politicians sprung enough petty cash to even buy me a parachute!" Jack was reminded of his dad's singular achievement every time they went fishing, as his father had managed to bring home the actual oil-damped globe compass retrieved from the wreck of the Zero he had shot down, which had been duly mounted in their boat to record the bearings of favourite fishing marks.

The military tradition of the family became a source of conflict between Jack and his father. Despite (or perhaps because of) his limp, Johnny Johnson was quite clear where his son's duty lay as soon as Australia entered the Vietnam War.

"I paid for your helicopter course, now you have the chance to use it for something better than making money mustering up north and pissing it all up against a wall. You must volunteer for Vietnam," was Johnny's edict.

The decision was not quite as clear cut for Jack. Unlike World War Two, where the entire Australian population was in support of the war effort as the Japanese came ever closer to invasion, the country was deeply divided whether Australia should go 'all the way with LBJ' and join the US intervention in Vietnam. Understandably, opposition to Australia's involvement was particularly prevalent amongst those of enlistment age!

After much soul-searching and a couple of stand-up rows at home, Jack refused to volunteer, which mortified his father. Unfortunately for Jack (although fortunately for their relationship), the national ballot decided the issue when Jack's birthday marble was drawn out and he was duly drafted. Following in his father's footsteps, Jack joined No9 squadron RAAF, flying combat-modified Iroquois helicopters. The RAAF escalated his training to qualify as a combat pilot in only two months, then dispatched him and his novice crew straight to the US Da Nang air base in South Vietnam to fly support and rescue missions.

Flying extraction missions, you didn't remain a novice for long. Either you became very good very quickly, or you became dead. Fortunately for both themselves and a number of grateful infantrymen, Jack and his crew became very good, very quickly – amongst the best Australia had.

While Jack was away, the country remained divided on Vietnam, particularly after it became clear that despite winning every battle, the allies were losing the war. Even Jack's best friends Dave and Julie, had joined the peace movement and marched in the 1970 Melbourne moratorium against the war along with over 100,000 other young zealots chanting: "*Hell no, we won't go, we won't go fight Uncle Ho,*" a stance of which they were unshakably proud and were happy to go to jail for. In Jack's opinion, the sheer unpopularity of the war was a major contributor to the alarmingly high suicide rate amongst returning Vietnam vets, two of whom he knew well. He himself had never fully come to terms with the deaths of Viet Cong and North Vietnamese combatants he had killed from the sky, even though they were shooting back. It is one thing to kill in the service of your country, but psychologically vital to know these actions are fully supported and that your cause is just. Jack's father, along with all the armed forces who went to New Guinea were defending Australia itself, so not only was the whole country behind them but their actions were much easier to justify to themselves. The Australians came home from World War Two to ticker tape parades and victory marches, whilst Jack and his mates came home from Vietnam after losing their war to virtually no recognition at all, with many at home voicing the opinion they never should have gone in the first place.

Apart from the small number of well-reported Victoria Crosses, there were few popular heroes returning from a war that Australia as a whole was trying its best to forget, but after demob, the DSO at least made Jack a minor celebrity within his immediate circle.

He rekindled old friendships in Melbourne's A-list in an only partially successful attempt to excise the five-year gap and its inevitable distancing effect.

Ariel had not waited in the story-book sense of the girl back home, but playing the field and fashion modelling had only added to the alure of the stunning beauty who had attracted Jack in the first place. He managed to return home just in time for the annual race week party at the Melbourne Club, but even though nobody could hear much over the roar of conversation, he managed to first find and second re-connect with Ariel. Even better, he managed to persuade her to leave with him by slipping an arm around her waist and shouting a well-timed "Let's get out of here" in her ear, as everything was winding down and the singles jockeyed for position in the traditional manner.

Conversation during the cab trip back to Ariel's South Yarra flat was somewhat strained, which was only to be expected with one passenger having ceased writing letters to Vietnam after only six months, and the other resenting not getting them. Even so, the magic words, "Would you like to come up for coffee?" were offered. Ariel experienced the first knock-back in her privileged life when Jack responded, "Better not; I have my first client pitch tomorrow and I'd best get home." This was essentially true, but on the basis that nobody ever really had any coffee when asked up for it, that wouldn't have stopped Jack for an instant. The real reason was he still had a week to go on the course of Flagyl he was taking to treat the drip he picked up from the farewell party at the unit's favourite Saigon cat-house the night before his unit pulled out. Homeward bound alone in the cab with its incredulous driver, who would have gladly given his whole year's takings for that invitation from that girl, Jack cursed Saigon girl-friend Lucy for her parting gift of the clap, nonetheless hoping she was attractive enough to survive the new regime.

As far as Ariel was concerned, Jack resolved to leave it a week until 'medically fit' so to speak, which turned out to be an irresistible challenge to Ariel, as ten days went by without his call. Thus, it came about a personal call was put through to Jack at the Agency at six o'clock the following Friday, right in the middle of end-of-week drinks:

"Hey, it's Ariel. I don't really drink coffee at eleven o'clock at night, you know."

"I know. It was just a bit too soon after everything," said Jack. Wondered how to slip in a dinner date invitation. Didn't have to.

"How about coming up to Chartwell for the weekend? Anthony Plunkett is going to christen his new ski boat on Lake Colac, and you get to drive me up just like in the old days."

"Do you still have the Porsche?"

She did. It turned up at Jack's flat next morning, with the top down.

Chapter 2
For Better or for Worse

It took five years before Jack and Ariel tied the knot. Jack needed all of that time to get over Vietnam; and Ariel was never short of dates during the gaps when he disappeared to go bush or search for surf breaks with Dave. But when they did happen, their times together were always good. Ariel finally left her string of disappointed suitors behind the night Jack popped the question, and she said "yes".

***

Resplendent in hired morning suits, Jack and best man Dave stood up the front of a packed St John's Church Toorak, viewing the sharply contrasting collection of wedding guests assembled on opposite sides of the aisle.

On the left, or bride's side of the church, were arrayed the cream of Melbourne and seemingly half Sydney society, starting at the front with the Governor and Premier of the State together with their wives, three knights of the realm, large contingents from the Victorian Racing Club and Australian Ballet committees, twelve company heads, most of Victoria's Western District, and a yet-to-be-disgraced Sydney entrepreneur along with the two stars of his latest production. Young guests included a selection of deb's delights, including two English chinless wonders who seemed to spend their entire life attending Government House parties and do no work, plus assorted debs modelling the latest in French and Italian fashion, teamed with designer jewellery.

Apart from immediate family, the right-hand or groom's side of the church countered with mates of Jack's dad from his mining adventures all over the world plus recent stints on Bass Straight oil rigs, assorted World War 2 vets including Ian Chomley still sporting his magnificent air force moustache and Charlie

Griffiths, who still ran the army disposals store he had stocked at the end of the war by hiring a fishing lugger in Darwin and sailing across to New Guinea to loot two equipment dumps left behind in the jungle by the retiring American army, and forgotten. This assortment of heroes, rogues and hard men were rubbing shoulders with an even stranger assortment of his mother's artist and musician friends presenting in an extraordinary selection of outfits, some of which had almost certainly come straight from the recent Sunbury Rock Festival, Australia's answer to Woodstock.

Jack's groomsmen included 'Hanoi' (bombed every night) Smith, his Iroquois helicopter door gunner, and Mongrel, the chief mechanic who had kept their chopper in the air with its guns working for four years, plus all the way from the US of A, Harry the Huey King, resplendent in his Air Cavalry captain's dress uniform, complete with campaign ribbons, Air Force Cross, and his Purple Heart won copping a ricochet in the shoulder whilst extracting Jack and his crew from their grounded chopper after the rear rotor was hit by an RPG during the battle of Long Tan. Filling the back of the right-hand pews were Jack's mates, including the centre line and three of the back six from his old Anglesea footy team, plus an assortment of surfers, their partners and girl-friends who made up for a lack of expensive outfits and jewellery with real (as distinct from bottle) tans teamed with bleach blonde hair; (some achieved naturally and some with the application of lemon juice, in lieu of the South Yara boutique bouffant displayed on the opposite side of the aisle).

Jack smiled as Dave's drop-dead gorgeous wife Julie walked to her place up the front, wearing a white cotton dress from the little shop on the Lorne strip that cost a tenth of the creations opposite, but which turned every head in the church. Smiled again when Jules gave him a big cheesy grin and a thumbs-up.

"I can still get you out through the vestry," Dave whispered, looking nervously down the high society line-up along the bride's side of the church, but before Jack could answer, "Wagner's Wedding March," struck up on the St John's organ, and Ariel walked through the door on the arm of her father.

Chapter 3
Tess

Five years later, I came into the world, apparently the result of an accident involving Mother forgetting to take the pill after a New Year's Eve party at Portsea. Although no longer modelling and with the clock ticking, Mother professed to not wanting to lose her figure having children, but after Dad talked her into going through with me, she need not have worried; she stayed stunning all her life.

I had a mixed childhood.

Mother's influence involved lots of baby photos involving frilly dresses, the passing down of her own Barbie collection with each Barbie still in her original cello-window box, my first designer clothes, private prep school for girls, dancing and horse-riding lessons, personal coaching at the Toorak Tennis Club next door, skiing at the family lodge at Buller, and ballet school; (the latter abandoned when it became clear I had grown too tall to make prima ballerina). Mother's social planning centred around the birthday parties of the sons and daughters of Melbourne society, topped off by weekends at Portsea involving tennis and pool parties at the sheep stations of the Western District; mostly involving horses.

Whenever possible, Dad reverted to his vastly different worlds of the beach, the bush and the outback. Although I enjoyed the fun and perks of high society, Dad's world was where my heart landed. Dad and Mother had an unwritten agreement that each weekend, we went to either her family's sheep station at Chartwell Downs or the clifftop house at Portsea; with Dad reserving the right to head to Lorne if the wind was offshore and surf was up. As soon as I could stand on a surfboard, I always went with him.

The first serious shots in our family's War of the Worlds involved my twelfth birthday. Mother had bought me white Rossignol skis, teamed with a matching ski outfit decorated with big silver snowflakes; whilst Dad's present was a tin of kero, four ball bearings still in their grease, and some timber. His unusual gift came about like this:

We lived in a big house in Balmarino Avenue, right next to the exclusive Toorak Tennis Club. It also happened to be the best billy cart hill in Toorak, with illegal road races after school most days. I knew twins Sam and Andrew Scott from school, and always up for any form of race, one day I fronted them at the start line, begging for a go.

"Tess, you're a mate, but The Ball Bearing Club is boys only, and we bet against the Stenson gang in pretty rough races," Andrew said, not unkindly but still firmly.

"You are only a girl and you'll get hurt if you crash out on Devil Bend," he said. "It gets pretty hairy out there and there is no way I'm going to risk my cart with a shiela."

Laughter from the Stenson gang.

"Okay, I'll be back with my own cart," I threw back at them all. "Let's see if you can handle losing to a girl."

More laughter from the Stenson gang.

I glared at everyone and walked home.

That night, I tackled Dad.

"Can you help me build a billy cart?" I said. "It has to have ball bearing wheels, as pram wheels are banned in our races as sissy."

Dad didn't turn a hair. He was that sort of dad. The next day being my birthday; he came home from work via the garage and wood yard, with two large and two small ball bearings still in their grease, a tin of kero, a wooden box previously used to pack brake linings, some timber, a two-inch bolt with lock nuts, two washers, and a skein of rope.

"You are going to build this yourself," he said. "As far as your mother's concerned I intend to take the fifth on the whole thing."

"Soaking the ball bearings in kero for at least three days is the key to getting rid of all the grease. Test them each day until they run free for at least thirty seconds. The big ones go on the back and the little ones go on the front. You'll need to steal one of the big Bushels coffee jars from the kitchen to soak them in."

"The long plank is known as the bally board; I don't know why. We're going to bash out one side of the box for you to sit in and nail it to the other end, with the rear axle screwed underneath."

Did that. Then drilled matching holes in the front axle and bally board for the steering bolt, tapped in the bolt, screwed up the lock nuts, threaded the steering rope through holes drilled in the front axle and tied on the steering rope. I had three days to wait for the kero to work its magic before rasping the ends of each axle and wedging on the ball bearings; plenty of time to paint my speed machine. Although now out of publication due to losing a trademark dispute with DC Comics; (the publishers of Superman), I had avidly read every one of Dad's prized collection of Captain Marvel comics; and Mary Marvel was my favourite superhero. I painted the cart Mary Marvel purple, with a yellow lightning bolt on each side, a big lightning flash down the centre of the bally board, and 'SHAZAM' emblazoned across the back. The gift for art inherited from Dad came into its own; my race cart looked wicked. I reckon it would have won first prize in a custom hot rod show!

Three days later, I was up with the first sparrow and down to the garage. Each bearing whizzed freely for its thirty seconds, so I dragged Dad out of breakfast to help wedge them on the axles to finish my masterpiece.

Thirty minutes later, we tested SHAZAM on the pavement out the front of the house, and boy, did she fly!

School dragged by at a snail's pace till that afternoon, when I fronted John Stenson and his two brothers, the Scott twins, Tony Ward, and two other guys from Bruce Street at the Balmarino start line, with SHAZAM tucked under my arm.

"I'm back, and here's my dollar for race one," I said, looking John Stenson in the eye and tossing the dollar in the betting cap.

"Okay, but you are meddling in men's business," Stenson said with a sneer. "No blubbing when you lose."

After I won four races in a row, the sneer was gone, and I was getting seriously rich. It would have been five in a row except a car arrived in the middle of the fifth, so even though I had rocketed out of Devil Bend in front, we had to pull over. I don't think the wins were entirely due to me. The trick seemed to be the combination of big roller bearings back, small ball bearings front, meant I broadsided better, plus the three-day soak in the kero for sheer speed.

I wondered how Dad knew about all that?

Anyway, who cares why?

Up at the start line before the sixth, the Stensons went into a huddle. John stared me down with a new challenge:

"How about you put it all up on the last against me and my brothers? Unless you're too scared, of course," he said.

Scared? I was on a high and getting better with each race.

"You're on," I replied with as fierce a look as I could muster.

Andrew Scott came up worried.

"Watch them, Tess," he warned. "They play dirty."

They did.

I was at the front three abreast as we hit Devil Bend, when John Stenson moved close in on my outside, blocking me from throwing my broadside around the corner. I looked across and saw him sneer, just before he deliberately turned straight into my front steering axle, leaving his brother Charlie clear on the outside to go for the win. They told me later the crash was spectacular, as my front axle hit the kerb and the cart somersaulted, with me flying over the nature strip to crack my head on the pavement and break my arm in two places. I only came to as they lifted me into the ambulance, surrounded by onlookers. John Stenson and Andrew Scott were being interviewed by the cops in front of a police car with its lights still flashing.

John Stenson's nose was bleeding profusely as a result of a punch from Andrew that had apparently been thrown during the ensuing fight between the Scott brothers and the rest of the Stenson gang, the first but not the last time in my life a guy was to defend my honour. The cops were busy taking names and addresses. Lady Drummond from the house opposite (who was the one to have called the cops) was hurrying in her front gate to place a second phone call, so I knew Mother would not be far away.

Dad got the blame.

Chapter 4
Jack

STREET FIGHT IN TOORAK

Not a good headline in *The Sun* newspaper, and not a good article accompanying it, either. Someone with a camera happened to be returning to his car after the Toorak Tennis Club men's final and managed to be in the right position at the right time to take a picture of the cop car, Tess being loaded into the ambulance, and the cops confronting Andrew Scott and a bleeding John Stenson, with the wreck of Tess's billy cart in the foreground.

It got worse. A photographer from *The Sun* happened to arrive at the Royal Melbourne Hospital to interview an injured Carlton ruckman and got a fine close-up of Tess and Ariel leaving casualty, with Tess's arm in a sling and Ariel glaring full on at the camera. It was probably the fact that they were both blonde and beautiful, plus Ariel being the winner of the Melbourne Cup Fashions on the Field, that caused what was a pretty minor incident to make it onto the front page of the paper. This also gave the editor the chance to champion the cause of 'Road Safety for Our Children', calling for the banning of billy carts on Melbourne's pavements in addition to its roads. Being an election year, the State government seized the chance to look good at no cost to the budget, and the ban was passed into law at the very next sitting of the Road Safety Council. Although this was probably a good thing when you think about it, try telling that to the kids who had lost another, (although minor) freedom to parental and government control.

I had my own problems with Ariel.

"This is the last straw," she said, pouring herself a second G&T, which she only ever did during a crisis.

"Take a good hard look at your daughter. Tess is a *girl*, not the son you never had," she said.

24

"I let it go when she came home in disgrace from the Village matinee the time the manager confiscated the water pistols and banned them all for a month."

"I didn't turn a hair when Tess and those Scott boys were reported by Mrs Stuart for shooting the dove with the air rifle."

"I knew Tess lied about blowing up the Stenson's mailbox with the double bunger, but I was a good sport and let that go."

"I even came to terms with her coming home with the cut on her head after the shanghai fight at the tip. That involved the Scott twins and the Stenson brothers too, didn't it?"

"But this is bloody well the end. She is going to boarding school to learn to behave like a lady."

I went into bat to keep Tess at her girls-only school in Melbourne, citing the importance of keeping her circle of friends at her age, but if I were to be honest, mainly because I would miss her too much.

Selfish, I know.

I lost.

Next term, she started boarding down at Geelong, at the most exclusive boarding school in the country.

Tess's letters home told a story of typical boarding school struggles, followed by quiet achievement and an education that seemed to be working. The first letter was pretty well as expected:

This place is worse than Pentridge, and the worst thing of all is the food. I still can't come at the pale-yellow cubes of so-called scrambled egg made from egg powder served up twice a week. The thing that really freaks me out is the water that squirts out the holes when you press down with your fork, so I go hungry each Tuesday and Thursday morning rather than attempt to eat the horrible stuff, or I'd be sick all over the table. Other delights include brains (Wednesday dinner), steamed flake that I am sure are sting ray flaps and not even real shark (every Friday) sinker (segments cut from long steaming rolls) and frog's eggs with boiled custard to name just a few delights. Can we have roast lamb the first night I come home?

But by her final year, they became more positive:

I just made tennis captain.

I just made swimming captain.
I just made House Captain.
They are starting rowing for girls, and I am going to try out for the first eight.

There was more I couldn't help but be proud of. Even allowing for a father's natural bias, by the time Tess hit seventeen, she had grown into the most beautiful girl I had ever seen. The electric blue eyes, natural blonde hair, and model's frame came from Ariel, but it was more than that. I like to think I had contributed in a small way, given that Tess insisted that every weekend exeat from school and most of the holidays were spent surfing, which I was only too happy to encourage; first coaching alongside her, flipping along on the boogie board that my smashed left ankle now confined me to, then acting as transport driver as Tess and Dave's son Ben followed the big waves to Bells, Southside, and finally Joanna. Regular, serious paddling plus her love of school sport built lithe athlete's muscle over her model's frame, and we ended up with a raving beauty; cross between a supermodel and a too-tall ballerina.

This started having an effect, as expressed in her letters:

I keep getting photographed. This time an official Robert Pockley photo for the school magazine cover; posed wearing my blazer beside school captain Alexander a 'Beckett, holding a book and looking studious (though I have never seen anyone actually studying wearing their blazer); another one emerging from the water in my speedo for the opening of the swimming pool, and yet another posed in front of the new girl's racing shell when I am not even in the first eight! Do you think I should charge them?

Not all Tess's letters were about school life and sport. This one arrived in the middle of third term:

Dear Dad,
Even though I won last year's art prize trying to paint like you I have decided I shall no longer endeavour to nail Streeton. I can never be that good, so am going full-on impressionist. Anyway Dad, your pictures from the Howqua got far closer to Streeton than I can ever hope to achieve, so I'll just leave him to you. When Mother goes to Paris at Christmas, can I go too? It is in the holidays, and I simply have to see Monet's garden...

Then a second letter came on the subject of Tess's painting. This one was not from Tess herself, but from her art teacher, Michael Collins, hand-written on school letterhead in his tiny, immaculate script:

Dear Mr & Mrs Johnson,

I am writing concerning Tess's painting over and above that which I put in my end of year report.

As you know, Tess has been improving each year, and was well deserving of last year's art prize; but this term her work has crossed the line into more than exceptional and I need to expand upon it.

Her last two oil paintings are done in a completely unique impressionist style; one entitled 'The Crash' involving billy carts (she told me the story!) and the other entitled 'First Wave' which is apparently a painting of a childhood memory. They are utterly amazing; by far the best student work I have seen in all my years of teaching art.

The point I am obliged to make as her Art Master is that an important part of the final school year is the selection of tertiary education courses and careers. Tess's results this year are in the top 5 percent in every subject, so barring a meltdown in next year's VCE exams, she should be accepted for any university course at any campus she chooses. Normally I would leave the process to take its course and for Tess, her teachers, and yourselves to arrive at the best career choice. I understand at this stage she wishes to take Physiotherapy at Melbourne University.

I must however implore you to discuss with Tess about seriously considering tertiary training in Fine Arts. Quite apart from the physiotherapy course she is talking about, she could be anything from a doctor (as I understand will be recommended by the school careers master as having higher earnings potential than physio) to a supermodel (as urged by her friends) but if I am any judge at all, in her painting lies a potential gift to the world. She is that good. Please come and see for yourselves next time you visit the school.

If it would be helpful, I will be happy to write a letter of introduction to The Paris College of Art, as I know the director well from my own time there.

I look forward seeing you again and showing you Tess's paintings when next you visit the school.

Yours sincerely,

Michael Collins
SENIOR ART MASTER

Two weeks later, we drove down on Speech Day to see Tess collect her second art prize, and Michael Collins took us over to the art school for a cup of tea and to show us her latest impressionist paintings.

I was glad he had written. Tess was already way better than me, and I have sold a number of my own paintings for big bucks plus won two Quill design awards judged against the best in the advertising industry.

What to do? After the long Christmas break, Tess went off to Paris with Ariel and a letter from Michael Collins to take a six-week introduction to impressionist painting at the Paris College of Art.

Following that, we still had all her final school year to work everything out.

Or so I thought.

Chapter 5
Tess

Boarding school is no picnic.

I remember unpacking my case, thinking, *the next time I see this case is when I go home again*. This happy thought was not enough to make up for leaving family and friends, and I joined many other girls having a quiet little cry that first night in the dorm.

News of the great billy cart crash had preceded me, and although I suspect this did not endear me to the teachers, I was at least able to start as a new kid on the block with minor celebrity status amongst my classmates.

Fortunately, I knew some kids from the Western District to start making new friends, but best of all, my surf buddy Ben Holt from Lorne was at the school, only one year ahead of me. Ben was a day boy, but just knowing he was around made it all okay.

Friendships at boarding school are hard won and come from all directions. So do enemies.

Apart from Ben, the first true friend at my new school was my physics partner, Arabella Jiou, a cute Chinese girl known to all as AJ. For some reason, our chemistry teacher Mr Arnold-Lester had it in for AJ, who he called 'Chairwoman Jiou', regularly humiliating her in front of the whole class with the hardest questions he could come up with. I reckon he was racist and had no place teaching.

Fortunately, he couldn't get enough of me, who he (followed by every kid in school) called 'Elle', (after Elle Macpherson), so our prac work got good marks, except for the time AJ added water to acid instead of the other way around and caused the explosion. I shared a study with AJ right through school and ended up in our final year helping her set up 'The Great Ant War', for which we sold tickets and made a fortune. This entailed making a large flat box in carpentry with a glass top and a removable divider, filling one side with the inhabitants of a big termite nest we found in a rotting tree, and the other with black ants from a thriving nest we found at the back of the main oval score board. AJ said it was essential to get both queens, and digging around in the nests amongst angry insects was pretty scary, even when you wore long sleeves, overalls, rubber boots, and dishwashing gloves. It took a whole term for the little kingdoms on each side of the divider to organise themselves into fully functioning colonies, then with all tickets sold, we got the bio teacher on side, set the box up on the big table in the biology lab, pulled out the divider and watched the battle as the natural enemies fought to the death. It took three days, but the ants won.

In later years, AJ ended up a world authority on entomology and the first Chinese fellow of the Royal Entomological Society. I just ended up being nervous around ants.

I encountered my first school enemy at the end of my first term, across the net in the Under 13 tennis final. Claire De Coursey was big and strong and the Junior School Girl's Champion, but she was slow. And couldn't handle my second serve kicker. Or my drop shots. Or losing.

Things started well for Claire when she aced me with her first serve, then wheeled down three more to win the first game to love.

"This won't take long," she declared loudly as we changed ends with a Stenson-like sneer at me and a thumbs-up to her adoring fans.

It didn't.

What Claire didn't know was first that I had lived beside the Toorak Tennis Club for six years and had been very well coached; second, that I had practiced both backhand and forehand drop shots for hours on the Chartwell Downs grass court, with Tom, a farm-hand who played A Pennant in weekends, slamming drives at me both sides, and third, that each of my returns of her big first serves had only missed catching the lines by inches.

Framing my shoulder-high second serve kickers was bad enough, but it was the humiliation of being stranded behind the base line as drop shot after drop shot died just over the net, long before she could lumber up to them, that really hurt. So did my 6-2 6-0 winning score.

Claire ended up red in the face and stormed off without shaking hands. I didn't realise I had made an enemy that day, one who would change my life.

This was not the only life-changing event that occurred that week. The second one occurred the very next Sunday, when the wind went around to the north, and Dad pulled me out for a weekend exeat to Lorne. Not only was the surf going to be glassy, but Ben had confirmed that the movie Big Wednesday was showing at the Anglesea Memorial Hall on the Saturday night.

Dad agreed that Big Wednesday was an essential part of my education, and so it was that Ben, Gillian, and I hitched a ride over to Anglesea with Jill's older sister Helen and her boyfriend Rabbit, in his '51 Ford twin spinner.

We girls bought our tickets, and then Rabbit's proven Memorial Hall seating plan swung smoothly into action. Jill went in to bag the back row before the Anglesea Clubbies could nab it, while I went and locked myself in the ladies' loo just inside the entrance door, carefully removing the six louvres from the window so the three guys could climb in for free, using Rabbit's little painting ladder he had brought along in the Ford's cavernous boot.

Helen ran interference, engaging the redoubtable Mrs Ward at the ticket box in an earnest conversation over the price of Jaffas and the weather, so she didn't notice as three males and one female emerged from the ladies' restroom. Worked a charm.

Cupid had hit our group during my weekends away at school, so I sat alone as the cuddly couples went at it. I didn't really mind, as fantasising about Jan Michael Vincent was every bit as good as the fumbling going on alongside. I admit I did sneak a look across at Ben and Jill, who at least came up for air to watch the good bits, but I reckon Rabbit and Helen only disengaged for the big wave at the end, even though they'd been sleeping together for months!

It turned out Cupid was still lurking at Lorne.

The next day was glassy, so Ben and I paddled out early at Lorne Point on what was definitely not Big Sunday (in fact, there had never been a big any day in the whole history of Lorne), but we were inspired by the night before and were happy to sit alone out the back, waiting for one of Lorne Point's trade mark small right-handers.

I looked across at Ben.

"Big wave last night. Had to be Hawaii," I said.

"But you guys had the best time. You got to pash on as well."

Ben broke into his familiar smile.

"I hate to see you left out," he said. "Let's see if we can come up with the world's first kiss on surfboards."

"Come over here."

I paddled alongside.

He reached over, put one hand gently on either side of my neck, and kissed me.

The kiss was light as a feather, tasted of salt, and lasted half a second, tops.

Then we fell off our boards.

But I also fell out of the friend zone.

WTF?

Ben was like a brother, for Christ's sake!

I'd known him forever!

He has a girlfriend!

This pivotal moment of my life was cut off by the arrival of a traditionally pathetic one-metre Lorne wave. Ben looked me in the eyes and said, "Now we're engaged," splashed me in the face, and paddled onto it.

He obviously didn't mean it.

I've read books. I've watched movies. I had a whole list of ways 'it' would happen.

Now that my big moment had come, 'it' was decidedly underwhelming.

No bolt of lightning. So much for SHAZAM!

No lingering looks across a crowded room.

No candlelight dinner.

No breakfast at Tiffany's.

No proposal in an iron-frame bed, with the sun coming up over Paris.

No two-minute tongue kiss in the rain.

The kiss that changed my life was probably the shortest one in the history of the world.

But it was 'it' all right. No bloody doubt about it.

"Fuck!"

Ben was seemingly unaffected. He paddled back out, splashed me in the face again, and uttered his first words as the love of my life:

"The crowd's starting to roll up. Let's hit the Arab."

We did, and that was that.

I was carted back to school by Dad that afternoon and cried myself to sleep yet again that night.

Why does love make you miserable?

Chapter 6
Jack

The year we sent Tess to boarding school was the same year Silas Silver talked me into going out on our own as Silver & Johnson Advertising.

I had put in twelve years at Australia's largest agency and was now one of the country's highest paid creative directors, with a swag of awards to my name and making the big bucks that went with them. I would have stayed on if it were not for the retirement of much-loved Managing Director Tom 'Knobby' Clark, who had hired me fresh from Vietnam with nothing to show but a little portfolio of war sketches. Nibby's retirement resulted in the arrival of Walter Ames Burns, the new MD from America who arrived with the pre-conceived idea that only proven US campaigns would work in Australia and who also clearly didn't like me.

Silas was very persuasive:

"You can forget making any creative decisions from now on. Walter is forming a new creative committee with himself as head, and that means we will be using American creative only on the big international brands. Hasn't he told you?"

He hadn't.

"Do you want to spend your life remaking US ads with Australian talent, or do you want to do your own thing?"

"Why make millions for the Yanks when we can make it for ourselves?"

"Since Walter arrived, I have been lunching with some of our biggest clients. If we hang up our own shingle, I think most of them will follow us."

"And I happen to know your best creative staff will follow you."

I suppose it was my time in the army, but although I recognised the business sense of it, Silas's last two points didn't sit well with me. Even with the toxic climate that was building at work, loyalty seemed to be part of my DNA, and that was hard to ignore.

I said I'd think about it.

Didn't think about it long, as Ariel made up my mind that same night.

"Jack, you are good enough to be Australia's own David Ogilvy, so for goodness's sake do it. It's not just the money; I want to prove Mummy wrong about you."

I didn't care what Mummy thought.

Except that I did.

So, I said 'yes' to Silas, and the die was cast.

He was right. Most of my clients came over within three months of us forming our new agency. Apparently, the creative committee Walter Burns set up at the big agency hadn't worked. True to the old adage, they were advertising Australian horses as US camels, and the horses weren't selling.

Ariel dragged me off to Henry Bucks and bought me a very expensive suit plus three shirts with matching ties and handkerchiefs; Silas made a string of bookings at Melbourne and Sydney's best restaurants, and after a number of serious lunches (each costing more than a new surf board), some big clients walked in the door.

The two best writers from my old creative team resigned and came over as well.

Walter was recalled Stateside and was never seen again.

By the time Tess reached her second year at boarding school, S&J Advertising employed forty people, and I was getting ready for the biggest pitch we had ever done: a proactive tilt at the worldwide Ford account.

It all came about only because during the previous summer, a Portsea sailor with more money than sense had managed to sink his couta boat *Lucy* during the Portsea Cup by gybing too hard in that day's strong wind. Lucy's leeward rail went under and so did *Lucy*, in less than thirty seconds.

She remained on the bottom for three months, during which time the owner managed to get a full insurance pay-out and ordered a brand-new couta boat from the Wooden Boat Shop in Sorrento, which he eventually got to sail equally badly, now only racing in light winds.

At Easter, a dive school group from Queenscliff managed to snag *Lucy* with their anchor, and she was raised by winch to be auctioned by the insurance company as a write-off. There was only one bidder, Doc Russell from Anglesea, who snapped up *Lucy* for the reserve price of one thousand dollars. The auctioneer hadn't even bothered to hose the mud off; I think any other potential bidders had been put off by the stink!

Doc, Dave, and I spent a whole year of weekends fixing her up. Doc was the mechanic who got the engine going again and machined the blocks and running gear. Dave was the master craftsman who steamed and moulded new ribs and riveted them in place, and Ben, Tess, and I, being unskilled, were the paint removers, fillers, and sanders. With the prep work finally completed, we all helped to apply the three coats of paint in *Lucy's* original colours and varnished her teak deck, mast, gaff, and boom. She looked magnificent. There is something about the workmanship in the old boats that is the stuff of dreams, and the varnish brought out the patina of her beautiful old timbers.

By the time she was finished complete with new sails, we each had to kick in another two thousand dollars, but we reckoned we had done pretty well, ending up with a classic Hanson-built couta boat for seven grand – not bad when you consider that the Wooden Boat Shop sold *Lucy's* previous owner his new couta boat for over a hundred grand!

We didn't restore *Lucy* to race her; we did it to go fishing out in Bass Strait in the old way. Up to the 1960s, couta boats were used to troll for barracuda to supply Melbourne's fish and chip shops. The fastest boat arrived dockside first to snare the best prices from the waiting wholesalers, so the gaff-rigged sails of the couta boat fleet got bigger and bigger for maximum speed, as rivals raced each other to the docks, thus creating what became the largest heritage yacht racing fleet in the world, and a true Australian icon.

Finally, the big day for the relaunch came, and Doc, Dave, and I took *Lucy* fishing outside the Rip. We were trolling along for yellowtail kingfish to the steady beat of Doc's reconditioned Thompson diesel when I hooked into one of the most spectacular game fish on the planet. Well, not strictly a fish, but a shark.

A mako shark.

It took over an hour to land him. We should have been warned by his marlin like leaps, but instead of tying him alongside by the tail, we were silly enough to gaff him aboard. He nearly chased us out of the boat! We dodged his razor-sharp teeth and thrashing tail for a terrifying five minutes until Doc managed to dispatch him with a well-timed blow with the fish billy. As the mako lay there, I marvelled at his magnificent iridescent cobalt blue on top and the pure white underneath and could not help but regret we had killed such a beautiful creature.

Getting soft.

Always the dreamer, I thought of my mako that night and experienced a 'light bulb' moment when I aligned his blue and white colours with the legendary blue and white Alan Moffatt Falcon GT, the Bathurst winner we all lusted after but none could afford.

I couldn't sleep.

S&J was going to talk Ford into building and launching the Mako sports car, America's answer to Jaguar, Porsche, and Ferrari and the next flagship of the Ford Motor Company!

We did it in an unusual way for an ad agency.

First, I rang a mate, freelance graphics guru Alan Perkins, who I had often used illustrating concept boards for creative pitches. Before becoming a freelance graphic designer, Alan had conceived and designed the Perkins Aurora, the now mostly forgotten but iconic RX-7 engined 1974 sports coupe that Alan and his mates had manufactured in Dandenong, until their money ran out.

I met Alan at the Botanical Hotel in South Yara.

Bought him a beer.

Showed him a photo of a mako shark.

Then a photo of the iconic blue and white Alan Moffatt racing Ford.

Bought him another beer.

Then, I put it to him: "Perkins, you and I are going to land the worldwide Ford advertising account. You are going to design them a new sports car called the Mako."

Alan carefully eyed the photos.

Sipped his beer.

Looked thoughtful.

Sipped his beer.

Looked at me.

Grinned.

Nodded.

Shook my hand.

Turned over his coaster and drew the little sketch that is still framed on the board room wall at the Ford head office in Detroit.

Like the great cartoonist that he also was, Alan had managed to capture the essential design in a couple of lines. His Mako looked a little like a '72 Dino

Ferrari and a little like a Perkins Aurora, except that it had four gill-like vents in the side and a pointed snout exactly like my mako shark.

"They already build the Ford-Cosworth engine plus the best performance gear boxes in the world. They could make a F1 Mako easily if they really wanted to. It's the side vents and the iridescent blue that will do the trick," he said. "Ferrari has its red. Mercedes has its silver. We'll have to talk Ford into selling the Mako only in Mako blue. Nothing else."

They will even be able to quote Henry Ford himself:

"You can have any colour as long as it's blue!"

And so it came to pass.

The little sketch on the coaster became a beautifully rendered concept design. The colour was a gleaming gradation from a special mix metallic indigo blue to become known as 'Mako Blue' through to silver-white starting at the bottom of the gill slit vents on the sides (the colour specifications forming part of the US and Australian Mako trademarks I registered in the car, clothing and surf board classifications).

Then we tested a concept pic of the Mako against the current line-up of prestige sports cars, using current owners who pretty well mirrored the guest list of one of Portsea's cocktail parties. Our Mako came out on top. Way on top. Probably only because we were careful not to include an e-type Jag or a 1972 Dino Ferrari in the study, but what the hell?

Alan drew twenty versions of the Mako bonnet badge before he got it right. Once we had that, I spent more of the Agency's money on a 3-D model and cast six chrome-plated bonnet badges.

The moment Alan and I saw the gleaming silver badges, we knew we were on a winner.

You just do.

The next step was to contrive a meeting with Ford's director of marketing, Winchester King III. Although supposedly ranking about the same degree of difficulty as getting an audience with POTUS; getting in Winchester's door turned out easier than we thought, as he had heard of our advertising success in Australia and reckoned we had to have something pretty good to leap-frog Ford's Australian entity and fly an idea all the way to Detroit.

I booked two return tickets.

We travelled light, as we didn't intend staying long. Our luggage consisted of a new leather briefcase containing ten bound proposals, including research results, a chrome Mako bonnet badge, plus an actual Mercedes star, Ferrari prancing horse, leaping Jaguar, and enamelled Porsche badges, stocked by Melbourne dealerships to replace the iconic emblems when kids knocked them off; a fine-lined pad and a blue Waterman pen; Alan's big flat artwork folio with his gel layouts; and two small suitcases of clothes. My suitcase contained my Henry Bucks suit with matching tie, shirt, and socks, plus a pair of five-thousand-dollar bespoke shoes by Lobb's of London (a honeymoon gift from Ariel), whilst Alan had splurged on an impressive outfit consisting of a tee shirt with little elephants on it, a New Zealand merino/possum wool cardigan with bone buttons, matching possum socks, and a new pair of Rockports, the totality of which made him look suitably creative yet uncharacteristically neat.

Winchester King's PA ushered us into his office, where Winchester himself emerged from behind an enormous glass desk to shake our hands, whilst the PA took orders for coffee, chocolate chip cookies, and Oreos.

Winchester took his black coffee with a chocolate Oreo in the saucer back behind his desk and got straight to the point: "Okay, what are we talking about?" Our cue.

Alan stood and propped his flip folio against the back of his chair.

I opened my briefcase catches, with two loud clicks.

I dipped my hand into the lid pocket and palmed the Ferrari bonnet emblem, just like we'd practiced.

Cue opening remark:

"Although Ford has built the most successful Formula One engine in history and your GT40s have won Le Mans five times, you have never succeeded in making a truly iconic sports car for the consumer market," I said.

Winchester's offended look was followed by the expected response: "What about the Mustang and the Thunderbird?"

"Both have been great cars, but neither has the aura of the Chevvy Corvette. Or of any of these:"

Onto the desk with the chrome Ferrari prancing horse.

Onto the desk with the chrome leaping Jaguar.

Onto the desk with the chrome Mercedes star.

Onto the desk with the enamelled Porsche bonnet badge.

"So, we have designed you a sports car that will finally give Ford the prestige market flagship you have always needed but have never quite had."

Onto the desk with the chrome Mako bonnet badge.

"Until now."

"The Mako."

"Alan?"

Alan flipped the folio cover, to reveal a spectacular close-up of an actual leaping mako shark. Same pose as our bonnet badge.

"This is a Mako shark."

"And this is the Ford Mako sports car."

Alan flipped the layout to reveal the Mako front closeup, featuring the chrome emblem which Winchester was now turning over in his hand.

Then the side, top, and three-quarter profiles, showing the four gill slits.

Then a page showing the pictures of each prestige sports car plus the Mako; in order of their 'like' scores in our group research. The Mako was there on top, with its 71 percent preference rating.

A 'Wow' look he couldn't hide came over Winchester's face as he rose and rounded the desk to confront the layout close up.

We knew we had him.

"If we were to look at this, what's the deal?" he said.

I dumped the ten proposals on the desk with a satisfying *plop*.

"It's all in there," I said.

"We are an ad agency, and as such are treating this as an advertising proposal. Bottom line is, we assign the automotive trademark and concept designs to you for no charge, provided we get the principal worldwide advertising account. We have included our group research results in the folder and have a number of creative concepts ready once you confirm its findings and go to manufacturing. We would retain the Mako trademarks we own for the clothing and surfboard classifications, and would licence all automotive merchandising back to you for the normal 10 percent royalty."

It was a good deal for Ford, and Winchester knew it.

It also helped that he had been heavily involved in Ford-Cosworth's Formula One glory days. The pictures of four historic F1 races were right there on the wall behind him.

He hadn't made it to top of Ford marketing by beating around the bush, and he didn't play games.

"I love it. We'll look at it, which will take a little time. Then we'll talk a deal," he said.

The next day, Alan and I were chauffeured to the airport; and not being into champagne, managed to get in bloody Marys and four beer chasers each before take-off.

It only took four weeks for the phone call, which came from Winchester King himself.

"We ran our own research on the concepts, and although the Mako rated under your numbers, it still came out on top," he said. "More importantly, the marketing guys and the board love it.

"We have lift-off!"

Three years later, the first Mako rolled off Ford's US production line, and S&J launched it worldwide as principal Agency.

And the money rolled in.

Lots of it.

Silas bought himself a Bertram 35 and Australia's first Mako (at factory price), bearing the personalised number plate MAKO1.

Dave and I took the wives and kids north to take delivery of my brand-new Robinson R44 Raven helicopter and go diving on the Great Barrier Reef with our Pommy mate Alistair Darnley. Alistair ran a dive school out of Palm Cove and was more than happy to contra scuba lessons for Tess and Ben against free helicopter rides to outer reef atolls inaccessible to his dive boat, particularly as we threw in the fifty dollars he still owed each of us due to England losing the previous Ashes series.

Chapter 7
Tess

Over the next four years, I got to quite like school. Although there always seemed to be challenges, my love of sports propelled me into the firsts in most sports and thence into the unofficial ruling class amongst my peers. I didn't mind schoolwork either, but my first love was painting, which was the realm of Art Master Michael Collins, who knew of Dad's work and always encouraged me with out-of-class study of both the old masters and contemporary artists. He even used his own money to take three of us to art exhibitions in Melbourne in weekends when sports fixtures allowed, squeezed into his ancient VW beetle.

The discussion was always the same, every time we stood together in front of a painting, invariably selected by Mr Collins:

"What is the artist trying to *say*?"

Even if we hadn't a clue, Mr Collins made us stand there until one of us said something he rated as passably intelligent. It was only years later I appreciated he was not only teaching us to paint; he was teaching us a painter's insight.

My love life was less exciting, by which I mean non-existent.

In the next four years, Ben went through three girlfriends, which meant our relationship got absolutely nowhere, either at school or Lorne. I hope my surfing didn't put him off. I had slowly become better than him and graduated to all the tricks on a short board, whilst he seemed happy sticking to big sweeping turns on his faithful mal. Dad claimed my seemingly magic ability to shred waves was in the genes, but I think it was more related to Mum's ballet classes. Jealousy in the surf was definitely not Ben's problem in missing every green light I threw at him; he always broke into his lop-sided grin as soon as he spotted me on the beach and always insisted, we surf together. So much so that his girlfriends invariably regarded me with some suspicion. Number three the most. I think she was onto me.

My only decent chance to get Ben without a girlfriend in tow came when our fathers decided to take us camping on the Howqua River, in Victoria's high country.

Back then, the Howqua was one of the best trout streams in the State, and both fathers were heavily into fly fishing whenever they weren't sea fishing with Doc, spear fishing or surfing. Dad owned a precious Hardy fly rod and reel personally fitted in person by Jimmy Allen at the Compleat Angler in Melbourne, whilst Ben's father Dave tied his own flies, and was always collecting the feathers of everything from bronze wing pigeons to chooks to tie his creations. He preferred his own flies to bought ones, and one day gravely explained this to us:

"Tackle shop flies are made more to attract fishermen than trout," he pontificated, extracting a factory-made Royal Coachman from his fly box and laying it down beside one of his own designs.

"As you can see, from above the Royal Coachman stands out better than the Dave Holt Bronzie," he said. "This is because I selected the Coachman looking down through the glass-top display at the Compleat Angler."

"But where does a trout see a fly from?" "UNDERNEATH," he answered himself, holding both flies above his head and looking upwards at them. "I design my flies from UNDERNEATH."

He then held both flies bottom up in front of our noses.

"*Now* which fly looks the most inviting to a trout?"

There didn't seem to be much difference to us, but our eyes met and we both politely chorused: "Yours!"

This meant one dad was heading to the Howqua already happy. Ben turned to me and fired off his special smile. I felt a warm, wet sensation.

Stop it!

We had two-man tents, but even though we had started out life having baths together like brother and sister, our fathers had not failed to notice Ben and I had reached a dangerous age, so each of us shared a tent with a parent, meaning an opportunity for me to blast Ben out of the friend zone once and for all went begging.

Bugger!

With our fathers close by, nothing of a romantic nature could happen during the day either. Dawn and dusk were taken up wading the river flicking flies, whilst the middle of the day was devoted to hiking up and down ridges, taking turns with the metal detector. The Howqua was a gold mining area in the gold rush days, and both our fathers were seduced by the lure of the yellow metal. Payoff finally happened at the creek bed under Eagles Peak, when the detector was set off by a nugget big enough to pay for both the next camping trip and a new generator to boot!

Sunday was hot, so not to be outdone, I went snorkelling the crystal-clear pools at the bends in the Howqua River with a little tea strainer, as I reckoned any gold at the banks would have been panned out long ago. I got a bit of alluvial gold out of a couple of sandy cracks to add to our horde, but even better was the look I got from Ben when I emerged from the river in my bikini. Definitely not brotherly. I'm old enough to know when a guy is checking me out.

Or I think I am.

I had a go at sneaking my hand alongside Ben's leg going home in the Toyota, but this ended up as yet another fish refusing to bite, despite the bait being presented right under its nose.

Was he pretending to be asleep?

Had I misjudged the look?

Seemed so. I went back to school with the love of my life still out of reach. Threw myself into sport and tried to forget about any romance with Ben.

Failed with that. Him being at the same school didn't help.

The September holiday involved both families taking a two-week trip to far north Queensland. Ben was between girlfriends, so things looked promising. Dad was going to fly his new helicopter out to snorkel some isolated coral cays, plus both Ben and I had each been given PADI open water courses for our respective birthdays, so were looking forward to learning scuba. Mother took six romance novels and a bikini to spend sun baking at the giant Sheraton Mirage pool but promised to come snorkelling 'only if the sea was calm.'

Our scuba instructor was a very correct Englishman named Alastair Darnley. Alistair had previously dived both the outer reef and Truk Lagoon with our dads and despite being a Pom had become a mate, so Ben and I scored private lessons at the best dive spots.

Alistair was a very strict instructor, which is what you want, but there was a fun side to him too:

"There are only three rules," he said, looking us up and down at the start of our first pool lesson.

"The first is you do everything I say."

"The second is that every time you refer to fins as flippers, you owe me a bottle of wine. They are fins, and don't either of you forget it!"

"And the third is you Tess, are to change to one-piece bathers for the pool sessions. Your bikini is drawing a crowd and is even putting *me* off."

The bikini was really to put Ben off, but along with taking an immediate liking to Alistair, I got the message and obeyed orders.

Visibility was perfect for the next four days, and Alistair was a fantastic instructor, so the lessons went like a dream. Ben and I became qualified open water divers by the weekend. During the final lesson, I purposely referred to 'flippers' four times, so we shouted Alistair two bottles of white and two bottles of red to share with us all at the celebration dinner that night. I wore my white handkerchief dress that showed off my tan and just about everything else, guaranteed to turn on even a guy who thought he was just a friend.

Mother got on well with Alistair and was in fine form. She drew Ben aside for a one-on-one chat, which was a good sign she was warming to him despite his being 'one of those rough Lorne surfies'.

After dinner, Ben and I left the five adults to their Cointreau-on-Ices and headed for the Saturday pool party at the nearby hotel. This was going to be a great night!

Except that it wasn't.

It started badly. Walking to the party, I took the plunge and went for Ben's hand, but he shrugged it off.

I had to have gone red, but it was getting dark, so I hoped he hadn't noticed.

It got worse.

I got the silent treatment all the way to the party.

What had I done?

As soon as we arrived, Ben left me stranded at the poolside bar like some wallflower and made a beeline for a cute sailboard instructor.

Didn't come back.

Hauled her onto the dance floor.

I was hurt, but more than that, I was pissed.

A good-looking guy wearing a Comancheros muscle shirt and tasteful barbed-wire tatts round biceps and neck was drinking just across the bar, and it only needed one smile in his direction to get me straight onto the dance floor too.

Slow number.

Ben moved in on his cute sailboard instructor.

I smiled at my partner, who I now knew as 'Big Dog.'

Big Dog moved in on me.

Went for a kiss on the dance floor.

I let him, looking across the floor at Ben.

How d'you like them apples? I thought.

The music stopped, and everyone returned to the bar. Three similarly tattooed mates joined Big Dog and his latest conquest.

Drinks.

More drinks.

Conversation getting louder.

Big Dog went to the Men's. Came back. Won an arm wrestle 'for me' with his pock-marked mate, Root Rat.

Spilled his drink.

Giggled.

Giggled?

Along the bar, Ben was looking worried; at least he knew I was alive!

"You're coming back to the room," said Big Dog proudly.

Ben got up.

Walked up to Big Dog.

"No, she's not."

I had always been able to handle guys, and Ben needed a lesson.

"Yes, I am," I said.

Big Dog and his three mates surrounded Ben.

"Piss off, college boy," growled Big Dog.

Ben was school middleweight boxing champion, so I knew he could fight. But not four of them. I started to grow scared.

Ben knew he couldn't win this fight either, but it didn't seem to matter. I had seen him angry at Bells when one of the Bra Boys down from Maroubra had dropped in and dinged his favourite mal, and the guy ended up having to have his jaw wired, but that never came close to the look he gave Big Dog. It was the look of a lion defending his mate.

He turned to me.

"They're all on drugs," he said.

"I need room," he added.

Then he picked me up and threw me in the pool, handkerchief dress and all.

Turned in one fluid movement and dashed every glass off the bar with an almighty crash.

Spun on his toes and hit Big Dog with a three-punch combination the bikie never even saw.

Big Dog went down like a sack of potatoes.

I emerged from the pool with what had become a clinging, see-through dress, much to the delight of many onlookers.

Security came from everywhere.

Big Dog got up, but instead of killing Ben, he and his mates disappeared into the bowels of the hotel; (obviously worried the cops were on the way).

Ben and I got thrown out and started walking back to the Mirage.

My anger at Ben had evaporated, and I started to cry.

"It's okay, Tess," he said kindly.

"I'll always have your back."

Put his arm round me.

But no kiss.

My big brother.

Shit!

The next day we flew home.

Chapter 8
Tess

Back at school, my one degree of separation from Ben became even wider. He always had a smile and often long chats with me, but also had a new girlfriend in tow only two weeks after the start of term.

The school boxing championship was also on his mind. Both our fathers loved their boxing, and their idol was 1960s Australian world featherweight champion Johnny Famechon. Dad returned from Vietnam in time to go with Dave to all Fammo's Festival Hall fights, and this, combined with the big televised Ali fights, seemed to qualify both of them as boxing experts in the endless pub debate of who was better out of Fammo and Australia's other world champion, Lionel Rose.

They kept dragging Ben over to O'Donoghue's surf break on the Anglesea back beach and making him run up and down its big sand dune to strengthen his legs, explaining that it was leg speed and evasion that made Fammo the greatest boxer of all time. I needed to strengthen my legs too, as I had only one more chance to make the first eight at the final selection, which was not going to be easy from the seconds bow seat. So, whenever we were down at Lorne, Ben and I sweated up and down the dune whilst our fathers caught their board and boogie waves opposite and made sure we kept going. Back at the house, Ben's dad employed my ballet training to teach Ben to move faster, a la Fammo. Ben would start with his back to the fence and have to get around me, while I threw jabs at him wearing training gloves. The upshot was Ben developed fast legs to combine with his surfer's shoulders, so we had him a shoo-in for his second school middleweight title in two years.

But there was trouble on the horizon. Trouble took the form of Meishai Rama, the new kid from Thailand. With his friendly disposition and ready humour, Meishai quickly became popular with teachers and kids alike. He only made the fourth eleven at cricket, but cricket was not where he would make his mark. In fact, he was probably the worst batsman ever to play for the fourths, which was somewhat of an achievement in itself! But failure to make double figures with the bat or take a single wicket with the ball was not the end of it for Meishai. Even though he couldn't catch a cricket ball to save his life, the hands that were useless in slips were soon to do his talking for him.

He chose boxing as his main sport. Middleweight. Built like a tank, he earned his nickname of 'Oddjob' (of James Bond fame) at his very first sparring session when he surprised everyone by knocking out Harry Jones, the previous year's finalist, with one punch – and this with padded training gloves! It turned out that while Ben had been surfing through our early years; over in Thailand, Meishai had been spending his time at the State-funded boxing academy. And it showed. Sparring partners for Meishai became hard to come by after the training knockout, and as championship week approached, he had firmed to favourite for the title; a hero in waiting for his house.

Sure enough, as the tournament progressed, a disturbing pattern emerged. Ben was boxing beautifully winning clear points decisions, but Meishai was winning all his bouts inside the first round! I think the referee was worried someone would get hurt, as he signalled each of Meishai's bouts over as soon as any opponent looked even slightly groggy, which was invariably quite early.

It was inevitable that Ben and Meishai faced off in the final. It seemed that the school had its very own Rocky movie on its hands, and the gym was going to be packed. I arrived early and bagged a ring side seat.

The big fight didn't disappoint.

I am too young to have seen Fammo fight (and anyway, I am a girl and wouldn't have gone), but I reckon after all our work, Ben's footwork and evasion would have run Fammo close. Meishai kept trying to cut off the ring, but Ben ducked and weaved and danced, racking up points with his lightning combinations. Round one to Ben easily.

Round two was going the same way when Meishai tied Ben up in a neutral corner and caught him with a huge right hook to the ribs. Ben went down but bounced straight up, so the ref allowed it to continue, which he wouldn't have done if it had been a head shot because Ben would have been dead.

As I said, I'm only a girl who has never boxed and cannot adequately describe rounds three to six. Suffice to say it was Fammo versus Oddjob, Meishai doing damage, but Ben's dancing feet and brilliant boxing evening the score.

At the final bell, the whole school went nuts as we awaited the announcement of the winner. In time-honoured tradition, the ref stood between the warriors, grabbing each of their wrists. Then he raised both their gloves aloft. We had just witnessed the first middleweight championship draw in the history of the school.

Ben was a complete mess, with blood seeping through the cotton wool in one nostril and a rapidly closing left eye. As soon as the ref released their arms, Ben grabbed Meishai's wrist and raised his arm as the winner as far as Ben was concerned, even managing a grin through a fattening lip. At that moment, they became friends for life. Ben spat blood, found me in the front row with his good eye, and gave me the thumbs-up with his free glove.

God, I loved him.

But so did his new girlfriend Mandy Morris, who climbed into the ring and went for the big embrace, which I later learned hurt Ben even more than it did me, as it turned out Meishai had cracked a rib when he decked Ben in the second round.

Okay, bugger it. I am not about to enter a monastery. I am going to have my own boyfriend, like everybody else.

As we girls tend to do, I discussed this at length with bestie AJ.

"With your looks you won't have much trouble Elle," offered AJ. "Every guy in the school would give his eye teeth to sleep with a supermodel."

Actually, this turned out to be wrong, or in any event nobody was queueing up to date me.

AJ said, "Trouble is, you're *too* beautiful. They're all shit scared," but I think it was more that my preoccupation with Ben had created the wrong impression, as I knew for a fact some guys referred to me as 'Frigidaire' behind my back.

That was about to change.

I really liked Will Thompson, who apart from being a keen artist like myself was both good looking and lots of fun. A minor problem was Tommo was already dating Claire de Coursey, who wasn't a huge fan, having lost yet another tennis final to me, despite her parents shelling out a small fortune for private lessons. To make matters worse, I had just been made school tennis captain ahead of her.

Who cares; AJ had told me Claire was the main mover and shaker in trying to change my nickname from Elle (which I was vain enough to like) to Frigidaire (which I most definitely didn't), so I was about to emphatically prove her wrong.

Everything fell into place due to the school play, this year, a production of the hit movie Grease. I found out Tommo (who was a tenor in the choir) had been selected for the part of Danny, so I put my hat in the ring for the part of love interest Sandy. Miss Whiteside, the Drama Mistress, gave me the nod, and stage one of my 'boyfriend' campaign was up and running.

We both looked the part, but there were two problems that Whitey needed to overcome. The first one was that Danny couldn't dance, and the second was that Sandy couldn't sing. Some serious coaching was needed, so Tommo found himself put to work with Mr Hollis-Bee, the play's choreographer, who taught dancing lessons in Junior School, whilst I sang Sandy's solos over and over under the supervision of Mr Cuthbertson, the Choir Master. I had an easier time than Tommo as I could just hold a tune, but Holly B had to simplify the choreography to accommodate Danny (except for 'Greased Lightning', which (strangely) he nailed perfectly).

In any event, we were more or less up to speed by the time rehearsals got underway, and it started to be good fun. Especially the finale, when Danny and Sandy get to kiss. First time up I really kissed him, and Tommo was not slow in kissing me right back.

"Cut! Cut!"

"For goodness' sake, someone pull them apart," Whitey said severely, as the rest of the cast fell about laughing.

"What just happened?" whispered Tommo, whose eyes had sort of glazed over.

"Don't know, but can't wait for next rehearsal," I replied, looking him in the eye with a most un-Frigidaire-like expression.

From there, things progressed apace. Next weekend, Mr Collins offered to take three kids from art class to see The Italian Masters Exhibition at the National Gallery in Melbourne.

"Can I come?" Tommo asked.

"Can I come too?" I echoed.

We were both thinking in terms of the back seat of Mr Collins's VW, but bugger me if Daisy King didn't beat me to it as our ride pulled up, which snookered our plans, at least for the trip up. Mr Collins knew something was going on, as he had almost never filled a quota to go to exhibitions featuring the Italian renaissance period, with its traditional, boringly religious paintings.

"What is it that particularly attracts you about Botticelli's babies?" Mr Collins asked me with a quizzical look, as the four of us stood in front of a painting of Madonna and Child. This was a pretty hard one to answer, particularly with Tommo pulling faces in the background.

"Nothing. I prefer Michelangelo's ones," I threw back at him.

I don't think I fooled Mr Collins for a moment. He had taught mixed classes for a long time and knew a budding love affair when he saw one. This was confirmed when we got back to the car park for the return trip.

Mr Collins turned to Daisy and made the wonderful suggestion: "Daisy, why don't you sit up front with me so we can discuss your change to water colour this year?"

Tommo and I dived into the back like a couple of rabbits down a burrow.

As we beetled along, I put my hand next to Tommo's leg.

Tommo put his hand alongside it.

Our hands intertwined.

I lifted both our hands and placed them in the middle of my jeans. Released my hand, leaving his right where it was.

His hand started stroking.

Mine undid the top button for easy access.

His hand slid under my pants.

I was soaked.

Two fingers slid in easily.

I moved against them.

God!

I came twice before the school turnoff. Thank goodness Mr Collins had the radio on!

After that, it was only a matter of time before I lost my virginity.

One day, to be precise.

That Sunday.

Tommo had got a Li Lo from somewhere and a condom from somewhere else, and straight after chapel, we sneaked into the scorebox on the main oval.

Tommo blew up the Li Lo while I unwrapped the condom from its little packet, ready to go. It was cleverly named 'Explorer 1', after the first US satellite.

We tore off our own clothes. Quicker that way.

'It' was much better than the books.

"You're no Frigidaire. You're hot," Tommo said, as we lay back after the big event.

"Nice to know you appreciate my beauty," I replied.

"Well, I do, but that's not it. You are *physically* hot," he said.

"Down there," he added, sliding in the same two fingers that had started the whole thing the day before.

I knew just what he meant.

Did I ever!

So, this was 'it'.

Wow!

Tommo and I were now officially an item.

Goodbye to Sandra Dee.

And hello to Portsea high society! Tommo's parents had a holiday house along the clifftop from Mother's family, and even better than that, his father was Culverton Thompson, head of Melbourne's biggest bank and Commodore of the Sorrento Couta Boat Sailing Club. Unlike her uneasy truce with Ben, Mother was all for Tommo, so it was easy to break it to her I needed to go on the pill. I was sent off to the family doctor for a prescription straight away. Dad liked Tommo too, so apart from plenty of sailing, we were always in and out of each other's Portsea houses, both of which had guest wings.

With beds.

Much better than the Li Lo!

Back at school, Grease was a triumph for me and Tommo. Our friends reckoned our big kiss at the end was far superior to Olivia Newton-John and John Travolta's effort, even if my singing and his dancing fell marginally short of their talent! Ben's dad had borrowed two cars, a rusty ute from a mate in the Lorne surf club and a custom hot rod that became the gleaming Greased Lightning from another mate in Torquay, so Ben was appointed stage hand in charge of the cars, with explicit instructions to orchestrate the magic transition from rust bucket to dream car and finally remove the lightning stickers and any adhesive from the precious Torquay car as soon as the play's run was finished.

Hope Ben saw the kiss he was missing!

My only regret was he was witnessing it side on from the wings, instead of full on from out front, in the full glare of the spotlight.

At least he appeared to appreciate Sandy's black Lycra cat suit, which I caught him checking out in a most un-brotherly way at the cast party.

"Are you really the kid I used to have baths with?" he said.

"Are you really the first guy I kissed on a surfboard?" I replied with my practised 'slutty Sandy' smile.

This could have gone anywhere, except that Whitey cut in to get Ben to roll Greased Lightning on stage for the cast party photo, and the moment was lost.

Anyway, I had Tommo now.

Sports-wise, there was one thing I still had to do, and that was to make the first eight. The weekend after the play, rowing coach William Willington (an ex-Cambridge stroke, known to all as Willy Willy) announced that all members of both the firsts and seconds squads would be tested on the dynamic machine the following Saturday, and then both eights would race the Head of the River course on the Barwon on the Sunday. He would post up his final selections for both Head Of The River crews following that race.

Thanks to my years of surfing and our massive O'Donoghue's sand dune knew I scored well on the ergo machine, which measured both strength and stamina. Willy Willy wasn't giving anything away though, and the next day we raced on the Barwon as scheduled, with the coach following up in his precious 1940 Chris Craft speedboat, checking our techniques through his binoculars. The race was close, with the firsts only beating the seconds by a canvas. We put the boats away and gathered anxiously outside the rowing shed, awaiting the final crew notices to go up. It was going to depend on the ergo tests, and I reckoned two or three of us seconds girls were in with a chance of an upgrade. But there was only one change to the first eight.

I had made the bow seat.

Hit the showers in a dream.

Which was to become a nightmare.

I was happily showering in the open booth, when the other girls in the firsts ran in with buckets of cold water: my initiation as the new member of the crew.

I spun as the bucketfuls of cold water hit me, hair and water flying everywhere. It was quite a sight, as I found out later.

That wasn't the nightmare. That was yet to come.

Claire de Coursey was in the first eight, but she didn't come in with a bucket of water like the others. She came in with her little Zeiss 35mm compact hidden in a towel and got a perfect shot of the exact moment of impact.

Which I knew nothing about.

Until six weeks later.

When I was summoned to the headmaster's office. Dad and Mother were there.

"Please sit down, Tess," Doctor Hogget said. "What is the meaning of this?" He pushed a magazine across the desk.

Australian Playboy.

It had a banner across the front cover, with a catchy headline:

THE GIRL IN THE SHOWER

With a little photo on it.

Me.

It had a centrefold, with the same headline:

THE GIRL IN THE SHOWER

Me.

It was all over the school.

It was all over Australia!

I couldn't look at my parents.

I couldn't speak.

But I had to.

"It's me. In the rowing shed," I stammered. "But I've never seen this before," I stammered. The tears were starting to come.

"Yes, I'm afraid you have," said the headmaster. "Your father's Agency contacted Playboy, and they confirm you submitted this picture with your written consent to publish it for a fee of a thousand dollars."

"I didn't," I said. "That was not me – this is the first time I have heard anything of this."

Mother was in tears too.

"If Tess says she didn't do it, she didn't," she said. "This must be a cruel trick by someone. You can't penalise our daughter for that. She is not to blame."

The head looked sadly at Mother and shook his head.

"It doesn't matter how it happened. The school has to uphold its standards, and we cannot be involved in this. I must ask you to remove Tess from here immediately. I am sorry."

We all stood up.

Dad put his arm around me and stared down Boss Hog.

"This isn't fair," he said quietly. "We didn't send our daughter here to be treated like this."

It didn't matter.

I was expelled.

I took Mother and Dad up to the dorm to help pack my clothes.

AJ and I went to our study to pack my books.

Friends piled in to say goodbye. Including Tommo and Ben.

Tommo held up well.

Ben cried.

Chapter 9
Jack

We were only home a week before the Melbourne Truth newspaper got into the act:

THE GIRL IN THE SHOWER REVEALED

The Girl in the Shower featured in this month's Australian Playboy centrefold is none other than Tess Johnson, daughter of Vietnam war hero and Ad Man of the Year Jack Johnson and Melbourne racing personality Ariel Johnson.

Tess has been expelled from Australia's most exclusive public school, at which she had just been voted a House Captain. The school made no comment.
Mother and daughter had previously made the front page of a Melbourne daily after the crash in Toorak that resulted in a Statewide street ban on billy carts.

Next morning, the doorbell rang. It was a Melbourne Sun journo and photographer. I told them to piss off and slammed the door in their faces.

"We've got to get Tess out of Melbourne," said Ariel. "The Portsea set will crucify her. I'll try and contain the damage down there, but you'll have to hide her away at Lorne until this blows over."

She was right, but it was going to take more than a safe house to pull Tess out of her misery. I went in to work and told Silas I would be taking time off.

"Mako is up and running now," I told Silas before going home. "Let the account and media guys do their thing, and ring if you need me."

When I got home, I collared Tess. "Pack your bag kiddo; we're going surfing!"

And so, we did.

Or to be strictly accurate, Dave, Tess, and Ben did, while I flipped along on my boogie board. Ben and Dave disappeared off to Dave's little surf board factory every now and then. It transpired they were shaping a short board for Tess, which they proudly presented to her only a week after we moved into Lorne. They had even got the Mako blue right.

"I want state right now I am not about to start making short boards," stated Dave. "I am a long board specialist and will only ever make this one-off shortie for Tess."

This time, it was good to see my daughter cry.

Lorne Point co-operated that day with a glassy right hander, so even the board christening turned out perfectly.

We made Tess catch waves till she could paddle no more, then we all went back to Dave's place for a chop on the barbie with Jules. I liberated my two precious bottles of Grange from my Lorne cellar, which was the least I could do.

After doing justice to the local chops, Dave, Jules, and I settled into deck chairs on the veranda with the bottles of Grange, whilst Ben and Tess went inside.

I hoped a very important part of her rehab was underway in there.

Jules obviously hoped so too. She opened the second bottle to make sure Dave and I stayed put on the veranda.

She needn't have worried – we'd got it.

Chapter 10
Tess

Ben and I sat on the edge of his bed and looked each other in the eye.

"I still haven't found out who it was," he said. "Although Claire is all over Tommo again. If I was a betting man, I'd put it down to her. She is mail monitor, so could easily have intercepted your mail and forged the Playboy form."

"Of course, it was her," I said. "You don't need to be Sherlock Holmes."

"If your dad could get hold of the authorisation form from Playboy, maybe we could match the handwriting on the signature and catch her out that way?" he said.

"No, this isn't a murder case, and anyway, the damage is done."

"I don't want to go anywhere near that bloody school ever again. I just want to move on."

"What do you want, Tess?" Ben asked sadly.

"That's easy. I want the world's first kiss on a surfboard to mean something. Can you ever love me now?"

Ben's response was not at all what I expected. He threw back his head and laughed.

"Ever love you? I've loved you all my life, you bloody idiot," he said. "Now more than ever."

I seemed to be blubbing an awful lot lately.

We got going on the world's best ever kiss *not* on a surfboard. It turned out the magic worked just as well on land, and apparently it got all the way to Mount Olympus.

SHAZAM!

My lightning bolt had been there all along. Zeus was just waiting for the right moment.

We made love.

Not just sex.

Love.

It's different.

I must have cried out.

"Quiet," Ben said nervously.

"They'll hear you!"

"They won't care," I responded.

They didn't. Actually, they did, but in a good way. That was made clear when we finally made it back to the veranda.

There were two seconds of awkward silence.

Then everyone cracked up laughing.

"Thought you two would never work it out," said Jules.

"Does this mean I don't have to pay for the surfboard?" asked Dad (rather unnecessarily, I thought).

The next day, Lorne lived up to its nickname 'Lake Lorne' so in the absence of waves, Ben and I cleared off for a low tide walk to Urquhart's Bluff with swims in the coves of Cinema Point and Sunnymeade whenever we were hot.

We had the chance to talk but didn't need to say much; long kisses in the crystal-clear water of the coves were far better than words. Ben is not a big talker, but when he did talk, he came up with two very important statements.

The first: "That day we nailed the world's first kiss on surfboards, I was gone for all money. That's why I fell off. I only wish it meant we really were engaged."

I think I had just been proposed to for the second time.

"We are, Ben. Have been ever since then, as far as I'm concerned. If you can put up with damaged goods, I'll marry you any time you want."

"Maybe finish school first?"

The second: "I've always felt badly about blanking you that night at Port Douglas. You had never looked so beautiful, but your mother caught me looking. She fronted me before we left for the party and said that her plans for you did not include me. I agree with her really. I still see you marrying into high society one day, whilst I do not fit there. Last night, I couldn't help myself. I hated seeing you so sad after the shower thing and couldn't stop the rest happening."

My turn.

"Do I really have to tell you what you already know? Even before the shower, I was never going to fit into high society, despite what Mother wants. She can have that. I only want a life with you."

That night, Dad had to go back to sort out stuff at work, and to have a serious talk with Mother (boy, wouldn't have minded being a fly on the wall for that little chat), and I was left behind at Ben's place.

"Haven't got enough sheets to make up the spare bed, Tess; you'll have to find somewhere else to sleep," Jules said with a perfectly straight face.

Bloody beauty!

Ben was back to school on the Monday, so with the sea still flat Dave and I launched his zodiac at the Anglesea boat ramp, and we went diving at the 'Block of Flats' his highly secret reef off Urquhart's, where there were good crays to be had.

Dave showed me the best (albeit highly illegal) way to catch crays using a shark hook with the barb filed off, screwed onto the end of a piece of dowel to reach deep into the crevices and pull them out. After only ten minutes in the water, I spied a pair of feelers poking out of one of the holes and with a deft piece of hook work, it was game over; although Dave might have told me crays grab your wet suit with their front legs while you are swimming up to the surface! Dave jagged another one almost immediately, so we headed back, as he never over fished.

The only downer for the day came when we were winching the zodiac back onto the trailer. Four Anglesea Clubbies walked past carrying surf skis, and two of them gave me wolf whistles. I am used to turning heads, but don't usually get that. Was my centrefold up in the Anglesea Surf Club?

Dave picked up on it, but soon got me smiling again on the way back to Lorne by chatting about my favourite subject: Ben.

Dad was back on Wednesday, this time with Mother in tow.

They brought my oil paintings plus the easel, paints, and brushes from school. Apparently, Mr Collins had driven them up from Geelong in his little beetle and left them with his good wishes, plus the offer to help in any way he could getting me a permanent place at the Paris School of Art, if that was what we decided was the best way to distance me from the Playboy fallout.

Dad didn't discuss his talk about Ben with Mother, who seemed to be in denial. She certainly was much nicer to Ben, so that was promising.

They also brought two letters addressed to me.

The first was a letter from Australian Playboy, enclosing a cheque for a thousand dollars, plus an offer of five thousand more to do a second centrefold.

Dad videoed me burning both the letter and the cheque, as he thought I may be able to use it sometime.

The second letter meant I didn't have to face a break-up with Tommo, which I had been agonising about:

Dear Sandy,

I hope you are getting over everything that happened at school. I still can't believe you are not here and really miss you – especially when passing the score box!

Some bright spark put the centrefold up in the cricket changing room. It only lasted a day until the traps found out, and you actually caused a special assembly in which Boss Hog laid down the law that anyone caught with a Playboy would be expelled. I wonder if that also applies to the teachers?

You also made Bug's sermon the Sunday after you left. You may be interested to know that God forgives you, even if the school doesn't. Nobody believes it was not you who sent the shower picture in to Playboy, despite anything I say. Your friend Ben has been carpeted for getting into fights with anyone he hears has been bad-mouthing you, but even he can't fight the girls, who are the worst. I am not a boxer like him, and I think it best we both move on.

I am seeing Claire again. I would rather you found out from me than from some cowboy wanting to hurt you. The parents have banned me from asking you to the yacht club dance at Easter or to even come over, and I think now we can't see each other at school either, we don't really have a chance anymore.

I am sorry it has had to end like this and am sure things will die down once the papers move on to their next scandal.

I will always love you and never forget our time together.

Love, Danny

Chapter 11
Jack

Ariel blamed me for engineering the latest development at Lorne but was not as angry as I thought she'd be. She had given up on Tess as far as Melbourne and Portsea society was concerned, accepting that ship had sailed, as soon as she saw how happy Tess and Ben obviously were.

"Things didn't go at all well at Portsea," she said. "We haven't been invited to Teddy Buckingham's fiftieth, and I'm sure Jane avoided me in the supermarket. Not only that, but I was not asked over to the Culverton Thompsons for their usual Saturday night cocktails, even though they had to have seen my car in the drive."

"You'll have to keep Tess here at Lorne."

"Don't let it get to you. I know what happened with Tess is bad, but at least it tells us who our true friends are," was the best I could manage.

"Tess herself is the most important thing," I added. "This has been a huge hit to her self-esteem. I will stay with her for as long as it takes for her to come good. Please come back to Lorne with me. Right now, she needs her mother as well."

Ariel came back to Lorne in her own car, with a promise to stay on until her next clothing shoot in Sydney.

It was the happiest week at Lorne I can remember. Ariel had always got on with Jules and Dave, and finally, she made friends with Ben – even apologising 'for getting it wrong'. Lorne had never failed to turn off the stress of work, and although Ariel had been rarely able to tear herself away from Portsea or Chartwell to come down to Lorne, this time the beach worked its magic on her as well. After all that had happened, I needed her as much as Tess did; it was a new experience for our busy little family to pull up the drawbridge on the world and spend quality time together. A wonderful time, right up to the night before Ariel had to leave.

We had blown my only two bottles of Grange, so instead of surf and turf on the barbeque, I thought it would be fun for Ariel to experience the Aireys pub.

My wife had contrasting tastes in drink. She drank only Gordon's G&T's, French champagne, or draught beer, and although French champagne was a bit thin on the ground this side of the bay and the Aireys pub almost certainly hadn't heard of Gordons, the draught beer was nice and cold. We grabbed an outside table under an umbrella, and a good time was had by all. Right up to when a bogan in a Mambo singlet came over and took a flash photo of Tess, right in her face.

Ben sprung up, grabbed the camera, and ripped the film out of the back. The bogan took a swing. Ben ducked it just like we'd practiced and decked him with a right hook that would have won him the school title.

Three more bogans weighed in, and all hell broke loose.

We bailed only five minutes before Anglesea's sole cop arrived.

Chapter 12
Tess

I've got to stop Ben hitting people.

I can handle myself.

"It's okay," I said in the car on the way home. "It's only a picture in a trashy magazine. It'll all die down."

But it didn't.

Not for a long time.

Three weeks later, what became the biggest selling poster in the world hit the shops; including the newsagent on the Lorne shopping strip.

Ben had always been the one to the rescue, but this time it was Dad.

The four of us had come in from surfing Lorne Point and were chilling out at the Arab, as I had refused to hide away anymore, provided Ben promised to behave.

Dad had something to say. "I've been so worried about the mess the shower picture caused you, I hadn't stopped to think of a way out of it," he began. "But flipping along out there, I think I've worked out what to do."

"This shower thing will never completely go away, Tess."

"So, I reckon you should use it."

"Use it? What do you mean? D'you want your daughter to become a porn star?"

"I don't mean the picture itself. But like it or not, you are famous, and like it or not, you are beautiful. I think you can make something of that."

He reached across the table like he was King Arthur, and tapped me on each shoulder with his long, iced coffee spoon, then dubbed Ben as well.

"I hereby bequeath to you, Sir Tess, the Mako trademark for clothing, and to you, Sir Ben, the Mako trademark for surf boards."

"Ben, you've already made the first Mako surfboard, the one you and Dave did for Tess, and Tess, you already have the four impressionist surf pictures you did at school."

"I know a firm in Melbourne who has perfected high res offset printing on cotton. We are going to produce four top-end *Mako Girl* tee shirts using your pictures, and when they are ready, we'll take them and the Mako board over to Wave Concepts at Torquay and do a licensing deal. Dave and I surfed with the founders back in the day, so we'll have no problem setting up a meeting."

We toasted our new business venture in iced coffee, and next day Dad headed back to Melbourne with the paintings.

He came back four days later, with some documents to sign, forming the Mako Surf Company, with the four of us as directors.

Print Horizons took only three weeks to produce the four *Mako Girl* tees, each with its 'Leaping Mako' swing tag. A Mako logo transfer arrived in the mail, which Dave glassed under my board, just in front of its three thruster fins.

Then we waited for a nice northerly and a clear blue sky. With the Bells Bowl in the background, I modelled each tee shirt with my favourite stressed denim shorts and also posed for Dad's Nikon, emerging from the surf in a blue bikini with the Mako board under my arm.

Dad disappeared back to the Agency to write up the Mako Surf Company proposal, combining the pictures we had taken with a cut-and-paste version of the clothing licensing deal S&J had produced for licensing Mako auto merchandise to Ford. He was back in three days, and we were ready to go, apart from a visit to the hairdresser in Geelong that Mother and Jules insisted on.

I dressed up for my role as a walking advertisement in what we reckoned was the best tee shirt, faded blue shorts, and bare feet, and we all drove over to Wave Concepts. The tee shirt must have looked okay, as everyone turned and stared as I padded through the showroom on the way to their boardroom with the Mako board once again tucked under my arm. Pure theatre, but hey, I'm a top Whitey-trained actress!

We were greeted by the two Surf Concepts owners and their marketing manager.

All guys.

First up, we got rid of the elephant in the room (aka The Girl in the Shower).

"You look even better in real life than in Playboy," said the founder of Wave Concepts, who had a bit of a reputation and wasn't about to pretend he hadn't seen my centrefold.

Probably had one in his study.

I took it as a compliment, not a slur, and fortunately so did Ben, who didn't hit him. We had bigger fish to fry.

The fish bit like tigers. Why wouldn't they? They gained fantastic products plus unpaid advertising leverage, straight up.

The Mako Surf Company ended up with everything we asked for.

Surf Concepts was awarded exclusive rights to Mako boards and *Mako Girl* clothing, plus the right to use my image in advertising and displays. Our only stipulation was there was to be no mention of 'The Girl in the Shower' or Playboy in any advertising, and I would not do media interviews.

The *Mako Girl* clothing test market was launched off-season, during the May holidays at the Torquay store only. The tees were priced at a hundred dollars apiece. At a hundred bucks a pop for a tee shirt, we were testing a completely new up-market category, but we need not have worried – all the test tees sold out within a week, with many customers buying all four! A big production order was placed to cater for a pre-Christmas launch across the entire Surf Concepts franchise, and I got going painting two more ocean-themed impressionist oils to build the set up to six. One of them was 'How to Kiss on a Surfboard', (which I predicted would become a big seller), and the other was a factually silly painting of a girl diving for crayfish in a blue bikini instead of a wet suit (don't try this at home, girls, unless home is in the Whitsundays, and if it is, make sure you hold the crayfish at arm's length when swimming up to the surface).

I did feel a bit self-conscious when two giant, back-lit billboards appeared above the entrance to the big Surf Concepts Torquay store, flanking an amazing centre billboard of a leaping mako shark. The first was the original shot Dad had taken for our proposal; me emerging from the surf at Bells, and the second was a subsequent Surf Concepts shot of me floating on a glassy swell, wearing the Mako blue bikini. What is it about girls with drops of water on them that's such a turn-on?

Dave and Ben had taken the same 'super premium' route with their Mako boards, which were exclusively sold in the Torquay store to serious surfers with two thousand bucks to spend. True to his calling, Dave only made mals and big wave boards, although Ben made some custom shorties for selected pros. Still in his last year at school, he could only shape boards in weekends, so they were of necessity rare. He loved doing them though, and with the help of his Dad, he became one of the most sought-after surf board designers in Australia, and later the world.

Although I missed study and my friends at school, life at Lorne was fine, with plenty to do. During the week, the painting was absorbing, and both new pictures came together well – in fact, my impressionist painting was getting better and better, thanks to the palette knife and broad-brush techniques added to my repertoire in Paris. Thanks, Mr Collins!

The weekends were all about me and Ben. Our parents drew the line at us sharing the same bed, but they feigned not to hear the creaky floorboard in the passage squeaking each night. The other spare room at Ben's place was often used by Meishai, who had become a mate and always came down to stay when he had any weekend exeat or holiday leave. It quickly became evident that Meishai was even worse at balancing on a surfboard than he was at cricket, so Dave got him a seat in the Lorne junior surf boat. This meant we found ourselves deigning to speak to Clubbies, which was previously unheard of for us Boardies.

With the school boxing program over, Ben was helping Meishai get ready to try out for the Thai boxing squad for the Barcelona Olympics, which were only two years away. In the best Rocky tradition, we introduced him to our big sand dune to strengthen his legs (which were like tree trunks to start with), plus he and Ben sparred each day in the back yard with training gloves – Ben's Apollo to Meishai's Rocky. I took the place of Rocky's famous chicken and danced around Meishai's bull-like rushes to get his feet moving. We even carted him off to the poultry farm on the Moriac Road to try him out on a real chook. He never got anywhere near catching it and just got sulky at us laughing. Either Australian leghorns are faster than Rocky's chicken, or they doped up the film one to slow it down. I reckon they gave it a shot of Valium!

Something had to have worked, as two years later, Ben and I became traitors to the nation when Meishai won the Olympic gold medal for Thailand, knocking out our Aussie middleweight on his way to the final!

Whenever he collected Ben for exeats, Dave would also bring AJ down to stay at our place, and you guessed it, she and Meishai got it happening. They were both so shy, we despaired they would ever even kiss, but it was lovely to watch them together. We weren't watching *all* the time, so they could have fooled us. Possibly in Dave's car, on the way back to school? AJ never admitted to a thing, but I reckon I saw mischief behind that enigmatic Asian smile.

The fallout from Playboy tapered off, just as Dad said it would; I suppose the bogans had new centrefolds with bigger boobs to lust after as subsequent issues hit the newsstands.

The poster was still out there of course, but it didn't seem to have quite the same notoriety attached to it as the centrefold. Ben and I were in the Arab having our usual iced coffees one day when a seventy-year-old lady walked up to our table.

"I couldn't help coming over," she said to me.

"We have your beautiful picture framed over our mantlepiece."

"You are a lucky man," she said to Ben.

I may just be a sex object to some, but to others, I was art.

Being a permanent resident of Lorne meant more time surfing. When the winter swells arrived, Ben and I hitched rides to Joanna to take on the big waves. Don't know why, but I got very good on them.

Very good.

This caused an idea to be born, which we put to our fellow directors over 'surf and turf 'on Dave's veranda.

"Every surf brand promotes itself via the pro tour, but we reckon that's becoming old hat," I said. "How many more ads are we going to see of short board re-entries and tube rides? They are all starting to look exactly the same."

"I reckon we can create something that will really resonate. How about Mako sponsoring 'The $100,000 Wave' in Traks magazine? A hundred grand to the best wave of the year, to be judged by Traks. It would undoubtedly be a big wave, and Surf Concepts would end up being able to use it in all their Mako promotions."

"Think of the publicity!"

Then the big ask to Dave: "And how about you build me a big wave board so I can enter?"

Both fathers had always been over-protective of me in the surf, so I was surprised when they agreed to not only design me a board but also mount a campaign to Hawaii.

Dave started talking tapered tails and concave front sections.

Dad started talking helicopter shots.

Ben started talking crystal clear lagoons 'after the shoot.'

He also went to work back at the office, and he and Silas Silver boosted the prize from a hundred thousand dollars to a cool million by presenting the whole idea to Channel 9's Wide World of Sports as a reinforcement to the Mako car media buy and to Ford as part of a potential future campaign: 'The Mako Generation'.

Surf Concepts agreed to help fund the travel and back-up as their contribution, and the Mako Million Dollar Wave Challenge was launched pre-Christmas on Wide World of Sports plus in Traks magazine, using me and Australian long board champion Peter Laird, who was already sponsored by Surf Concepts. Peter had won the national title using one of Dave's Mako custom mals, so I could see the Marketing Manager's eyes light up at the thought he could win it.

But he wasn't going to.

I was.

Chapter 13
Jack

Tess was going to be okay.

More than okay.

In Mako, she and Ben had a project to get their teeth into, and best of all, in Ben she had a soul mate, and I reckoned it was for keeps. Even Ariel was on side, both with the relationship with Ben and our plans for the Mako Surf Company. A former catwalk model herself, she was very proud of how *Mako Girl* was shaping up, although as far as the Million Dollar Wave was concerned, we dodged a bullet and had not fully revealed the dangers of big wave surfing, which was fortunately in its infancy and had not yet attracted much media attention. We just told Ariel, "The waves in Hawaii are better, and the water is warmer."

Ever since the Pipeline and Waimea trip Dave and I had done the year before Vietnam, I had never been scared of big waves, and although I feared more for Tess than I would for myself, I diverted that energy into helping her train. We ordered some little emergency breathing cylinders that had been developed for commercial divers, but I was determined Tess would have the best possible chance if anything went wrong, so also made her train for big wipe-outs the old way: walking into the water carrying a stone and holding her breath as long as she could. She never shrank from training, and her lung capacity increased to the stage we started to worry if she would ever come back up!

Dave and Ben were hard at work shaping gun board designs that Tess would try out whenever we could find big waves. The prototype ended up with a concave front section, pointed tail, and two radical hydroplane steps. Long and thin for maximum paddling speed, it's skeg design was completely radical too. Dave and Ben were inspired by the winged keel on Australia 2, winner of the 1983 America's Cup, and experimented with using one fin with wings instead of a traditional single island fin or a tri-fin thruster. There were a number of failures involving spectacular wipe-outs before they got the position right by moving the fin backwards and forwards in the skeg box, plus interchanging fins of different rakes and shapes. The final board ended up with a deep single fin with narrow raked wings, sited much further forward than traditional longboards and glassed right through to the centre stringer for strength. The winged fin was designed to help the board rise evenly onto its hydroplane steps as the speed increased, to save Tess's legs from the pounding they were sure to get on the face of seriously big waves, which we foresaw as the main problem she would face in Hawaii. In the end, we got a setup that seemed to work, at least as far as we could tell on the waves we were able to test it on.

The finished board was, of course, Mako blue and white, with four gill slits in the side that were entirely non-functional – only there for branding purposes. My contribution was a stylised graphic of shark jaws showing plenty of teeth plus two evil eyes, an idea 'borrowed' from a restored WW2 Mustang fighter I had admired at the Avalon Air Show. We graphic artists are always stealing each other's ideas!

Dave and Ben made three of the new boards in case of breakages, and Tess posed with one for *Traks* magazine, wearing her Mako blue bikini. The guys at the shoot reckoned she would win without even having to get in the water! But of course she was going to have to, so we kept building up her paddling power, and practicing with the test board wherever big swells arrived.

One weekend, we even carted Tess and the board over to take on Gunnamatta Beach on the so-called 'Dark Side'. The high society of the East Coast seemed to have collectively forgiven Tess's *Playboy* appearance, probably because half the girls in Portsea and Sorrento were now wearing Mako Girl tee shirts.

The Portsea A-list seemed to have forgiven Ariel too, as we discovered an invitation to the Culverton Thompson's New Year's Eve party in our letterbox.

Ariel and I went by ourselves, as Tess flatly refused.

Tommo came up as soon as we arrived. He seemed put out that Tess hadn't come and said: "Hi Mr Johnson. Couldn't Tess make it?"

I wasn't about to let him off lightly.

"She wouldn't come," I said.

I pointed out to the fishing boats bobbing out in the bay.

"Tess and Ben are out there with Andrew Scott in his little putt-putt fishing for flathead," I continued.

"I don't think she'll come near any of you ever again. I know we are guests tonight, but I need to tell you something for your own good. If some scandal had erupted around you like that what happened to Tess, she would never have deserted you. Never. I hope one day both you and your parents learn that loyalty is a far more precious thing than social standing."

Tommo didn't reply. He just went red, turned on his heel, and walked away.

At least I was able to pass on to Tess that Tommo was at the party with Sue Grimwade. Claire de Coursey had apparently been dumped in an ugly scene at the end-of-year school dance.

Ariel was back in her element. Come midnight, we stood in the admiring throng as Culverton ceremoniously lit the fuse on his ancient naval culverin and fired his traditional and highly illegal cannonball off the cliff into Port Philip Bay, fortunately not hitting anyone or blowing himself up.

In the end, we didn't go to Hawaii to chase our big wave, due to a surprise phone call that came only two weeks before we were due to book the flight. It came from Dazza Dare, an old surfing mate of ours who had actually gone and done what we had all threatened to do back in the day – make enough money to buy his own catamaran and head off around the islands, chasing waves. He ended up losing a wife and two girl friends over this somewhat selfish choice of lifestyle but found some amazing waves, incredible diving, and lots of big fish.

Dazza had heard of the Million Dollar Wave challenge and had seen the picture of Tess in Traks, so was moved to make a sat phone call to me, direct from the cockpit of his catamaran.

Which happened to be anchored three miles south of Namotu Island, off the southwest coast of Fiji, next to a reef break the locals called Tabua (Fijian for 'whale's tooth'). Years in the future, it was destined to be known across the surfing world as 'Cloudbreak'.

We dispensed with the preliminaries, as old mates do:

"Bloody hell, Jack, is that really your daughter in Traks?"

"How can an ugly bastard like you father something like that?"

"Are you sure she's yours?"

Yeah, yeah, yeah.

Then the clincher:

"Tess is a goofy, isn't she? Right now, I'm sitting at the stern, looking at a glassy left-hander the pro tour doesn't even know exists."

"It's big."

"*Really* big."

"Like the Pipeline on steroids."

"The wind has gone 'round to the south west and should blow for a week, so if you want Tess to win that million, get over here."

Dazza may have gone feral, but he knew big waves better than just about anyone on the planet. A brief chat with Dave, and we changed our campaign from Hawaii to Fiji. The vital thing was getting Tess, the boards, and a helicopter to Namotu while the big swells lasted.

Fortunately, Dazza still owed me one from back in the day when we were three broke surfers living on bananas and stale bread on Hawaii's North Shore. I had loaned him my spare board when he busted his attempting what he boasted was the world's first attempt to ride Back Door Pipe, only to see him smash mine up trying it again three days later. I had never hit him for the money but now called in the favour, asking him to make for the Port Denarau marina to pick up our assault team. He agreed, "Only because I want to check out that daughter of yours," pulled the pick and started north under both sail and engine.

I made two more calls. One was to the office, to get Silas to talk Channel 9 into lending me a Wide World of Sport cameraman for two weeks. That ended up being no problem, as they saw Tess as a big chance to increase their female audience. The second was to Chip Young, a gung-ho former US Air Cavalry pilot and Saigon drinking mate, now chief pilot for Island Helis out of Nandi.

Chip was a little taken back when I hit him to borrow one of their precious new Robinson helicopters for two weeks, but after reminding him of the time two of us Aussies had saved his 'ass' during a memorable dust-up with the bouncers at Saigon's most notorious cat house, he said he reckoned he could swing it. In the end, it was a good deal all round, as we agreed to give Island Helis an associate sponsorship of our wave challenge, plus the right to use all our footage in their advertising.

A Robinson Raven would be waiting when we arrived, fuelled up and ready to go.

Two days later, the team lined up at the Port Denarau marina. Dazza was there as promised, waving from the deck of his travel-worn, fifty-foot catamaran 'Between the Sheets', sporting not only a magnificent gold beard but also a very attractive crew named Lauren, who had to be fifteen years younger than him. Dazza hadn't changed a bit!

Tess, Ben, Dave, and the three boards were loaded aboard, and Dazza chugged out of the marina, heading south for Namotu. Kev the cameraman and I headed for the Denarau Yacht Club bar. We were to stay near the helipad with one of the sat phones to await the call that it was 'on.'

Didn't have to wait long; at first light three days later, the sat phone went off.

"*Between the Sheets* to *Flyboy*. This is Dazza. It's a glassy thirty feet and barrelling. We don't have the luxury of practise; today has got to be the day. We are sitting off the shoulder as I speak, so get here pronto."

I wasn't nervous for Tess until I flew over and saw what she was facing. Huge sets were marching in, and Tess had already left the zodiac and was paddling way out to the west of the break, with the zodiac trailing our rescue belly board making for a pickup point that looked to be impossibly far from the boiling white water. If Tess wiped out, it would be very, very nasty.

I zoomed in low over everyone and waved encouragement.

Now it was time to test my angle of attack to film the wave, then go on a hover to wait for Tess to make her attempt to ride it.

She started paddling onto a huge swell way off the break zone, and I couldn't believe she'd get up enough speed.

But she did.

My incredible daughter did.

We filmed her magnificent ride all the way.

She stood up as the wave built and the board started to run. We opened up with a perfect long shot: a tiny, golden girl in a blue bikini powering down one of the biggest waves I had ever seen, with a huge rooster tail spouting from the pointed tail of Dave's gun board, which was planing perfectly on its hydroplane steps.

By the time the wave peaked and Tess dropped into the tube, I was hovering close in at the end of the monster barrel, with Kev focussing all the way from front on long shot to three-quarter close-up, getting every move she made, from the screaming bottom turn to her desperate drive out of the tube.

The finish was reminiscent of the Pipeline left-hander, only far, far bigger. The wave literally spat Tess out the end of the tunnel in a plume of spray, and she ended the ride with some nice cross-over footwork and a spectacular flick-off, just for show.

She'd done it.

I radioed Dazza.

"We got it all. No need for another run; for Christ's sake, pull her out of there before I have a bloody heart attack!"

"I think I just had one myself, and Ben has been sick over the side. I think he quite likes her!"

The swell was too big to argue, so even Tess was happy to go back to the island without taking on another monster.

I was waiting at the little jetty when *Between the Sheets* arrived and must admit I teared up when Tess leapt off the boat, threw her arms around my neck and whispered, "Thanks, Dad," and then just clung. All fathers of daughters treasure one father/daughter moment above all others. This was mine.

That night we all got very drunk on kava.

I had to get the chopper back to Chip and Kev back to work at Channel 9, but we made time for one more day on Namotu. The next morning, the swells were smaller but still better than anything any of us had ever surfed, so Tess and Ben took a couple of the gun boards out with Dazza, his new fiancé Lauren (Dazza had proposed the night before and although I don't think it counted as they were both sky high on kava, it was good enough for Lauren), and Dave using a selection from Dazza's quiver of state-of-the-art longboards to take on the big sets. I rode shotgun with the zodiac, which fortunately was not needed for any white-water rescues.

Kev was not a surfer, but seeing as he had been certain he was going to die flying into the monster barrel the day before, he deserved a treat too, so that afternoon I landed the two of us on the sand of a little atoll for some spear-fishing on its pristine coral reef. We came back with three big coral trout and a painted cray for dinner, all speared by Kev, who insisted on me taking a photo of him grinning over the catch, 5kg cray held triumphantly aloft. As far as I am aware, this picture still graces the coffee room wall at Channel 9.

Next day, Kev and I left Dave with both engaged couples on board *Between the Sheets* and flew out.

Chapter 14
Tess

I have known many surfers; some famous and most not. Young or old, they can all describe the best wave they ever surfed (some ad nauseam). I can only describe the start and the end of my speed blur, as the memory of the time in Tabua's massive tube has largely been blanked out by fear.

The hiss when the speed built up and the silence as the Mako rose on its hydroplane steps is still with me.

So is the almost vertical swoop down the face.

Then a blank. Try as I may, I cannot recall the critical bottom turn I had to have made.

I remember the tunnel. A shining emerald-green room with an elliptical window to the blue sky, way in the distance.

And in the middle of the window, my guardian angel.

Dad.

Hovering impossibly close in to the giant tube, in his little helicopter.

I was never going to make it out to him.

But somehow, I did.

Spat out in a squirt of spray as the tube closed over, I remember cross walking back on the board and flicking off, using the speed to kick the Mako high into the air. It was really all over by then, but I have always been a show pony, given half a chance.

Every daughter has one moment with her dad she treasures above all others. Seeing the tears in his eyes as he hugged me dockside is mine.

When in Rome, do as the Romans do. That night, we followed Fijian tradition and drank far too much kava to celebrate our Million Dollar Wave entry now in the can. Dazza and Lauren woke up next morning engaged, and Ben and I woke up on a beach towel, with me feeling like I had been ravaged all night by some Fijian chief. No wonder they like kava so much!

Dad and Kev could only stay one more day, but we made the most of it. By next morning, the swell had died down to a still-awesome fifteen feet, it was great that Ben and the others got to surf this magic place as well, which we did till our arms could paddle no more. Come afternoon, Dave and the newly engaged couple dived the fringing reef, as Dazza wanted to get a cowrie shell just the right size to grind down for an engagement ring for Lauren. My Fijian chief had need of sleep, and I obliged by spooning up beside him under the palms. Don't know whether it was the release of all the tension or the after-effect of the kava, but we both went out like lights in about ten seconds. Dad and Kev disappeared in the helicopter to go spear fishing and came back with some fresh coral trout and a big painted cray for the team's last night together, whilst the others returned with cowrie shells of varying sizes. We placed them on an ant's nest to be cleaned out overnight.

Ben selected a nice one to grind down to make an engagement ring for me as well; after all, we had been unofficially engaged for months, and he had now finished school!

The next morning it was sad to see Dad lift off, but Lauren and I were happy to go to the resort workshop and watch our respective fiancés grind the ends off our cowrie shell engagement rings. In my opinion, mine was every bit as valuable as any Portsea socialite's ring from Hardy Bros or Tiffany's. I hoped Mother would agree.

The next two weeks went by in a flash, and the time to go arrived all too soon. I looked out the window as our plane flew out and managed to pick out the little white dot of *Between the Sheets* continuing its travels on the blue expanse of the Pacific. Dazza and Lauren had found their answer to happiness; ours was destined to be far more complicated.

In the end, the wave of my life didn't win the million dollars, but it came close. I came second in a split decision, with two of the three Traks judges giving the nod to Hawaiian big wave legend Lance Harrison for a wave far better than mine. I reckon my judge must have just liked girls in bikinis!

I would have voted for Lance too. Like us, he had been experimenting with board shapes to increase his paddling speed, but being stronger, his board ended up shorter. He planned to paddle into one of the biggest waves in the world at Pe'hai on the north shore of Hawaii, the wave now known as Jaws. As if paddling into Jaws was not enough of an achievement in itself, he was working on a move that had never even been thought of, let alone attempted. Instead of levelling out from his bottom turn and driving to beat the break the way I did, he was going to keep his upwards momentum and 'bust the tube' as it came over. His board needed to develop speed, then transition to a high-speed vertical turn, and to this end, they had developed a mid-length pintail 'twinnie' instead of a gun board, this one with little straps to secure the feet during the death-defying manoeuvre they had planned.

Lance's wave was truly awesome; and in my opinion the most spectacular ride ever achieved or ever likely to be achieved; a monster wave with Lance smashing through the top curl instead of out the end of the barrel. Instead of the now tame flick-off of which I had been so proud, he became totally airborne and disappeared straight down the falls, still standing his board with arms extended in a swallow dive pose; somehow living to tell the tale and win himself the million bucks.

Channel 9 sent me to Hawaii as Mako Ambassador with our favourite cameraman Kev to film me handing over a jumbo-sized Million Dollar Wave cheque to a happily smiling Lance, who later described many harrowing wipe-outs that would have drowned anyone else before they got it right. I didn't feel so bad losing to the best big wave surfer ever; it was fantastic to meet him and also hear him admit he had been every bit as scared as I was!

Lance also seemed happy to meet me and offered a number of comments:

"You surfing Tabua in that blue bikini was the second sexiest sight I have ever seen. Now I have *two* posters of you up in my pool room."

"I suppose you realise you would have lost the top and possibly the bottom as well had you wiped out?"

"If I was one of the judges, it would have been a tie for the million bucks."

You can't get mad at a guy like Lance. I just told him *The Girl in the Shower* was my twin sister and left it at that.

I did, however, manage to bring home a hundred grand, this being what Lance paid the Mako Surf Company for one of our gun boards and the right to use variations of the hull and fin designs. That only left us with the board I had ridden for filming, as we had given the number two board to Dazza and Lauren as an advance wedding gift, along with a suitably wrapped bunch of dried kava, "not to be opened until the big day." Lance and some of his Hawaiian mates were starting to experiment with tow-in surfing on big waves using modified jet skis, and he wanted to look closer at the hydroplane steps and see if our winged fin could be developed into a full hydrofoil. History was later to prove that hydrofoils worked on both surf boards and the yet-to-be-invented stand up paddle boards, making hydroplane steps unnecessary; so sadly, our Mako gun board with its hydroplane hull never made it into mass production. Instead, it ended up relegated to the wall of the Torquay Surf Museum, where it remains to this day.

In any event, missing out on the million-dollar prize didn't matter. My wave ended up making us much more than that.

By the time we arrived back in Oz, my wave appeared as a panorama of three back-lit billboards across the front of every Surf Concepts outlet in the world, with the film footage looped on TV monitors inside in their showrooms. Dave and Ben had already started talking to Chinese factories about going mass market with an extended clothing and wet-suit range plus entry-level Mako surf boards and boogie boards, whilst Dad was having a fine old time designing fierce mako shark graphics for them. Come Christmas, I reckon a Mako boogie board under the tree was going to scare Santa straight back up the chimney!

Publicity was roaring along. In addition to headlining the winner's announcement, Traks produced the second (and thankfully last) centrefold of my career. This time of the Tabua wave, which was subsequently published as yet another poster entitled 'The Girl in the Blue Bikini'. It never achieved anywhere near the sales of the first one, but I was gratified to learn that whilst my first centrefold had ended up displayed in sometimes questionable areas, the second ended up in many girls' bedrooms and studies, so hopefully I had proved girls could surf big waves, instead of just lying around on the beach looking beautiful and watching their boyfriends in action. In addition to featuring them on Wide World of Sports as per our contract, Channel 9 had syndicated both waves internationally. Mine received enormous additional exposure on normal news programs just because I was a girl; all in all, millions of dollars' worth of free advertising.

Best of all, I came home flashing my new cowrie engagement ring. Dad convinced Mother that Ben and I were serious, and we booked the little church in Lorne for a June wedding. I was even able to tell Mother that the way things were looking, I was going to marry Ben for his money. Who needs a merchant wanker from Portsea when your husband shapes the best surf boards in the world?

With a wedding in the wings, our story should have ended right there, with...*and they all lived happily ever after*.

But it didn't.

Chapter 15
Jack

As I saw it, the Million Dollar Wave was not a quest for the million dollars at all; it was therapy for Tess to get back her self-respect.

And it had worked.

She no longer looked scared in public.

The smile was back.

The laughter in those blue, blue eyes was back.

The love of life was back.

Best of all, Tess was back, flashing Ben's little cowrie shell on the third finger of her left hand.

Ariel was happy for her too, taking in her stride Tess's wish to have her wedding at the little weatherboard church overlooking Lorne Point instead of a grand society affair at St John's Toorak. With an enthusiasm only mothers of brides can muster, she ordered an enormous white marquee to be erected at our house on the cliff at Cinema Point. This involved a masterpiece of engineering and some death-defying excavation by Doc Russell, cutting a level into the hill with his backhoe suspended by winch and chain. The council never knew a thing, and Doc had yet another cliff-defying excavation to add to his legendary earth-moving achievements along the coast. I don't know what I was going to say if someone from the council ever walked down from the road sometime in the future and came upon our car park. Perhaps I could convince them it had been an ancient meteor strike?

Most weddings are happy events, and Tess's was no exception. The surfers and tradies of Lorne got on surprisingly well with the members of high society, probably due to the eighteen-gallon keg of free beer mixing well with the truckload of French champagne. Even the Lorne Clubbies behaved themselves, possibly because Meishai looked more like a bouncer than a groomsman in his tight black silk suit and possibly because the junior Lorne surf boat with Meishai as sweep had beaten Torquay at the Anglesea surf carnival the weekend before, for the first time in ten years. Meishai would have been useless as a bouncer anyway, as he spent the whole wedding holding hands with Tess's friend AJ and looking smitten.

There were two surprise presents to top off the occasion. Despite pleas from Ariel, the Culverton Thompsons had not been invited, but nonetheless a DVD of *Grease* arrived in the mail, signed only:

'Be Happy, Sandy. Danny'

Maybe Tommo had learned something from our little talk after all.

The second gift was an air mail parcel from 'Dazza and Lozza Dare', postmarked Tahiti. It contained twelve big cowrie shells with the ends ground off to make serviette rings, plus a large bunch of dried kava that had somehow evaded customs.

The Monday after the wedding, I went back to work.

I didn't know it then, but I had only three months of happiness left in my life.

Chapter 16
Jack

Just as well I made it back to work when I did, as the Mako creative had gone completely off the rails.

It was immediately evident that Melanie Wright-Smith, the expensive hot-shot Silas hired to stand in for me as creative director, was not working out. She had ignored the client-approved strategy I had left in place and completely changed the creative, apparently against the advice of the account service team. Melanie had overruled the '*Built for Le Mans. Built for you*' positioning we had planned for the worldwide rollout and was pushing a supposedly 'award potential' outdoor campaign that was clever, but way off strategy:

Prey

Mako. The Prey Hunts You.

24 sheet billboards with this banner were to feature a girl in a silver cocktail dress perched on a stool at a nightclub, gazing longingly across the bar at a man with a tall frosted glass of Peroni, beside which on the bar top lay a silver Mako Sports key ring.

Melanie had supported her change of direction with concept research from Ad Ratings International (ARI), but frankly I didn't believe the results. The 'like' score was amazingly high, even with women, and my gut feel was that the numbers were way overstated. In any event, it was far too early to use image advertising for Mako, which was still to establish itself as a serious performance sports car. I called an immediate halt to production of the outdoor billboards, fortunately just before the twenty-four sheet posters were printed. That left the problem of Melanie herself. It was clear she had lost the confidence of all the account service and production guys with her 'my way or the highway' style of management, combined with too many long lunches and missed meetings. There was nowhere else to go; as my first task back at work, I was going to have to fire her.

I have never claimed to be a good businessman, as I have no courage when it comes to firing anyone, an action I had mostly managed to avoid by hiring good people in the first place. I agonised for a week over 'doing the deed', but in the end had to confront it.

It did not go well.

I gritted my teeth, called Melanie into my office, and laid it on the line. The exit interview was an unusual one. Melanie justified the long lunches/no returns by claiming she was doing the Agency a service by having an affair with the Mako Automotive Marketing Manager and thus 'helping cement the client relationship'. I have never been a saint myself and am all for consenting young adults going for it provided nobody gets hurt, but Melanie had lost the confidence of the entire account group, and her reason for the long lunches did nothing to change my mind.

Nor did the flood of tears.

Nor did the offer of sex.

"There is nothing wrong with cementing relationships, Jack. I know your wife is a looker, but I'm twenty years younger. How'd you like to live a little?"

Fortunately, I had the presence of mind to hit the intercom and summon Anna Cheng, Melanie's only real friend in the Agency, to 'take Mel home' before things got out of hand.

Which nearly happened, as Melanie had already undone the top button of her shirt and had started on the second by the time Anna knocked on the door. I ducked around Melanie to open it, with some relief.

Now confronted by both of them, I said how sorry I was that Melanie hadn't worked out. Although true, I don't think either of them believed me.

I had just dodged a bullet.

Or so I thought.

I went and had a couple of double whiskeys with Silas, and we resolved we would stick to approved practice and never do an exit interview again without another person being present. I also took issue with Silas over letting the outdoor get as far out of control as it had. He pontificated, justifying his decision by quoting the strong research results; but I questioned those, as I just didn't believe the extraordinarily high purchase intention rating and upon close examination the research design looked distinctly flaky. Group discussions do not typically quote purchase intention percentages as with quantitative research; they were usually only done to highlight negatives or positives in positioning or communication. Something was off, and I resolved to raise my concerns with both Anna Cheng and Harriet Jones of ARI.

We agreed to disagree, but although Silas had a dicey meeting ahead to mollify the outdoor contractor, at least Mako was back on strategy.

Our campaign came together exactly as planned with US Marketing. Ford managed to secure ex F1 World Champion Jorge Marantz to drive the Mako at Le Mans, and as covered in his contract, he was signed as star presenter in our launch TV commercial:

60 Second Tvc – Mako

Voice Over: 'This is the Ford Mako. Built for Le Mans.'

Opening Shot: *Mako race car with Le Mans number 3 and sponsor livery.*

Super: **Built for Le Mans**

Cut to Jorge powering around the Le Mans circuit at Pays de la Loire in the racing Mako with its engine screaming as only a flat-out V12 can.

Super: **Built for you.**

Cut to rush hour in Trafalgar Square, London. The racing livery Mako has morphed to the production version, Jorge's race suit has morphed to a white tuxedo, and the screaming exhaust note has morphed to a purr. Supermodel Jennifer Bryce graces the passenger seat wearing her famous little black dress.

Cut to our Bond-like couple pulling up at foyer of the London Savoy, attended by a uniformed Doorman, who opens the passenger door. Jorge gets out of the driver's side, walks around the front of the car to scoop up Jennifer, and heads

into the restaurant with his arm around her waist. A uniformed porter drives the
Mako off to park it.

SFX: Production car exhaust note.

Cut to three-quarter shot of race and production cars side by side.

End frame: *Silver Mako key ring*

End Super: **Built for Le Mans. Built for you.**

Best of all, Ariel and I scored a European holiday together following the Mako TV production around, even ending up having a real dinner at the Savoy together with Jorge, Jennifer, and the film crew.

A simple 'presenter' commercial like this was never going to win awards, but it sold a helluva lot of Makos.

So many that out of the blue, Ford appointed us Principal Agency for the worldwide launch of their new city car, more than doubling the size of their account.

We were becoming seriously rich.

I took Ariel on a two-week Kimberley cruise on the *True North* to dive with whale sharks, swim in island lagoons, and eat five-star dinners.

Silas stayed in Melbourne and started hiring the new account group.

But that's not all he did.

Chapter 17
Silas

I was very angry at my meeting with Jack, but hid it well. Maybe he was a good Creative Director, but how dare he question my decisions? S&J had always been *my* Agency, and although I had to admit it turned out Jack was right in sticking to strategy on Mako, the Agency had grown big enough to function without him. I could now afford to hire top creative talent and no longer needed or wanted his 'gentleman larrikin' presence or, more importantly, him having a half share in the business. Something had emerged from our exit meeting on Melanie that warranted further examination.

The research results.

I realised that for the past year, we had exclusively used the same research company originally introduced by Anna Cheng to support all our creative concepts, and on thinking it over, it was unbelievable that we were always given the exact results we wanted. We pride ourselves that our creative is good, but was it that good? I decided to run a company check on Ad Ratings International and unearthed something very interesting.

Very, very interesting.

ARI was registered in the State of Victoria, with only two directors. The first was Harriet Jones, the ARI executive who had always presented their group discussion results. The second was Anna Cheng.

I checked the total billings for ARI.

$253,759.32.

Then I called Anna into my office.

"Hi, Anna; we have just had a client query on the Mako research. They want to expand on it for a trade article and would like to hear the actual master tape of the group discussions and maybe interview a couple of the respondents," I said.

"Don't have them, I'm afraid," she replied. "I asked ARI to destroy the tape once they had lodged their report, and they don't keep respondent details."

"Did this happen with all fifteen of the creative research reports ARI has done for us?"

"Yes. No point in keeping them."

"Anna," I said. "No legitimate research company ever does that. There never were any group discussions, were there? You and Harriet concocted the reports yourselves. And in the past two years, you have defrauded this Agency and its clients of more than a quarter of a million dollars."

She knew she was caught and didn't even try to get out of it.

"What are you going to do?" she asked.

"There are two things I *can* do. The choice is yours."

"The first is I can call the fraud squad, have you both thrown in jail, and retrieve all the money I can."

"The second is that you and Harriet get to keep it all, plus leave the Agency with a further fifty thousand dollars. Would you like me to tell you how?"

"Yes," she replied.

"As you know, Jack is always joking around and flirting with his favourites. I need you to push that one step further. Friday night is the Agency party to celebrate winning the new Ford city car account. You need to set up a believable sexual assault allegation against Jack, bad enough for us to call the cops. If you can make a sexual assault charge stick, the Agency will pay you fifty thousand dollars compensation when you leave, as you will obviously have to do. And I mean leave the country."

She didn't hesitate for a second.

"Okay, I'll do it."

In the event, it was ridiculously easy.

Chapter 18
Anna

What with the promotions and new hires that had been going on, by Friday, the whole Agency was in festive mood for the big celebration party.

I made two important preparations. The first was to engineer an obvious hickey on my neck that morning, compliments of my puzzled boyfriend, then cover it with Clinique skin-tone foundation. The second was to break out my thin strap handkerchief dress for the party and lose the bra.

The boardroom kitchen was where we always set up the bar, and that was where we would lay the trap.

I waited until the party was in full swing, with music pumping and drinks flowing. Silas made sure Jack was in the board room, where he was waxing lyrical to a couple of entranced petrol heads about his new F1 mate Jorge Marantz, Mako test times for the coming Le Mans 24-hour race, and the real-life beauty of Jennifer Bryce in her little black dress.

I hung out in the kitchen pouring drinks, waiting until I was alone.

Then it was time to rub off the makeup from my neck with hot water to reveal the hickey and spring the trap.

"Hey Jack, I can't budge this champagne cork," I called into the boardroom. "Can I borrow those muscles of yours for a minute?"

In he came, like a lamb to the slaughter. He took the bottle and twisted off the cork with a 'pop.'

As he turned 'round I slapped him hard in the face, ripped off the shoulder strap, and screamed my head off.

"No!"

"Don't!"

"Please don't!"

People came from everywhere.

Jack stood there frozen, with a nice red slap mark developing on his cheek. Nobody knew what to do.

Well, someone did. Silas slipped straight into his office and called the cops.

The St Kilda Road police patrol took less than five minutes to arrive.

I went right on crying.

"He tried to rape me," I blurted between sobs.

Jack seemed to be in shock, as you might expect from a rapist who had just been caught out.

"No, it wasn't like that," was all he could manage. That wasn't going to get him out of a trip to the police station.

Once they had taken down everyone's names, a cop led Jack to the lift in front of a horrified staff, while a female cop escorted me away.

Back at the St Kilda Road police station, I spun a harrowing description of the whole sordid incident, posed for photographs of my neck bruise and under detailed questioning managed to impart the clincher that I had set up: that to my knowledge, Jack had also indecently assaulted both ARI research exec Harriet Jones and ex-employee Melanie Wright-Smith; the latter only two months previous. When you play the sexual assault card, the more accusers the merrier!

They took Jack's no-doubt-perplexed statement in an adjoining interview room, and then the nice female cop drove me back to my flat. I don't know what happened to Jack, but I reckon I knew what was going to happen. There was no way he was not about to be charged.

As soon as I got home, I rang Silas, who had wound up the party and was awaiting my call.

Twenty minutes later the doorbell rang, and there stood Silas.

I told him everything that had transpired at the police station, and he seemed pleased. But that was not the end of the night.

Not by a long shot.

"Everything's going according to plan," he said. "But you will be interviewed by the media shortly. I've decided you need work on some genuine outrage."

"Take off your clothes."

I did everything he wanted.

Chapter 19
Jack

Back at the St Kilda Road Police Station, I was ushered into a bare, grey-painted interrogation room by the two uniformed cops, sat down at a matching grey metal table on a small metal chair, and left to cool my heels for two hours.

Finally, a male and a female cop came in, each carrying their own chairs. Obviously, my interrogators.

They sat down opposite, and the female cop turned on a small tape recorder:

"Interview commenced 7.38 pm on Friday October 4th, 1993. Sergeant Mary O'Halloran, Constable Clive Trudgett, and Mr Jack Johnson present."

I was then Mirandized just like in the movies:

"You have the right to remain silent. Anything you say can and will be used against you in a court of law. You have the right to speak to an attorney, and to have an attorney present during any questioning."

I never even thought to demand a lawyer be present. I was innocent, for Christ's sake!

After an hour's good cop/bad cop questioning I signed a statement denying Anna's allegations, but I could tell neither of my interrogators believed me.

Once they finally let me go, I rang Silas on his mobile, but he was not picking up.

That left getting a taxi home to break the news to Ariel. We had been through many ups and downs during our marriage, but nothing remotely like this. I was still struggling with the reality of it all, but Ariel was far more logical.

"She's after money," was her immediate response. "We're going to have to pay. It's no use trying to defend yourself. You can't afford even a 'he said/she said' impasse; if even a whiff of this gets out, it will ruin your career."

"As it is, I don't see how you can turn up for work tomorrow. You'll have to get Silas to hold the fort until you are officially exonerated."

It was midnight before I finally got onto Silas.

"After what just happened, I won't come in tomorrow," I said. "You will have to announce that this is an attempted extortion by Anna and that I am seeking legal advice."

The response from Silas absolutely floored me: "I don't know how any of us can work with you after what you just did, tomorrow or any other time. My job is to protect the Agency and its staff; as far as I'm concerned, you're on your own."

"What? You can't believe I actually did what she said?"

"I believe my own eyes and my own ears,'" was the astonishing reply. Then he hung up.

It got worse.

The next day, I got a call on my mobile from Tom Donovan, news editor at *The Sun*. Although Silas acted as Media Director for S&J, Tom and I had a good relationship dating from interviews on the Million Dollar Wave and our Le Mans campaign.

He got straight to the point:

"Jack, we've just received a media release emailed by Silas Silver, accusing you of sexual assault. What on earth happened over at S&J last night?"

"What did the email say?"

"I'll read it out. It's pretty short:

'S&J Advertising would like to extend the sympathy of everyone at the Agency following last night's sexual assault of Research Director Anna Cheng. We will be giving Anna every support. Both Anna and S&J Creative Director Jack Johnson will be taking leave of absence until the police investigation has been completed.'

"That's it."

I couldn't believe it. Far from supporting me and working to contain the damage to my reputation, Silas was hanging me out to dry.

"It's total bullshit, Tom. Anna Cheng is trying to set me up on a false sexual assault charge. No doubt she is going after compensation."

"I'm sorry, Jack, but given your high profile, this case is going to be big news, whatever the outcome. We always publish without bias, but the women's magazines are going to tear you apart. For what it's worth I believe you, but if I were you, I'd lawyer up right away. This is going to get nasty."

"I had no idea Silas was going to make any disclosure to the press on this scam, which should have stayed internal. I'll get onto a lawyer right away. I am completely innocent, but I know there have been cases in England and America where guy's careers have been destroyed, even when there were open findings. I can't believe this is happening to me."

"Thanks for letting me know, Tom. I'll be sure that The Sun gets first look at any press announcements we make."

"Good luck, Jack; I think you're going to need it."

First thing Monday morning, I called Rachel Cohen, S&J's solicitor.

Rach and I had always had a good relationship, and Ariel advised if I were to be charged, it wouldn't do any harm to be defended by a woman.

Rachel cut me off straight away.

"I'm sorry Jack," she said. "I can't act for you, as there would be a conflict of interest. We have been retained by S&J to defend the Agency position and possibly also issue civil proceedings against you personally."

She couldn't help herself, adding: "Did you do it?"

"Of course I bloody well didn't," I said and hung up.

I needed to find a new lawyer.

It was Ariel who recommended Kate Lee act for me. Kate was a young Melbourne barrister had built a good reputation winning some well-publicised cases in the fashion industry, two involving sexual harassment. We made an appointment for later that day.

I had only just hung up when the landline went crazy with phone calls from the press: three dailies and three women's magazines.

As advised by Kate, I answered each one with a "No comment."

Next day came a call came I had to respond to. It was from the St Kilda Police, requesting I present myself at the St Kilda Road police station immediately.

I took Kate with me.

Anna had obviously been convincing, as the thinly veiled hostility was still there, and the same interrogation team was waiting.

We were ushered into the same bare room, and I was sat down at the same grey steel table, with the two cops opposite. Mary O'Halloran turned on the tape recorder as before.

"Interview commenced 2.30 pm on Tuesday, April 6, 1993."

"Sergeant Mary O'Halloran, Constable Clive Trudgett, Mr Jack Johnson and solicitor Ms Kate Lee present."

"Mr Johnson, do you have anything further you wish to say following our interview last night?"

"On the advice of my attorney, I have nothing to add," I replied.

"We are obliged to ask you the following questions," Sergeant O'Halloran responded. "On July 2, 1993, during the Ad Ratings International lunch in The Willows restaurant, did you uninvited put your hand up the dress of Harriet Jones sitting next to you and attempt digital penetration?"

"No, I did not."

"On the advice of my attorney, I have nothing further to say."

"On September 5, 1993, at the Silver & Johnson advertising Agency premises, did you uninvited approach from behind and fondle both breasts of Melanie Wright-Smith and as a result of her refusing your advances, did you demand her dismissal from the Agency that same day?"

"No, I did not."

"On the advice of my attorney, I have nothing further to say."

"On October 4, 1993, at the Silver & Johnson Agency premises, did you uninvited approach from behind and fondle both breasts of Anna Cheng whilst biting her on the neck and pressing your erect penis against her rear?"

"No, I did not."

"On the advice of my attorney, I have nothing further to say."

"My client is innocent of each of these allegations. We have nothing further to add," said Kate.

"Interview terminated 4 pm, October 4, 1993."

Kate explained our 'no comment' strategy in the cab.

"The reason we must always state 'no comment' is that as you have done nothing wrong, there is nothing you need say. The onus is upon the prosecution to prove you guilty, not upon you to prove your innocence."

Maybe so, but this was far worse than I had imagined. There were now three women making sexual assault claims against me, not just one. I was escorted out of the police station and drove myself home. Ariel had already changed both our Melbourne and Lorne phones to silent numbers, but that didn't stop the press; by the end of the day, we had shut the front door on two reporters, and it was clear that whatever the decision of the police to prosecute, I was to endure trial by media.

Monday's meeting with Kate Lee was short, as apart from confirming my innocence and relating everything that had happened at the Agency party, I could not supply any concrete information on the other two charges, over and above what the police had outlined, basically because they had never happened. Kate took down everything on a yellow legal pad and then offered her preliminary advice:

"The critical thing is whether the police are going to prefer charges. They will undoubtedly take detailed statements from all three girls making the accusations before they act further, but we should assume you will be charged on at least one criminal count of sexual assault."

"Even if you are not charged with a criminal offence, we have to assume both you and the Agency will be facing compensation claims from both Anna Cheng and Melanie Wright-Smith, as they both left employment as a result of events and will no doubt mount cases for loss of income, almost certainly including punitive claims for psychological damage. As you have said, money is what this is all about."

"Either way, you must not return to the Agency until the legal position becomes clear. We have to avoid any suggestion of you attempting to influence witnesses, plus it is also clear you don't have the support of Silas Silver, who we have to assume is hostile to our case."

"If the police are going to charge you, it will not be long, so we'll just have to wait."

"I'm so sorry you are going through all this. When a man is innocent of this sort of charge, it is a horrible situation for a family to face. You need to prepare for some very bad fallout, not least from the media; so as far as they are concerned, keep responding with simply 'the accusations are untrue, and I wish to make no further comment on legal advice', whatever the temptation to further protest your innocence."

The main thing I gained from meeting with Kate was that I could read in her face that she believed me. After experiencing the grilling by the police and media, my confidence had been badly shaken, and knowing that an experienced litigator was fully on side and not just mounting my defence for a fee meant a lot. There was a cafeteria on the ground floor of Kate's building, so I took Ariel in for a coffee.

Far from being shattered as I had feared, it turned out that she was far tougher than I thought, and quickly brought me down to earth.

"It's no use planning our defence until we know if you are to face court," she said. "We need to go straight down to Lorne and tell Tess. She must hear it from us rather than read it in tomorrow's papers."

We headed for the coast as soon as we had finished our coffees, not even stopping to go home and pack.

Tess was over at Torquay with Ben when we arrived, so breaking the news to them had to wait until their return later in the afternoon. In the meantime, we went over to Dave's and filled them in. Dave looked bemused, but Jules burst into tears and wouldn't stop crying. This was going to affect our friends too.

When Tess and Ben arrived back at Cinema Point, Tess took one look at us and knew something was up.

"Why are you down on a week day?" she asked. "Is something wrong?"

Away I went, leaving nothing out. I had to finish with: "I'm afraid this is going to affect you as well."

"We have already seen what the media can do, and this is going to be much worse than anything we faced last time round. None of us is going to escape attention."

Just like Ariel, Tess surprised me. She didn't tear up like I expected; she just got mad.

"Don't worry about me," was her response. "Those fucking, greedy bitches. We are going to beat this, because truth is on our side."

If only it was that easy, I thought, which was confirmed the very next morning. There was page one coverage in two Melbourne newspapers. Not only that; whilst Ariel and I had been driving to Lorne, Anna and the others had been busy at the Agency, giving a full-on media briefing.

My trial by media had begun, and I had already lost. Tom Donovan had promised fair reporting by *The Sun*, but even their article following the S&J media release was damning:

WAR HERO DENIES SEX ALLEGATIONS

Vietnam war hero Jack Johnson has denied workplace sexual assault allegations from three Melbourne women, two employees from Melbourne ad Agency Silver & Johnson and the third the Research Director from Ad Ratings International, a strategic partner of the Agency.

Allegations from the Agency staff follow the same pattern, with both women accusing Mr Johnson of attacking from behind and fondling their breasts. Anna Cheng, attractive twenty-five-year-old research director of the Agency, issued the following statement:

"Jack Johnson had been forcing kisses on me for some time. Then last Friday, he attacked me while I was alone serving at the bar in the board room kitchen. He came up from behind and bit my neck, running both hands round my body and down the front of my dress, fondling my breasts. I slapped his face, screamed and ran for it. Mr Silver called the police."

Ex-employee Melanie Wright-Smith had a similar story, with the alleged offence occurring only ten days previously in Mr Johnson's office.

"Jack Johnson had called me into his office to discuss a contact report. He closed the door, and while I was putting the report on the desk, he attacked me from behind, fondling my breasts," she said. "Fortunately, he had not locked the door, and Anna Cheng came in before he could go further. I was fired later that day," she said.

Ad Ratings International Director Harriet Jones alleges Jack Johnson had sexually assaulted her at The Willows restaurant, where she was having lunch with both S&J directors and S&J Account Executive Bill Robinson.

"I had to come forward after hearing what had happened to the other two girls," she said. "Back in July, Jack Johnson was sitting beside me at a client lunch and assaulted me, putting his hand up my dress on my bare thigh, then moving higher, attempting to burrow up under my pants. I should have said something but just pushed his hand away, as I did not want to jeopardise our company's relationship with an important client."

Police have interviewed witnesses and expect to lay charges.

The other daily reported the same announcements, but went one stage further and came out with a page one editorial, tying the allegations against me to an attack on the advertising industry itself, calling for an end to 'overpaid ad men behaving badly'.

With this editorial, I even managed to edge a gangland murder in Carlton off the front page – obviously, sex sells more papers! If the dailies were going this far, the women's magazines were going to have a field day.

They were not the only ones.

Mid-afternoon, there was a knock on the door, and there stood a Channel 7 TV reporter with mike in hand and cameraman beside her. They had tracked me to Lorne.

"I'm sure you know why we are here, Mr Johnson. Care to comment on today's papers?"

"My only comment is that I did not do any of those things. I have no further statement to make, on legal advice. Goodbye."

I shut the door.

"Well, that'll be on tonight's news," I said.

Ariel took charge.

"Tess, you and Ben are going to have to disappear over to Dave's. Now that they have tracked Dad to the beach house, the media will be queuing up here."

"We'll go back to Melbourne, which should draw their fire."

Ah, my air force wife! That must have come straight from one of my letters from 'Nam, but she had a point.

We hugged Tess and left for Melbourne.

The mind plays funny tricks. Driving over the West Gate Bridge into the city haze, I felt the same as I did flying into the smoke over the Battle of Long Tan, this time with Ariel as my door gunner and Kate as my mechanic. I started whistling, "Last Train Out of Sydney."

Apart from easily deflected media inquiries (now including two radio stations), there was a two-week lull in which the only thing of significance was a big article in Australia's leading women's magazine with photographs of everyone (Anna showing her neck hickey), boosted by commentary from an internationally famous women's rights activist, demanding I be made an example of: "To protect the innocents and encourage other abused women to come forward." She was also interviewed by the shock jocks of Melbourne and

Sydney's largest radio stations, so I was now a pariah across a good chunk of the country.

The police had been busy as well, and at the two-week mark they came to the door, demanding I surrender my passport. I was also served with a notice from the Director of Public Prosecutions (DPP) requiring I present myself at a committal hearing. The trial process was underway.

A committal hearing was set before a Melbourne magistrate only four weeks later; so we didn't have long to prepare a defence.

Under the rules of discovery, Kate obtained full disclosure of each accusatory deposition. She asked me to read each statement carefully, and then write down everything I could think of pertaining to the dates in question; particularly any weaknesses I could see in the girls' claims.

Writing everything down was actually quite therapeutic.

Apart from claiming the whole thing was a money scam by all three women, I could only put forward theories.

The first was that Melanie Wright-Smith carried an obvious grudge from me firing her, which added 'revenge' as motivation in addition to money. Her statement of Anna fortuitously 'coming in as I attacked her' looked weak, as surely if I had intended to make a sexual advance on Melanie, I would have just pressed the lock button on my door when I closed it to make sure we were not disturbed. I had always insisted staff knock when coming into my office, so the claim of Anna coming straight in could also be challenged. The outside offices were open plan, so nobody could have seen her walk in unannounced, as claimed.

The second theory came after thinking it all through. I decided that the weakest link in the prosecution's case was Harriet Jones. In going over her involvement with the Mako campaign, I remembered telling Anna that I seriously questioned ARI's research results, not only on Mako but other creative research as well. I was now convinced ARI had fudged results to give us what we wanted without proper process, and if Anna had informed Harriet of that, she would be aware that ARI would also certainly have been fired.

A lot of dollars were at stake there, maybe enough for Harriet to make a pre-emptive strike (there I go again with another military analogy) against me by playing the sexual assault card.

As far as Anna Cheng was concerned, it was the incident itself that surely didn't hold water. I had read a bit and heard a bit about sexual predators misusing their power to have their way with women, and I reckoned one thing in common was they all sought to have their gratification yet get away with it. Me supposedly attacking Anna at a party with twenty people in the next room just didn't make sense. Why would even a true sexual predator be that stupid?

I wrote all this down and took my notes along to the next meeting with Kate. She read them through and looked quite pleased with the defence that was starting to take shape. Or maybe she just wanted to cheer me up. Anyway, apart from my insights, Kate had come up with another fact that could be used to shake the prosecution's case: In addition to the victim videotape made on the night of the party, the police had supplied their photograph of Anna's neck hickey as part of the discovery process. The photo was a high-resolution colour shot that showed three upper and two lower teeth marks coming out in well-defined bruises. The date and time the photo was taken was recorded on the lower margin; forty-nine minutes after the alleged attack, to be precise. Kate had obtained a medical opinion that bruising to that extent could not develop nearly that quickly, and that the bruise pictured was more than eight hours old.

We resolved to take further action on two fronts.

The first was, I was to have my dentist make an impression of my teeth. We wanted to compare my bite pattern against the one on the police photograph. The second was, Kate and I were to go into the Agency and secure the files of all the ARI research projects I had kept in my filing cabinet. We were going to have an independent forensic assessment done and were confident they could be shown to have been fudged.

I acted on both the next day.

The morning trip to the dentist was easy. He even found I needed two fillings, which he duly did after the bite impression had been taken. We were to get the model of my teeth back within a week.

The afternoon was less successful. At three o'clock, Kate and I walked into S&J together and headed for my office.

A red-faced Silas emerged from his office next door and challenged us, saying: "What are you doing here? I thought we agreed you were not to come in again." He moved to block us from my office door.

"I am joint owner of this Agency," I replied. "And I will come in whenever I bloody well like."

"Get out of my fucking way."

I read the desirability of adding an assault charge to the list conflicting with physical cowardice cross Silas's face. Cowardice won out, and he stood aside.

Kate and I went into my office and I unlocked my filing cabinet, but someone had been there before us. All the ARI research reports were gone. Nothing else had been touched.

Back to Silas, still hovering in the passage.

"Who has been rifling through my office?" I asked. "And where is my laptop?"

A flustered Silas replied, "The police have your laptop, and I know nothing about any files."

"I didn't mention files. How did you know that's what I meant?"

Silas reddened and said he was not obliged to answer questions from me.

Kate gave a small shake of the head that meant that as my lawyer, she would definitely not approve of me taking a swing at him, so that left only one thing to do before we left. Not directly related to the case, but it needed to be done. I walked into the passage and buttonholed Bill Robinson, who was on his way to the coffee machine for his afternoon caffeine fix.

"Robbo, can you please get everyone into the conference room? I have something to say to you all," I said.

"No worries, Jack," Bill replied and bolted off to round everyone up, which seemed to take only seconds.

I stood at the head of the familiar boardroom table and looked sadly over the sea of faces in front of me; most of whom I had hired and many I had worked with directly for years.

I started:

"It's nice to see everyone again."

"You will have all read the papers, heard the radio, and seen the TV, so I imagine everyone here will know of the sexual assault charges made against me by Anna Cheng, Melanie Wright-Smith, and Harriet Jones. I wanted to look you all in the eye and tell you these charges are complete bullshit. I did not do any of these things, and I intend to prove that with my day in court. I will not be returning to the Agency until that is done, but I look forward to seeing you all again then. Meanwhile, thank you for your good work while I have been away. I know you will carry on fine without me and wish you the best of luck. Some of you have had the kindness to ring me with your support, and I apologise for being short on the phone. The reason is that my lawyer, Kate here, advises me I cannot discuss the case with anyone who was at the Agency party, as any of you could be called as a witness in court, so I'm using today's meeting to thank you all as a group. Thanks for listening, and I look forward to coming back and hearing your news as soon as I have cleared my name."

Someone started clapping, then the whole room joined in, bringing tears to my eyes. It seemed Kate and my family were not the only ones who believed in me.

I waved my workmates goodbye and walked out with head held high and Kate at my side.

"As your lawyer, I have to say that was not the best idea," said Kate.

"But I wish the magistrate had seen it."

"I'm glad I saw it, too. You were just found innocent by a jury of thirty people, and all I've got to do is convince one magistrate. We're going to win this."

She sounded very like our Anglesea footy coach all those years ago. I had always believed him, so now it was time to believe her. Trouble was, the Anglesea Roos usually lost!

I suppose the day had given me confidence, because that night I took Ariel to the Toorak Tennis Club for dinner.

Big mistake.

Every head turned as we walked into the members' dining room. You could cut the air with a knife; and not one of our friends greeted us or came over to our table. This was bad enough, but it quickly got worse. Dining at the next table with half the ladies' A-pennant team was Lucinda Everton-Rice, the lady captain. Lucinda had never had much time for Ariel. Something to do with never being invited to the sponsor tent at the Melbourne Cup, partly because she never talked about anything else but the rights of women in tennis and was thus incredibly boring, but mainly because Ariel just didn't like her. This was Lucinda's chance to not only establish herself as a champion of the sisterhood but also put Ariel in her place, once and for all. She got up, marched over to our table, and threw her drink in my face. I stood up and uttered the last words I would ever speak in the Toorak Tennis Club:

"You. Stupid. Ignorant. Fucking. Bitch. Come on, Ariel, we're leaving."

You could have heard a pin drop as we walked out.

Ariel surprised me yet again. No tears, just a quiet rage behind those sapphire eyes.

"We are resigning from that bloody club," she said. "Even when you are cleared, I want nothing more to do with any of them."

"They'll probably kick me out anyway," I replied.

And they did. The letter only took four days.

It didn't stop there. In an effort to cheer Ariel up, I rang to book the usual table at our favourite South Yara restaurant, and was told it was not available that night. Or any other night.

Sex was out. We were both wound up like springs, and each had too much respect for the other to fake it.

"We have to get out of Melbourne," I told her. "You shouldn't be around me, and neither should Tess. You go to Chartwell, and I'll go bush with Dave after I square things away with Kate."

After a goodbye kiss that seemed like forever, Ariel rang her parents and left for the family farm, while I tried to focus on my defence for the upcoming committal hearing.

I never did make it to the mountains with Dave, as preparations for my defence had to take precedence.

I met Kate for our scheduled meeting the next week. She had been busy delving into Ad Research International and was quite excited by what she had found:

"After we left the Agency last week, I got to thinking," she said, (Rather proudly, I thought).

"I've been through a lot of trials and pride myself on being able to read people's faces. Back at S&J I thought Silas Silver looked more than just concerned for the Agency's reputation. When you accused him of taking the research files, he looked positively scared. Got me to wondering if he has an undeclared financial interest in ARI or was complicit in fudging the results for the Agency's benefit, so I checked their company details."

"Look what I found."

She placed a printout of the ASIC company listing for ARI. There were only two directors: Harriet Jones and Anna Cheng.

"This could be the link we've been after. We still need one of the original ARI reports so we can challenge it forensically. Although the Agency copies are gone and Cheng and Jones have undoubtedly shredded everything at ARI, all the clients must still have their copies."

The client that owed me the most was Mako Automotive. Also, they had the advantage of being US-based and hopefully had not yet caught up with the local media coverage. I didn't have my passport anymore, but Tess did, and she had already met Mike McFarlane, Ford International Marketing Director, in Hawaii. That night, I rang both Tess in Lorne and Alan Perkins, now heading up the Mako design team in Detroit.

First call:

"Tess, can you pack your bags and come up to Melbourne? I need you to fly to Detroit to get hold of a research report that is vital for my defence."

Second call:

"G'day. Is that the filthy rich Alan Perkins?"

It was.

"Hi thar, good buddy."

These days he even *laughed* with an American accent!

"Al, have you heard what's going down over here?"

He hadn't, so I filled him in with a quick version. He was horrified and, like any man would be, highly sympathetic.

"Jesus Christ! What can I do?" was his immediate response, his pseudo accent gone.

"Tess is coming over, leaving tomorrow. I need you to look after her and if humanly possible, get her an audience with Winchester King, or if not him, Mike McFarlane in international marketing. She has already met Mike in Hawaii last year. We need to get hold of the ARI research doco on Mako. To be usable as evidence, it must be the original, not a photocopy."

Alan promised he would do what he could, and I promised I would email Tess's flight details as soon as I had them.

Chapter 20
Tess

I put down the phone and turned to my brand-new husband.

"Dad needs me to go to the US to help get evidence for his court case. I have to leave tomorrow, but should only be gone four or five days."

"Surf Concepts approved the new tee shirt and beach dress designs yesterday, so all you need to do while I'm away is stitch up the ex-factory prices and delivery schedule and then forward the electronic art files for production."

"No worries, Tess. You know what I think? I think it's glassy on the Point today, and we should get the boards out. I want to propose again before you go."

A girl never tires of this sort of stuff, so down went the paint brushes and on went the wet suit.

A bad thing happened out there, one that really brought home to me the trouble Dad was in.

Being a Sunday, Lorne Point was crowded. Fortunately, there were only a few mals out the back, but a heap of short board heroes congregated closer in, blocking our run. We tried a couple of rides, navigating through the mob of shorties with our 'first on the wave' right of way, but still leaving them plenty of waves. Even so, I managed to piss off Dirty Dick Symes, who was a good short board surfer (but not nearly as good as he thought he was) and hated any other surfer who came anywhere near him, mals, grommets, and female surfers, more or less in that order.

I picked up the last wave of a nice set. Apparently, Dirty Dick liked the look of it too and tried to drop in, so I held my line, grabbed the tip of his board on the way through and flipped him. He was waiting in a rage as I paddled back out.

"You fucking mole! Fuck off home and have a shower with Daddy," he shouted.

Fortunately, Ben was out the back and didn't hear, or we would have had Lorne's first beach homicide to contend with along with everything else. I just wanted to go home after that, but wasn't going to give Dirty Dick the satisfaction and made Ben stay out until sundown.

And yes, we did manage the world's longest tongue kiss on surfboards. Kept it going even after we fell off!

I didn't tell Ben about Dirty Dick. He just put my tears that night down to the mess Dad was in, which was pretty right anyway.

I didn't tell Dad, either.

He briefed me on what was going on with the research. If we could prove it was dodgy, that would be a motive for the actions by Harriet Jones and Anna Cheng to discredit him and remove him from the Agency.

I got off a plane at Wayne County Airport, Michigan, two days later, looking for Alan Perkins. This proved to be no problem, as he was not only carrying a sign with 'Tess Johnson' written on it, but instantly recognised me.

"Picked you straight away from your poster, even with your clothes on," he drawled with an evil smile as we threw my bag into the tiny boot of his Mako sports car.

He had certainly acclimatised himself to America.

Not only did he sound American: "How was the trip from Mel-burn?"

He *looked* American. *More* than American – a living, breathing relic of the Wild West, circa 1850.

He was wearing an outfit that would have done John Wayne proud, consisting of a Buffalo Bill Cody leather jacket complete with tassels, a belt with a huge silver buckle embossed with crossed Colt 45's, and hand-tooled cowboy boots. The only concession to the modern world was a Detroit Lions cap in lieu of a Stetson. I took an instant liking to him.

He had his very own Mako sports car waiting in the short-term car park.

"Can you actually drive this thing, pilgrim?" I asked with a grin.

"Sure you don't have a couple of pintos hitched up round the back?" Serve him right for the poster wisecrack.

Al roared with laughter.

"Well, actually ah do, but ah thought we'd better use the car. I've never met a supermodel yet who could ride a horse, and your pinto isn't broken in yet."

Two instant friends headed for Dearborn, in the beautiful car one of them had designed himself.

"Have you managed to line up Winchester King?" was my first question after we shoehorned ourselves into Al's car.

"No, I steered clear of him," was the reply. "On thinking it through, I reckoned it was too risky to approach Winchester himself. He is both highly religious and very protective of the company, so could easily refuse to get involved in a scandal, even on the side of good. I lined up Mike McFarlane instead, and he was more than happy to help. His only condition is that seeing you refused his invite to dinner in Hawaii, he gets to take you to lunch tomorrow! I told Mike what we needed the research for, and fortunately for us, defence of a sexual assault claim is something his department had experienced only last year. Apparently, a girl in the sales force accused two colleagues of having uninvited sex while she was passed out drunk at a marketing conference, and the company had to come up with a big settlement, despite both men swearing the sex had been consensual. Anyway, he's getting Head of Research Hans Neidorff to prepare a report that should cast doubt on ARI's credibility if what you say is true. You're staying with me tonight, and tomorrow, I'm driving you into the marketing offices for an eleven o'clock meeting with Mike and Hans."

That being settled, I got to spend a very pleasant evening with Al in his amazing pad, which was decorated like a high-rise version of a dude ranch with an incongruous dream kitchen tacked on. He proudly showed me his collection of guns, which included the still-working pearl-handled Hopalong Cassidy cap pistol given to him by his father for his tenth birthday (which started his lifetime love of the Wild West), plus some valuable real guns, including a silver-plated Colt .45, a Buntline Special (apparently the favourite weapon of Wyatt Earp), and a Winchester repeating rifle circa 1860 ('the rifle that won the West'). I must have overdone my polite interest in the Wild West, as the evening's entertainment consisted of longhorn steaks in front of El Dorado, a favourite from Al's complete collection of John Wayne movie classics. He boasted of having seen it a hundred times; now a hundred and one.

At eleven o'clock the next day I was ushered into Mike McFarlane's ultra-modern office. Mike greeted me like a long-lost friend, then introduced me to Research Director Hans Neidorff. Hans placed our original ARI Mako research folder, an even larger one from US-based Concept Research Group Inc, and a DVD on the desk in front of us. He got straight down to business in his clipped German accent:

"Vinchester King passed on ze ARI Mako research to evaluate before ve decided to proceed viz ze development. I did nicht like zere process at all unt said zo. Ze main thing in qvestion vas ze numbers. ARI hat done two focus groups of just tventy respondents, unt, after discussing ze new Mako design compared to existing classic sports cars, used a ten-point preference scale to determine vere ze Mako came out. Giffen ze strong brand loyalties ve know exist viz prestige car owners, I do nicht believe ze Mako design could possibly score thirty-vun percent ahead of ze nearest existing car; ze Porsche 911. Zere iss no vay to put zis politely. I haf to say zat in my opinion, ze results ver cooked to support ze proposal."

"Ve vere asked to run our own research using ze same visuals, viz ze same target market. Ve ran it viz a hundred respondents instead of tventy, unt ze Mako still vun, but by a factor of only four percent over ze Ferrari unt ten percent over ze Porsche 911. Zis vas still a very gut result for a new design unt brand vich hass hat no marketing or sales support, but it proves beyond doubt ze ARI results ver cooked."

"Ve ver asked to keep our results confidential from you, as ve still vanted to proceed, but did not vant to spoil ze Australian relationship by qvestioning your honesty. You vill note zat since zen, ve haf insisted on carrying out all ze advertising research ourselves, unt zis vos vuy."

"Here ist my report, plus ze original ARI one, unt a recording of my summary of ze situation."

This was everything we needed. I thanked Hans for his frankness, and after we all had coffee, he stood up to leave, almost clicking his heels together.

I experienced a disturbing vision of Sergeant Shultz and couldn't supress a giggle.

Mike scooped the reports and DVD into a transparent blue plastic document case.

"Now for our lunch," he said with a smile of his own.

"Let's go."

Mike also drove a brand-new Mako; what else?

It purred to a stop outside the Eagle Tavern, a rebuilt stagecoach stop specialising in traditional American fare; even featuring waiters in historical garb. I was stepping from the latest Ford Mako sports car into the past of Henry Ford himself.

Mike was a gracious host, insisting I had the traditional local delicacy of whitefish, and as I emerged from the bathroom before we left, even produced two glasses of Dom Perignon at the bar. The champagne was icy cold, just like it should be. It tasted just like Dom should taste, even with the little white pill dissolved in it.

The little white Rohypnol pill.

The date rape drug.

By the time we got to the car, I was away with the fairies.

"My place is just around the corner. We'll go back there and check out Hans's DVD on my system," he said.

That seemed fine. *Everything* seemed fine.

"I hope I can concentrate. I think I'm being hit by jet lag," I said.

I only just made it up the steps of Mike's converted warehouse and onto the couch. Mike got straight down to it. He took the plastic folder out of his briefcase.

"In this folder is everything you need for Jack's case in Australia," he said.

"But I want something in return."

"You."

"Be nice, and you get the folder."

Nice? "Mike, you are an attractive guy, but I can't go to bed with you. I just got married. See?"

I showed him my wedding ring, as if that settled everything.

"This may come as a surprise to you, Tess, but plenty of married women go to bed with men who are not their husbands. If it makes you feel better, you can take the ring off."

Dad was not going to jail. Meaning I was not going to leave without the folder.

What the hell?

I rose unsteadily to my feet.

"Where's the bedroom?"

Like any bachelor pad worth its name, the bedroom opened right off the lounge. It was decorated with seduction in mind. Red carpet, black walls, mirror on the ceiling, and a king-size bed with black silk sheets already turned back, ready to go. Over the bed, an enlarged, spot lit poster in a black frame.

The Girl in the Shower.

Bloody hell.

I walked in and kicked off my shoes. Then turned around so he could unzip my dress.

It fell to the floor, and I stepped out of it on unsteady legs.

He peeled down my pants and I stepped out of those as well.

For some reason, tidiness seemed important. I scooped up my clothes, laid them carefully on the red leather chair beside the bed and turned to face him.

"God, you're gorgeous. Beach girl tan *and* shaved pussy," he said, his voice becoming distant and fuzzy.

He took off his own clothes and threw them on top of mine. Already erect, he cupped my breasts like a lover, and kissed me.

"Not good enough. Show me you want it."

"Open your mouth when I kiss you."

I opened my mouth.

"Lie down."

I lay back on the bed and started to zone out. Just floated and tried to dream it was Ben.

I'm lying on silk.
Tongues kissing.
My nipples are being sucked.
My body reacts.
His voice: "Spread your legs."
I part my legs.
Fingers ready me.
I'm wet.
He enters.
Starts slow.
I meet his thrusts.
In and out.
In and out.
Now faster.
Now deeper.
Is that me moaning?
I come.
Nothing.

I wake to the noise of a blender coming from the main room. I had a roaring thirst and a headache, but at least I could focus. He was gone, and his clothes were gone. In their place, a fluffy white dressing gown. I swung my legs off the bed, shrugged on the gown, and walked into the lounge.

He greeted me from behind the kitchen island bench as if nothing had happened.

"Drink this. It will make you feel better," he said, handing me a big tumbler of fresh orange juice.

Then he passed me a box of Tylenol. "Toss down a couple of these as well."

He's done this before.

"I know you like showers. There's a towel in there."

"Thank you," was the most I felt like saying.

"For the orange juice."

I gulped it down with two Tylenol, had a shower and then got dressed. He even came in and zipped me up. The perfect gentleman.

It was dark by the time he dropped me back at Al's place, complete with the blue folder, as promised.

"I hope you win your case," he said.

Then an unexpected question:

"You loved it, didn't you?"

We may need more from him. I got out of the car, turned, lowered my eyes demurely, and turned on a shy smile.

"Yes," I whispered.

"I really do hope you win," he repeated.

I felt his eyes on me all the way up the steps. I turned around at Al's door and smiled. After all, I'm a consumate actress as well as a slut.

Strangely, I felt no shame.

My marriage vows were intact. My body had rebelled and given him what he wanted, but I hadn't given anything of myself at all.

I had just done what I had to do.

I will never tell Ben.

Lunches don't normally take eight hours, and I was still pretty spaced out. Al had been around, and I'm sure he suspected what had gone down, but had the good grace to pretend he didn't. He offered me coffee with his John Wayne smile, but the eyes were the giveaway. So was the comment that came with the coffee, his Wild West accent now gone:

"You are an amazing daughter, Tess. Don't worry, things will be fine."

I didn't feel fine.

I felt like shit.

But we were going to win.

Chapter 21
Jack

Tess returned from Detroit with more than we had hoped for; not only the original ARI proposal on Mako but also the forensic challenge we needed, compiled by one of the biggest research companies in America, topped off with Hans Neidorff's audio-visual presentation – just the thing to play to a magistrate untrained in market research. It was drawing a long bow to make a link between the precariousness of the ARI research contract and Harriet Jones's effort to discredit me, but at least now we had some concrete evidence to support motive.

Added to that, an unexpected witness came out of left field – Robbo. He rang Kate direct with a bombshell statement that he was prepared to swear to in court.

As would be expected, the whole Agency had followed the case avidly in the media. Robbo had read Harriet's quote in *The Sun* accusing me of "moving my hand up her bare thigh, trying to burrow under her pants", at the Willows lunch. Fortunately for me, Robbo was an unashamed leg man and distinctly remembered admiring Harriet's long legs as she walked into the restaurant ahead of him: her long legs encased in black panty hose, with little silver butterflies embroidered on them. No 'bare thigh' or panties to burrow under! Here was a witness statement that blew her accusation out of the water.

We supplied copies of Robbo's deposition, the ARI research results, and the Hans Neidorff DVD, together with my contention of fraud to the police under rules of discovery, and guess what? Harriet withdrew her charge next day.

"The witness now states she is too traumatised to face her attacker in court," was the reason given.

Yeah, right.

One down, two to go!

We assumed there would still be a trial and got ready.

First, Melanie Wright-Smith. I listed Amy Hiddlestone, the Account Coordinator occupying the desk immediately outside my door to be called as a defence witness and also purchased a Gainsborough doorknob with centre lock button, exactly the same as the one on my office door, to show the magistrate as an exhibit. This could just be enough to discredit Melanie's accusation.

As far as Anna Cheng was concerned, it was all going to hang on the result of Kate's cross-examination on the day. We didn't have any hard evidence to support my denial, but the police had an additional exhibit to support the case for the prosecution. Silas and I had shared our respective computer passwords, and that gave the police access to every internal and external email on my laptop. They presented a chain of emails between Anna and I that taken out of context looked damning. At one of our regular Friday drink sessions, Anna had got a laugh relating how her new boyfriend had taken her to the Como ball on their first date, but had not had the courage to kiss her goodnight. The following week, I had sent the first of the emails straight after an important client meeting. The email was a joke to congratulate her about her presentation that had helped us get the pitch across the line:

Best yet, gorgeous – here's the kiss you missed out on last week! Jack x

From then on, we started signing off emails to each other with an x, just for fun.

No trouble, Jack; anything for the team. Anna x

Meeting 9.30 tomorrow. Jack x

Your turn to bring the donuts. Anna x

Anna had signed a deposition that I had groomed her by email and then started demanding real kisses whenever we were alone – the prelude to my supposed sexual assault at the party. This was surprisingly reinforced by a signed statement from Silas that I had made 'locker room comments' to him about Anna and my intention to bed her. This was complete bullshit, of course, but there it was, signed off in writing by my male partner no less.

Significantly, the prosecution had selected Outlook file copies of only one-to-one emails. Kate demanded access to my laptop as vital to my defence, and we got it.

A search of all my Outlook files against anna.cheng@sandj.com.au showed more back and forward emails between Anna and I where other staff had been openly copied – hardly the action of a sexual predator secretly grooming his prey! Significantly, some of these emails were from Anna to me, also signed off with an x – hardly supportive of a supposed 'reluctant victim of sexual advances.'

Despite being based on a blatant lie, Silas's deposition was much more concerning. I wanted to march straight into the Agency and confront him, but Kate advised against it.

"He obviously has his own agenda to see you convicted," she said. "Confronting Silas would be seen as intimidating a witness, especially if you were to lose your temper and hit him."

Kate is a bloody good lawyer. She can read minds.

The DPP was successful at the committal hearing, and my trial before the magistrate was set for 11 am at the Melbourne Magistrates Court, in only five weeks' time.

This was literally my 'day in court', where the defence is able to present exhibits plus call and cross-examine witnesses.

I refused Kate's advice to wear my air force uniform and DSO medal to court. The air force had been another part of my life, and I would not allow something like this to be associated with my unit in any way. So, despite my protest that they made me look like a drug baron, Ariel made me wear my tailormade charcoal suit, shot silk tie, and black bespoke shoes from Lobb's of London.

Ariel, Tess, Kate, and I went in straight from Kate's office in a cab, which pulled up right at the courthouse steps. This didn't save us from the media circus though, and we had to run the gauntlet of press, TV, and a noisy contingent from the women's liberation movement. I held Ariel's hand one side and Tess's on the other. Both hands were squeezed when the jeers and cat calls started, whilst Kate just turned and shook her head at the lynch mob.

The court was full to overflowing. I looked up into the gallery and saw a number of Agency colleagues and Air Force mates, as well as Ben, Jules, Dave, Doc, and all my regular golf buddies. At least my friends were there for me.

The trial pretty much matched TV courtroom dramas I had seen. The DPP team sat down on one side and we sat opposite, waiting for the magistrate to appear; which she did on the dot of eleven. The clerk announced the case, and the DPP Prosecutor was called to present the sexual assault charges against me by the two women.

The Prosecutor read the charges.

She followed with the police videotapes made at the station, statements from the questioning officers, subsequent depositions, and in the case of Anna Cheng, the large colour photo of the bite marks left by my alleged attack as Exhibit A, and the police transcript of my emails, marked as Exhibit B.

She then called a succession of prosecution witnesses.

First to the stand was Melanie Wright-Smith, who looked nervous. Not because she was facing her attacker in court, but because she was lying. The DPP Prosecutor gently coaxed her through the elements of her police video interview. Obviously rehearsed, but still a good performance by Melanie; she even managed convincing tears when she got to the part where I had caused the Agency to sack her for rejecting my advances.

Kate ripped her story to shreds.

Regarding the alleged attack itself, she called me to the stand to explain why, as a creative writer, I always locked my office door so people wouldn't walk in on me all the time and disrupt my train of creative thought. On her prompt, I pulled the Gainsborough knob out of my pocket and demonstrated how easy it would have been for me to lock my door as we entered the room, should I have planned to sexually assault Melanie.

We produced testimony from three witnesses that the day I had given Melanie her exit interview, Anna had knocked before entering in the normal manner. This supported our contention that Anna had not "happened to come into the office in the nick of time to save me", as Melanie had claimed.

The prosecution didn't realise it, but on the week before the party, I had talked to everyone in Melanie's account group, and it was common knowledge that she was about to be fired, not to protect a breast-fondling boss but because of poor performance combined with a loss of confidence by her entire Account Group. This was confirmed by our first witness, Mako Account Director Terry Coulter.

When Kate cross-examined Melanie on this she stumbled badly, and this time her tears were real. The Prosecutor made some mileage out of the lack of warning letters prior to dismissal being an illegal procedure by the Agency and myself as a director, but Kate even turned that back on the prosecution in her rebuttal:

"However, it was done, even my learned friend has accepted that the sacking of the complainant was in fact a performance-related issue, which she conveniently failed to mention."

Next the prosecution called Anna Cheng, who stuck to her "grooming followed by uninvited sexual contact followed by sexual assault" story; with the Prosecutor tabling the police neck hickey photograph Exhibit A, and reading out the transcript of the so-called "grooming emails" from their Exhibit B.

Although Kate seemed to score with our challenge against the emails, Anna survived cross-examination relatively unscathed, even ending with some realistic tears of her own. How do women do that?

Then it was Silas's turn. He stood there on the stand, lying through his teeth as the Prosecutor led him through his testimony.

"Did you witness the sexual assault?"

"Yes, I did. I was at the boardroom table when I heard Anna say, 'No Jack, no', from the bar. I looked up and clearly saw Jack Johnson and Anna through the kitchen archway. Jack was behind Anna, biting her neck with both hands down the front of her dress, which had one strap broken and off the shoulder. Anna screamed, broke free, and slapped him."

"Was that the only time you witnessed inappropriate behaviour by the defendant towards Anna Cheng?"

"I never saw him actually do anything else, but he often made unsought comments of a sexual nature to me about her."

"And what were these?"

"I don't remember the exact words. Comments like 'Can't wait to taste Chinese', when Anna left the room. Things like that."

I saw the magistrate frown. *Nice going, Silas; you've just managed to brand me a racist as well.*

Silas also survived Kate's cross-examination unscathed; sticking to his story with feigned righteous indignation at the "appalling behaviour of my Partner of seven years".

Silas was stood down, and the prosecution closed their case.

Kate opened the defence by challenging the prosecution's bite mark photograph with Rumpolean finesse. She showed the court the model of my teeth, then lined up a same-size photo beside it, showing a Plasticine bite impression supported by the dental model, clearly showing the demonstrably different bite pattern of my incisors versus those in the Exhibit A police photo.

Of equal importance was a second bite pattern photo made after me giving a Styrofoam store head a bite on the neck from the front, not from behind, labelled as Exhibit C. We had highlighted the teeth impressions in the white Styrofoam with a black Sharpie, which stood out nicely. Our front-on Styrofoam bite arc showed a mirror image of the arc pattern on police Exhibit A, clearly demonstrating the police had their bite mark round the wrong way!

Next, Kate drew the magistrate's attention to red figures on the margin of the Exhibit A photograph, confirming the date and time the police photo was taken: forty-three minutes after the alleged assault.

Next, she called our medical witness, who gave his expert opinion that based on the extent of bruising, the bite on Anna's neck could not have happened at the time of the alleged sexual assault, but at least eight hours earlier.

The prosecution tried to challenge his credentials, but they got nowhere on that as Kate had been careful to use a highly qualified expert, not a 'dollars for testimony' medico.

Back on her feet, Kate went for the jugular.

"Corroborating evidence demonstrates the complainant is lying about being bitten on her neck from behind during the alleged assault, and we contend she is lying about the whole incident, no doubt playing the sexual assault card to go after a nice, juicy compensation."

The Prosecutor leapt to her feet.

"Objection! The defence is making an accusation against this poor girl with not a shred of evidence to support it."

"Objection sustained. Ms Lee, you will refrain from grandstanding at the complainant's expense," admonished the magistrate.

Kate didn't back off.

"The complainant is not a 'poor girl'. She is a consummate liar who is trying very hard to become a *rich* girl via a spurious and criminal claim against my client."

Laughter in the court.

"One more comment like that, and I shall find you in contempt," was the angry reply from the bench.

Kate may have overstepped the mark, but in refuting the prosecution's photographic evidence, she had clearly established an inconsistency in Anna's testimony that had to have registered with the magistrate, angry or not.

Both prosecution and defence summed up.

The Prosecutor stuck to the basic allegations from each complainant, contending that *two* women could not both be wrong in making very similar accusations and emphasising the eyewitness evidence from Silas of my sexual assault of Anna.

Kate was more specific:

First, she emphasised that there were originally not two complainants but three, the first one withdrawing her allegation of sexual assault as soon as her allegation was seriously challenged and her research for S&J about to be exposed as fraudulent, and in conjunction with the primary complainant Anna Cheng.

Kate also highlighted that Harriet Jones and Anna Cheng had not declared their interest as sole directors of Ad Research International to their major (and only) client, plus that I had given Silas Silver notice I was about to fire ARI as a supplier and Anna Cheng as an employee, which would have resulted in considerable loss of both income and reputation for both complainants.

Regarding Melanie Wright-Smith, Kate quoted the witness statements that Anna had knocked on my office door before entering on the day in question, and did not "fortuitously come in unannounced and rescue Melanie" plus the corroborating evidence from her Account Group she was to be fired for performance reasons; predating the alleged sexual assault.

Regarding Anna Cheng's sexual assault allegation itself, our defence relied on refuting the physical evidence of the 'coercive bite on the neck', the out-of-context emails, and the sheer unbelievability of me sexually assaulting Anna right next to a room full of people.

Summations over, the magistrate called a recess for lunch, after which time she would hand down her decision.

By 2.00 pm we were all seated again, everyone waiting on the magistrate. She didn't take long.

"Will the defendant please stand."

I stood.

"On the charge of the sexual assault of Melanie Wright-Smith, I find the charge unproven."

"On the charge of the sexual assault of Anna Cheng, including both coercive assault causing injury and sexual contact, I find the charge of coercive assault causing injury unproven, but the charge of sexual contact proven."

"I have therefore decided to record a conviction of the lesser offence of sexual molestation. There are clearly extenuating circumstances surrounding this case, and it is also clear there has been some dubious embellishment by the complainants, but that does not alter the evidence of the sexual contact charge sustained beyond reasonable doubt."

"Sentence will be passed at the next available court date."

Whatever the sentence, my professional life was effectively over. I still didn't know why Silas had turned on me, but swore one day I would prove he had perjured himself and clear my name.

The two women I cared about most in the world were shattered, and even Kate went pale.

I hugged Ariel, gave Tess my smart silk handkerchief to wipe her eyes, and shook Kate's hand.

"Thank you," I said.

"You did great."

"We were never going to beat Silas's evidence."

"No, we weren't," she replied.

"I'm only sorry we never got to the bottom of why he did it."

Somehow, her handshake turned into another hug. Who said lawyers have no heart?

Ariel rang Silver Top Taxis on her mobile. We still had to barge our way back through the media scrum reach the safety of the cab.

The whole experience was horrible, particularly for Ariel and Tess.

I remember the sea of faces, the battery of cameras, and a large woman with a bright yellow buzz cut, screaming, "I hope you burn in hell."

I was too stunned to do anything other than shake my head.

I remember Kate facing the forest of microphones with her last comment for the day: "He didn't do it."

I remember telling Tess not to cry.

I remember Ariel lifting her bag to hide her face.

I remember getting home and holding her close.

With sub judice no longer a factor, the media went to town.

That night, all four TV news channels featured my conviction, with footage from the courtroom steps. Kate's "He didn't do it" could clearly be heard, but that didn't matter; the media had already convicted me out of hand, and the trial result only confirmed it. They even made mileage out of Ariel hiding her face.

Convicted criminals did that, and one editor's note "Jack Johnson is guilty and even his wife is ashamed" was used by one paper as a footer to their courthouse steps picture and 20 point 'GUILTY' headline.

The next morning, we woke to 'RAPIST PIG' sprayed on the wall of the house. I got two litres of graffiti removal fluid from the hardware store in the Village and scrubbed it off. Some photographer even managed to take a shot of me doing that.

The same day, a woman confronted Ariel at the Safeway supermarket checkout queue:

"You poor, poor thing. For goodness sake, leave him!"

"I would," agreed the checkout chick.

Ariel glared at them both.

"He didn't do it," she said for the benefit of the queue.

She's tough alright. Didn't cry until she got to the car.

Next morning, 'RAPIST PIG' was back. I scrubbed it off again.

This was killing Ariel. I came in from scrubbing the wall, got her favourite cappuccino going on the machine, and put my arms round her.

"I must stay here until sentencing, but you should leave for Chartwell today. Your parents haven't even called. You must go to the farm and tell them the truth; and it will also get you away from the wolf pack."

"Yes, I'll go. I can't take any more of this," she whispered into my shoulder.

I kissed her goodbye.

No 'RAPIST PIG' the following day; the spray can must have been empty! I didn't need more aggro, so stayed indoors watching old movies and hiding behind our silent number.

Rang Tess at Dave's place. She was still seething but otherwise seemed okay.

Then finally, something good emerged from the shit. My mobile went off, and it was Robbo from the Agency.

"Hi, Jack. I'm round at the Botanical with a few of the guys. Can we buy you a drink?"

A drink with my work mates sounded a hell of a lot better than sitting at home feeling sorry for myself, so I went. To my great surprise, 'a few of the guys' consisted of most of the Agency.

My PA, a lovely girl called Jane, led the goodwill charge. She came straight up, threw her arms round my neck, and kissed me full on the lips.

"I've wanted to do that for years," she said.

"Just don't go me for harassment."

Everyone cracked up laughing. Humour in the face of adversity is the Australian way, and it was therapeutic to see it was alive and well, that night in the pub. Nobody avoided the elephant in the room; one after another, my workmates came over and shyly stumbled over their support for me and their belief in my innocence. On a more serious note, I found out that Anna had become 'persona non grata' over her accusation (which nobody believed) and had stopped coming in to work. It would never have been usable in court, but ad agencies are funny places; affairs amongst staff are invariably common knowledge almost before they even start, and any vibes regarding Anna and I had never been picked up by the Agency gossip machine, which had never been known to fail.

Added to that, Silas had remained in his office with the door shut ever since my trial. The bean counter in advertising agencies is seldom popular, but as Joint Managing Director he had been expected to make some internal announcement, and the lack of one had diminished him in the eyes of the staff.

I made sure I talked to everyone individually and then excused myself, placing two hundred dollars on the bar for the last shout I would ever give them. I waved goodbye with the parting words:

"Thank you for inviting me tonight; it means a lot. For God's sake, don't anyone go over the limit. Now the cops don't have me to chase any more, they'll want to make up their quotas with *you*."

Shades of Richard Nixon.

Laughter.

Good for the soul.

I waved jauntily from the doorway and then walked back to my car, parked at the edge of the Botanical Gardens. The fruit bats had settled in the acacia trees, the sky was clear, and the stars were out, just where they had always been.

That was good for the soul too.

I reckoned the best thing to kill time awaiting sentencing was to keep busy. The tennis club was out, so I decided to go down to the golf club for the Thursday men's comp I usually had to miss because of work.

In my group, the draw for partners always occurred over lunch, so that was going to be a test. As it turned out, the reception from the men's golf group mirrored that from my work colleagues: rejection of the conviction coupled with sincere sympathy, although I did note that two committeemen at the table remained aloof. They say one's golf often reflects one's state of mind, and this was certainly true that day. My golf was shit, and Austin Carlan and I lost the money six and five. It was still good to have come and enjoyed the company; at least it was until we repaired to the bar for post-game drinks.

As soon as our four sat down, the two committee guys got up and left, refusing to meet my eye. Worse than that was the reaction from Sue, the long-time bar attendant, who knew all our names and always collected our drink orders with a friendly smile and good-humoured tolerance of our endless golf banter. There was no smile for me and no request for my order; I may as well have not existed. I justified the committeemen's attitude as related to their duty of care for the club's reputation, but Sue's reaction hurt, as we had always got on well.

She thought I was guilty.

I did not know it, but this was the last time I would ever attend the golf club that my father had so proudly put me up for all those years ago. I was glad he and my mother were no longer alive to see it.

I had told Ariel and Tess to stay away until the day before sentencing, to protect them from the flak, but underneath, I hoped Ariel would come back early. She didn't, and she didn't phone either – worse than that, whenever I rang her, our conversation was strained, whatever tack I tried.

Tess was the opposite; she called every day trying to cheer me up with long conversations about the most trivial things, insisting on putting both Ben and Dave on one after another as well. It must have driven them nuts, but I found myself waiting each day for that call – a drowning man clutching at his straw.

Finally, the day before sentencing arrived and my family came home. I knew what I needed that night, but Ariel did everything but claim a headache, so nothing doing there.

Sentencing day.

We drove to Kate's office and then shared a taxi to the court. Kate didn't have much to say, apart from briefing us on the procedure, but at least volunteered the encouraging words that she was confident of a non-custodial sentence for the lesser conviction I had ended up with.

When we arrived at court, it was like the day of the trial all over again.

Big media presence.

Demonstrators.

Ariel in one hand, Tess in the other.

Jeering crowd.

Hands squeezed.

Ariel hiding her face.

Unlike the trial, sentencing was brief. In fact, it took under ten minutes, including preliminaries.

"Will the defendant please rise."

I rose.

"Jack Johnson, you have been convicted before this court on the charge of sexual molestation. Do you have anything to say before sentence is passed?"

"Only that I am not guilty, your honour," I replied.

"Your guilt or otherwise is no longer at issue. There may be extenuating circumstances surrounding this case, and as I have already stated, there has clearly been some embellishment by the complainants, but that does not alter my ruling on the criminal charge of sexual molestation, proven beyond reasonable doubt. It is therefore my decision that you are sentenced to one year's prison, which shall be suspended subject to a Good Behaviour Bond for the period of one year from today. Although your conviction will be recorded on the Victorian register of sexual offenders, there will be no fine imposed by the court in addition to the Good Behaviour Bond."

That was it.

I called Silver Top Taxis, then we ran the gauntlet of media and protestors and cabbed it back to Kate's for her final instructions.

Taxi drivers are a pretty well-informed bunch, probably because they listen to the radio all the time while they wait in line for fares. Our guy, Chris, was no exception and expressed sympathy from at least one section of the public:

"I just wanted to say that me and the other guys on the cab rank reckon you were shafted, Mr Johnson. We hope you will be okay after this bullshit case."

Nice of him.

We had a last cup of tea with Kate, and then I drove us back home, hoping the worst would be over after the next couple of days of media attention surrounding the verdict.

But the backlash had only just begun.

Two solicitor's letters arrived the next week, both unexpected.

The first was from the solicitors for Silver & Johnson, arriving by registered mail in a big buff envelope. It contained a copy of the original Partnership Agreement I had signed with Silas seven years previously, plus a short letter drawing my attention to a very important clause. I had 'left the legal stuff to Silas' and was about to pay the penalty for my lack of attention to detail in not retrieving and reading our original Agreement through properly. Clause 12.4 was the killer:

12. Termination

12.4 Should either partner be convicted of any crime or criminal fraud against the Agency, his shareholding plus that of any of his nominee(s) shall be declared null and void, and shall revert to the remaining partner and/or his nominee(s) without cost to the surviving partner and/or his nominee(s) or to the company.

Silas's solicitor was very efficient. Stapled to the letter was a share transfer form already signed by Silas transferring my fifty units in the trust – my half of the Agency – to him. Under our partnership agreement I was to sign and return it. A prepaid return envelope addressed to the agency solicitor was provided.

So *that* was what it had all been about. Silas had perjured himself to steal my half of Silver & Johnson.

I wasn't signing anything. Fuck him!

The second solicitor's letter was delivered by hand later the same day.

To Ariel.

She answered the doorbell and came back bearing a large envelope.

"Now what?" I said.

She burst into tears, and her reply hit me like a blow:

"Jack, I'm so sorry. I want a divorce."

I think all I said was, "Oh, no." Something like that.

I should have seen it coming. There had been a widening gap between us ever since Ariel had gone to Chartwell, and it was clear her parents had got into the act. But it was not only that. Ariel had obviously rehearsed her next words:

"It's got nothing to do with us as a couple, but everything that has happened means that we can never have a normal family life again. I can't drag my family and Tess into this anymore. I know you're innocent, but you should never have let yourself get into this position."

"I don't want any money from you, as I have plenty of my own. More than that, I still love you and don't bear you any ill will. This is not one of *those* divorces."

"I just want this house, which is already in my name. You keep Lorne, unless you decide to leave the country or something."

"We don't need to go and contest anything in court, as I am not trying to go you. I'm sure the terms will suit us both."

"It's all in here."

Ariel opened the envelope and pulled out two copies of the divorce settlement; drafted by her family's solicitors. They even had little red plastic tabs showing where I should sign, just like when you buy a house.

Then she started crying again.

I had blocked divorce out of my thoughts, like a pilot avoiding a threatening cumulus cloud, but knew in my heart of hearts there was nowhere else for us to go. There was no other way to protect my family from the shame and hurt that I would inevitably bring down on them.

I didn't even read the divorce settlement; just walked over, picked up the pen we kept by the phone, opened the pages with the little red plastic tabs, and signed my name. Then I put my arms around my soon-to-be ex-wife.

"Darling, I know you are right, and I know this is what we must do."

"I'm so sorry," I heard myself say.

"We'll go down to Lorne and tell Tess together."

"I couldn't handle coming back here after that," said Ariel.

"I'll go straight back to Chartwell from Lorne."

It was as if a great weight had lifted from our shoulders. The tension between us was gone, and all that was left was our love and our sadness.

Ariel looked up and kissed me.

Just like she used to.

"Come to bed," she said.

We went.

Just like we used to.

When we got down to Lorne, I summoned Dave and Jules round to our place and broke the news of the impending divorce to all four of them at once.

Tess's response was exactly as expected.

"No, you can't let them do this to us."

"You can't let them win."

"It's your whole life we're talking about."

I had rehearsed my reply to her even more thoroughly than my statements on the witness stand:

"This divorce is something your mother and I have decided upon together. It is the only way to call off the media from wrecking everyone's lives, which neither of us is prepared to let happen. Even cutting me loose won't work by itself. As soon as I can get organised, I am going to disappear. I'm going to do what we talked about those nights around the campfire up at the Howqua: I'm going to take the chopper into the desert and find Lasseter's Reef!"

Dave's response was both practical and typically laconic.

"You're going to need the metal detector," he said. "And a good dirt bike. A KTM is the best."

Tess's response was also straight to the point.

"We're coming too!"

"No, Tess, this time you're not invited. Disappear means really disappear, even from you. It won't work any other way."

She tried reasoning.

She tried tears.

She tried storming out and slamming the door.

But she came back, like I knew she would.

I put them all at ease as much as I could.

"It's going to take a couple of years for this to die down, but I'll be back. And when I do, I'm going after Silas Silver and Anna Cheng. Now we know what Silas was really on about, it opens up a whole new can of worms. It is quite possible he did a deal with Anna or threatened her with exposure for the research fraud. I have always got on well with her, and even allowing for the fraud angle, I don't think she would have done what she did unless there was some coercion by Silas."

It was better not to draw out the farewells, so Ariel and I left next morning, sadly headed in our different directions.

Dave remained practical. He rose early and hunted out the metal detector and the canvas gun bag containing his precious Browning .233 hunting rifle, the Kahles scope that went with it, a ramrod, and a cleaning kit. With the canvas bag came four boxes of Remington Centrefire ammo.

"The Browning will be perfect for Roos, and it will easily stop a dingo if you need to," was the comment.

I tried to refuse the rifle, but he wouldn't hear of it.

"I don't go roo shooting anymore," he said. "And it will only rust in the sea air."

Nothing of Dave's had ever rusted. There was nobody on the coast who looked after oiling and servicing his gear like he did, from his fishing reels to his ancient Partner chainsaw, which had gone through about a thousand chains yet still ran perfectly. No; this was my best mate giving me one of his most precious possessions, without a second thought.

Jules sent me on my way with a kiss. A real one. I have a theory about first love. Even if you move on, it stays with you the rest of your life.

Tess surprised me yet again. No girly tears, just a practical 'au revoir'.

"Just in case the unheard of happens and you don't find Lasseter's Reef, while you're away we're going to turn the Mako Surf Company into the most successful surf brand in Australia. There will be plenty to come back to, I promise you that."

Tess gave me a most un-girlie hug as I got into the car and had to get my breath back before I could put on my seat belt. Tess is very strong.

Then it was back to Melbourne, to pack up and get ready to disappear.

I managed it in four weeks, which was good going, as there was plenty to do.

The first week's packing was interrupted by visits from one TV station, one radio station, and two newspapers. Their questions were all the same, and so was my response:

"Mr Johnson, have you any comment on your conviction?"

"Yes. I am completely innocent. And one day I will intend to prove it. Goodbye." Shut the door.

So much for them.

That week, I also went into Kate's office to line up a good corporate solicitor. I wanted an opinion on the Agency agreement, and I needed to write a will in case I ended up dead like Lasseter.

Not good news on the Agency Agreement. Apparently, it didn't matter whether I signed the share transfer or not; Clause 12.4 would still apply, and unless I got my conviction overturned, Silas owned the Agency. Solicitor Don Kennedy was pleased I had not signed the transfer, as that could have been presented in the future as me implicitly agreeing that my conviction was valid. We left it at that, with me assuring Don that one day, we would be taking civil action to restore both my ownership of the Agency and my reputation.

Don also helped start the process of changing me from an ad man with a cushy city job into an outback gold prospector. He arranged to purchase a shelf company to be registered as Mako Mining NL, with the same directors as the Mako Surf Company. A courier was sent to Lorne to obtain the other signatures, as I was starting to unravel a bit and couldn't face them again.

My will was also simple.

I left my entire estate to Tess, except for the WW Greener shotgun, Hardy fly rod and reel, Zeiss binoculars, and my proudest possession, probably the only undamaged Gordon Woods mal in existence, to Dave, and (if they ever found me) my Rolex Sub Mariner, which I bequeathed to Ben.

That done, I had to get ready to go.

Most days were spent reading. I bought every book and copied every press article I could find on Lasseter's Reef. I studied them all using Sherlock Holmes's proven method:

"Once you eliminate the impossible, whatever remains, no matter how improbable, must be the truth."

Not quite as easy as that, of course, but well worthwhile working over the maps of all the previous expeditions to eliminate areas before selecting a search grid and the site for my base camp.

There were many theories on the location of Lasseter's Reef, which of course had never been found, plus an equal number of theories that Harold Lasseter was a con man and the reef didn't actually exist, but I reckoned if it was out there, my helicopter, dirt bike, and metal detector gave me some sort of shot at finding it; much better than the 1930 expeditions by the Central Australian Gold

Exploration syndicate using camels, a huge six-wheel Thornicroft truck, and two Gypsy Moth biplanes. There were graded roads cutting through the desert these days, so access to the search area would certainly be much easier than the early expeditions had to contend with.

The Raven was at Essendon airport already, so all that remained to be done in Melbourne was source up-to-date maps, including existing mining exploration leases, plus purchase and set up a sat phone.

I was going to be using a helicopter and dirt bike, so needed to get special lightweight gear. I would buy a new dirt bike and find a good second-hand Toyota Troopy and an off-road trailer in Alice Springs, plus hire a driver to transport the heavy stuff to my selected base camp; on the basis that the Troopy had a basic engine far better suited to where I was going than a modern, computerised 4WD that could strand you if you fried a computer chip.

Meanwhile, shit continued to happen. A letter arrived from the Secretary of the golf club, cancelling my membership under Rule 22 of its constitution regarding criminal convictions. More friends cut off. Ten members and both teaching pros rang with their condolences, which was nice, but I was never to play golf with any of them again.

Apart from the media coverage announcing my conviction, all four women's magazines got into the act, each with articles featuring extensive 'in-depth' comment from the usual storm-troopers of the women's movement, making Anna look like Joan of Arc, sacrificed to the desires of yet another rapacious male from the Ad industry. Just as well I was not going back to the coffee shop at Lorne; they also sold women's magazines, and my picture was on the cover of all of them. I was glad of these articles, in a way. They vindicated both Ariel's decision and my solution. Once I disappeared, the fire would be starved of fuel.

Bugger them all.

I was off to find Lasseter's Reef.

I wrote a last note to Ariel and propped it on the mantelpiece.

Don't be too sad.
Look after Tess.
All my love, Jack

PS I shall miss you terribly, but should you find someone else, I will understand.

A lie.
But a good lie.

Chapter 22
Jack

Only two more things left to do.

Under the terms of my Good Behaviour Bond, I had to advise the police I was leaving the State for 'Country NSW', and would notify them on my return.

I also had to apply to the NSW Aboriginal Land Council for permission to fossick on aboriginal land, giving my Lorne address on the form. If I do strike it rich (such as finding a fabulous gold reef five miles long), I would need to peg out a lease and open up a whole new lot of negotiations to obtain mining rights, but decided to leave those complications until I had actually found something.

If only!

The big day came: blue sky and a twenty-knot southerly to push me north.

The Raven (now with its back seats removed) was serviced and fuelled up. Apart from the gear to stake her down and a special vent cover to keep dust out of the intake, I had bought a service manual and full set of tools; (although I am only a bush mechanic at best, and God only knows if I could fix anything major).

Maps, tent, swag, first aid kit, metal detector, pin pointer, spare batteries, large and small rock picks, geologist hammer, plastic bags for samples, Dave's Browning rifle and scope, my Greener shotgun, rifle and shotgun ammo, field glasses, spotter scope, compass, generator, paints and easel, digital camera, laptop, and portable printer are all stowed. Given the Raven's 500kg load limit, it was obvious I would need a Troopy with off-road trailer and driver to haul the heavy stuff (mainly extra petrol) out to base camp. Quite a logistics problem for a two-man expedition, but just the distraction I needed right now.

A last phone call to Tess:

"Hi. Kiddo; it's me. I'm about to fly off into the never-never; and this is the last time I'll be calling for a while."

"I have a goodbye present for you and Ben. I know you both have always wanted to learn to fly the chopper, so I have paid for pilot's courses for each of you at the Queensland Helicopter School in Redcliffe, just north of Brisbane. While I'm away, they can qualify you in a Raven 2 just like mine, so when I *do* come back, we'll be able to share it. They're mailing you the receipt so you can take the lessons any time."

I worried I'd get more tears, but her response was good. I think she needed a distraction, just like I did.

"That's fantastic, Dad," she said.

I detected a false cheerfulness, but that was better than tears.

"While you go for gold," she added, "we'll hunt out some nice atolls on the outer reef to dive on when you get back. I reckon we'll head up to the helicopter school soon, as the whole of Lorne is into the latest Johnson scandal, and it's starting to get to Ben."

She didn't say it, but it was obviously getting to her too.

"Good luck, Dad. Be safe," were her final words. This time, with a catch in her voice.

As I started the pre-flight checks, I was glad that I had at least managed to do something to make up for the shitstorm I had brought down around their heads.

I sighed and powered up to start the long journey north. It was nice to be back at the controls; the instrumentation of the Robinson Raven is very similar to the military choppers of the 1960s, so the familiarity went back a long way, plus the very act of flying was therapeutic. I got into Alice Springs airport without incident, bedded down the chopper, and headed for the Todd Tavern to have a beer and get a room.

They say luck evens itself out, and I was certainly due for some good luck. It came only half an hour after I arrived at the Todd. I had gone straight to the bar as was my wont, and after two schooners of XXXX was talking to the barman about finding a good used Troopy to buy. That's when the luck kicked in.

"Mate, if you're going prospecting, you might want to chat with Danny Cooper over there. He's still got his brother's Troopy and off-road trailer, all set up for the desert."

Danny was a big, fit-looking guy of about thirty, drinking with some mates at the other end of the bar. Schooner in hand, I sidled up and waited for a lull in their conversation, which seemed to be mainly about the upcoming AFL season.

I picked a gap, tapped Danny on the shoulder and got straight to the point.

"G'day. I'm Jack Johnson. I'm new in town and heard you may have a Troopy for sale."

"Not really," he said. "I'm taking it into the desert again shortly. If you want a good used Troopy, you should talk to Peter Kiddle Motors. What do you want one for?"

I told him I was about to become a greenhorn prospector, using a helicopter and dirt bike, but need a reliable 4WD, an off-road trailer to lug the petrol and stores and a driver to help set up my base camp.

"I'm willing to pay well for a driver."

"We should have a beer," said Danny.

We did.

In fact, we had a few.

And a fruitful conversation.

Despite recent events, I pride myself that my time in the military had made me a good judge of men, and I took an immediate liking to Danny, who seemed straight as an arrow and a good bloke to boot.

Our conversation was more than interesting; it changed my whole strategy.

It turned out that Danny was even more famous in Alice Springs than I was, meaning we both had stories to tell over our beers.

Danny's tale was fascinating. It turned out that his brother was George Cooper, the Alice Springs concreter turned prospector who had disappeared without trace in the Great Australian Desert only nine months previously. George and Danny had made a killing pouring industrial slabs around The Alice, and instead of buying a Gold Coast unit and a big boat like his wife wanted, George had spent twenty grand of his hard-earned dollars on a fifty-hectare gold exploration lease in the Peterman Ranges, despite much ribbing from his mates and a monster row with his wife, Brie. She gave him a year to realise his childhood dream; after which time he was to come back, "Forget this gold nonsense once and for all," then sell up and move to the Gold Coast, where she had set her sights on an 'off-the-plan', canal-front house complete with its own jetty.

George never came back.

The brothers had been out on the lease for three months and had made some progress. They had set up their first base camp under canvas at the north west edge of their lease, about fifty kilometres south-west of Lasseter's cave, but in

134

prospecting on the eastern ridge of Mt Curdie, they had found a second, hitherto undiscovered cave large enough to set up camp in; much cooler than their tent and even more importantly containing a pool of seepage water, which out in the desert was more precious than gold.

It was George who discovered it. Scanning the ridge for quartz outcrops, he noticed a number of zebra finches disappearing behind a large rock; the bushman's sign of water. On climbing up to the rock, the brothers found it hiding the entrance to a big cave with a pool of crystal-clear water and a sandy floor of white-weathered quartz. Not only that, but on the walls were some perfectly preserved aboriginal cave paintings that had been there thousands of years; a wonderful discovery in itself that the brothers dismissed as not particularly exciting. Of much more relevance to them was half a day's drive from this cave, they found a large quartz outcrop, which looked promising. After three weeks' work with the metal detectors, they had made an exciting discovery – a miniscule show of actual gold dust in one of the quartz rocks: of no commercial value, but at least the auriferous quartz definitely confirmed the presence of gold in the Peterman's in general and on their lease in particular.

The day after the find, George disappeared.

The generator had been playing up, and Danny, being the better electrician, had stayed behind to strip it down whilst George, being impatient, headed off in the Troopy to continue attacking the gold hole.

He failed to make the scheduled midday sat phone call to Danny.

Danny tried calling him.

No answer.

Tried again at 2 pm.

No answer.

Again at 4 pm.

No answer.

Checked with emergency services. George had not called in or activated his EPIRB emergency beacon.

Waited overnight.

No George, and no contact.

At first light, Danny filled in the destination log in case George turned up, loaded up the dirt bike with sat phone, map, compass, GPS, spare tyre, bananas and lots of water, then rode off to find the Troopy, which had to be somewhere between base camp and the gold hole.

Apart from having to spike a puncture, the ride out was uneventful, and Danny found the Troopy right where it should have been, standing out stark white against the red ridge, just below the gold hole excavation site.

The Troopy was just sitting there, but no George.

Danny got in, turned the key, and noted the starter motor failed to fire. The battery was dead, drained by the air conditioner that was still turned on. More than unusual. As a matter of habit, the brothers always turned off the air con when leaving the Troopy, to prevent draining the battery. Apart from George himself, the only things missing from the Troopy were one of the metal detectors and George's geology hammer. Could he be up on the ridge with a broken ankle?

Danny climbed up to the dig. The hole looked exactly the same as when they left it; with the large quartz rock they had been trying to dislodge still stuck in the bottom of the hole. There was no sign of George ever having been there. Danny spent the rest of the day walking the area but found no trace of his brother.

The next day, he topped up the dirt bike from the jerry can in the Troopy and widened his search perimeter.

George was an experienced bushman and knew not to travel too far on foot. The brothers always used the Troopy or the dirt bike to push out a search anything over a kilometre, but Danny quartered over a five-kilometre area surrounding the dig, just to be sure.

Still nothing, so he called in the Northern Territory Emergency Services to send their long-range rescue chopper.

Danny cleared and marked a landing square free of stones, and then waited for the arrival of the emergency search team. While he waited, he got to thinking.

Quite apart from there being no sign of George, some things didn't look right:

1. The air con in the Troopy was still on, totally against normal procedure.
2. George had left excited about moving the big rock in the bottom of the hole, where they were getting a both a spike reading and sound blip on the metal detector. There was no reason Danny could think of he would start working anywhere else, yet he had apparently left camp with only the small geology hammer instead of the large pick and the jemmy: the obvious tools needed to dislodge the rock, which still lay undisturbed from when both brothers had last been there.

3. George's favourite one litre double-wall aluminium water bottle was still in the Troopy's Engel car fridge, full of water. He would not have left for the gold hole or prospecting walk without it.

4. George's compass was still in the glove box. He would definitely have taken it if, for some reason, he had decided to explore.

The long-range emergency chopper arrived from Docker River the next morning and spent four hours on an aerial search with Danny aboard as guide.

Nothing.

Danny related the anomalies he had noted to the search team, but these were really no help to the search; just mysterious.

Search complete, Emergency Services left with no result, leaving Danny to stay at camp in case George came back.

He didn't.

Danny waited two weeks.

While he was waiting, he spent some of the time at the gold hole. He finally dislodged the big rock, but no more visible gold or metal detector spikes came of that.

Finally, he left all the canned food and bottled water plus George's sat phone and EPIRB emergency beacon in the cave, packed the bagged quartz samples they had planned to get assayed in the Troopy, and drove back to Alice Springs.

That was three months ago.

I saw a real opportunity to talk to Danny about going into the Peterman Ranges together, but I didn't want to start our relationship with a lie, so for starters, I related the whole story of my conviction in Melbourne. My case had been the subject of some speculation around the bar at the Todd, which more or less came out along gender lines: most of the men believed me and most of the women believed Anna. The important thing was that Danny was one of the ones who believed me. He had gone through two sessions of police questioning over George's disappearance where "they treated me like a bloody murder suspect," followed by some local press speculation along similar lines, so he knew first-hand what being an innocent man accused felt like. The main thing was that he believed me, and even more importantly, he was highly interested in the potential of my helicopter in both extending the search over the sections of impenetrable mulga scrub, for what must now be George's body and for other quartz outcrops on their lease. Apart from the one sample from the gold hole, all the assays had come back negative, but Danny was determined to make one more try at prospecting. If he found gold, George's widow was going to get her fair share.

Three beers later, I found myself invited home for a barbeque.

I was introduced to Danny's wife Jo, who turned out to be an unexpected ally once it was explained who it was hiding under my new beard. It appeared that the women of Alice Springs had followed my case much more avidly than the men (in fact, Jo reckoned it came a close second to the Azaria Chamberlain case, as far as her friends were concerned), and Jo was one of the minority of local women who came down on my side. She was the receptionist at the Ross River Resort and had herself been groped by a guest, a problem she had solved then and there by kneeing him "where it hurt most". Her attack had happened late one night with nobody else around, and she was convinced there was no way a sexual predator would have tried much the same thing right next to a room full of people. At least someone believed our defence submission, even if the magistrate hadn't!

That solved, Danny and I worked out a deal which suited us both. Basically, we would share the base camp installation, Danny's Troopy and off-road trailer, with my dirt bike and helicopter. Danny's family company Pioneer Mining would retain mining rights to any gold discovered on George's lease, with me free to range further afield in the chopper to do my own prospecting. The last expedition and assay costs had run Danny short, and he didn't want to ask Brie for money, so apart from the chopper, I was to kick in for the repairs from mulga scrub damage, a new water pump, a major service, and eight new Cooper off-road tyres for the Troopy; new bearings for the off-road trailer, an extra generator, an extra Engel camp fridge, new traction mats, and all the food.

Allowing for the usual delays on old car parts plus new springs and heavy-duty shockers, bringing the Troopy up to scratch was going to take four weeks at least, which gave me a chance to go for a medical check-up with Danny's doctor. I was getting gripes that wouldn't go away and didn't want to head out into the desert without getting that seen to and treated.

It turned out badly.

I was sitting in front of the doc talking through my symptoms when he noticed a little purple spot on my head, just above the left eyebrow. As an Alice Springs GP, he had seen plenty of melanomas, and he was looking at one right now.

He got out his magnifying glass, but didn't really need it.

"Jack, you have a melanoma on your head that needs immediate specialist treatment, and I don't like the sound of those persistent pains. I'm going to have to send you to Sydney. We'll run some blood and urine tests here for you to take with you, and in the meantime, I'll give you something for the pain."

He took the samples, gave me a prescription for the painkillers and made the Sydney appointment for me four days hence.

I flew commercial to Sydney, and that's when the shit hit the fan.

The melanoma was well advanced. That we cut out, as a day procedure.

The pain was pancreatic cancer. That was inoperable, as it had spread around my aorta.

Basically, a death sentence. The only unknown was 'how long?'

It came down to my decision on how I wanted to play it.

If I opted for no treatment, nine months to a year.

With radiotherapy and chemotherapy, maybe twice that, ending with palliative care over the final months.

I had experienced the heartbreak of my mother dying of bone cancer. Dad and I had sat at her bedside for two years while she battled the pain, the wasting, and the closing down of her wonderful mind.

Dad had died of cancer too. A chain smoker ever since the war, it was lung cancer that killed him. He chose not to have treatment except for the pain, and both he and I agreed that his was the better way to go. He had what he described as 'a three-month cocktail party', attended by an endless procession of practically every friend he had ever known, and it was only the last week the pain finally beat him, and he floated away on a cloud of morphine.

Way to go. Stock up on morphine and die in the desert. Even without my conviction, I would not have wanted Tess and Ariel to sit beside a hospital bed watching me slowly die, so in one way, things were turning out for the best.

And I still had a good nine months to find Lasseter's Reef.

Glass half-full. There's got to be a pony somewhere, under all this shit.

Back to Alice Springs, where I had to break the news about the cancer and our now somewhat shorter-term deal to Danny. He was stoic about the situation and also most helpful. He and the local doc were mates from way back, and we both went in to show him the specialist's report. I explained I needed a prescription for increasing levels of painkillers, ending with a good supply of morphine for my last hurrah. I expected some resistance from the doc but got none; in fact, he confided in me that he would make the same choice given my situation. Danny went one stage further and, after a number of beers at the footy club, introduced me to one of the trainers who sold me a big bag of marijuana and a bong, 'to use as needed'.

Danny also had some interesting news of his own. George's wife Brie had a visit from two Chinese men in suits and ties (unusual in Alice Springs, where most business is conducted in shorts). They were from 888 Mining, a mysterious Chinese-based exploration company who seemed to have unlimited resources and were already test-drilling on a large lease in the Peterman's, just south of Danny and George's holding. They offered Brie twice what George had paid for their lease. Brie politely refused to sell until Danny's upcoming expedition was over, but took their number. The long and short of it was Danny and Brie agreed they would sell if he failed to find either George or viable gold this time round.

Danny may have only been a simple concreter, but he was as sharp as a whip and probably should have been a police detective.

He came up with a disturbingly plausible conspiracy theory.

Danny was highly suspicious of 888 Mining. Apparently, they had bought a Peterman's exploration lease off another widow, Ida Postle. Widowed when her husband Ian had 'got drunk and crashed his ute into a tree'. 888 Mining had bought his mining lease three weeks after the funeral. Not suspicious in itself, except that Ian, like the Cooper brothers, was a member of the Pioneer Footy Club, where he caught the gold bug around the same time as George. They had often shared drinks together after (and sometimes contrary to coach's instructions, the night before) a game, and although Ian would have a drink, he was not a drinker; he always drank light beer and only ever stayed for one round, despite pleas from his mates and regular good-natured ribbing of being 'under the thumb'. On the night he died, he had left after his one round, cheerful as usual, and had been found on a back road, dead in his burned-out ute with a charred bottle of Teachers whiskey on the seat beside him.

The finding was 'accidental death due to alcohol', but Danny had never known Ian to drink whiskey or any other hard liquor, and he was well known in the club as a happy family man with heaps of friends, which seemed to cut out suicide. That being so, what was he doing driving a back road with an expensive Teachers Highland Cream whiskey traveller instead of going straight home?

What if 888 had killed Ian for his lease?

What if they had killed George for the same reason?

Not enough to go to the cops, but enough for us to be careful out there.

Two weeks later, everything was ready, and George set out in the Troopy, with me following in the Raven, having arranged to land next to the Troopy for more petrol where the road ended and the mulga started.

As I flew over the endless red desert, I thought of Harold Lasseter himself. Like many before me, I wondered about the man behind the mystery. I marvelled at anyone prospecting this unforgiving land, carrying supplies by camel train, and pondered his last days and lonely death. Was he a con man, or did he really find Australia's El Dorado? Danny and I were using the latest in technology and transport, and even then, the whole idea was daunting. I had experience in the bush, but survival in the desert was going to be a whole new ball game.

We made it out to base camp with only one fuel stop as planned. Everything was just as Danny had left it, but still no sign of George. Danny didn't really expect to find his brother there, but I hated seeing his hopes fade. I cheered him up as best I could, getting all the improvements squared away in the camp (which I am sure Lasseter would have regarded as complete luxury), plus also volunteered to fly Danny over his lease to fossick on any promising areas without compensation – after all, gold wasn't going to be any use to me, and Ariel and Tess were already in good financial shape.

Then the stars of the outback came out for the first of many nights at base camp. We lay back on our camp chairs and shared ice-cold beers out of the drinks Engel. Only two, as we were going to reserve our precious stock for celebration purposes, such as the day we found Lasseter's Reef! I didn't need to dip into my stash of weed, as the cancer was behaving itself for now.

Before worrying about gold, we went looking for George (or George's body, to be realistic). First up, I flew Danny at low altitude out to the gold hole, and then radiated out from there duplicating the search pattern taken by emergency services. Danny had built a cairn marker where he had found the empty Troopy as a starting point for the original search, and we again quartered the ground in a grid pattern out from that, eventually landing back at the cairn so Danny could show me the gold hole itself. Lifting off for camp, I happened to look down and noticed something unexpected. The Raven's rotor had blown sand away from the underlying rock at the landing point, which now stood out from above as a neat circle.

The unexpected thing was there was a second, larger circle close by, that like ours was far too precise to have been made by a dust devil. A second helicopter had landed *beside* the marked landing area, yet Danny confirmed that he and the emergency services guys had landed as we did within the marker stones.

Detective Danny Cooper was right onto it: "What if 888 landed one of their choppers here and killed George to get hold of our lease?"

Quite a 'what if?' but it did fit the 'chain of evidence', as Danny insisted on calling it.

We resolved to sell our lives dearly if 888 came calling. I had grown up in the Western District, popping rabbits with a .22, and had been known in my cups to describe myself as a crack shot as well as a gun surfer, but Danny clearly needed target practice. Like me, he and George had set up for shooting game with a nice BRNO hunting rifle teamed with a good scope, but Danny ruefully admitted he had missed all five rock wallabies and two rabbits he had tried for, and that George had been the great white hunter of the pair. We tried shooting rocks as targets but quickly established Danny 'couldn't hit the side of a barn from the inside', as we shooters say. We decided that if an 888 gunman took me down, Danny's best bet was to stay in the cave and let fly with the shotgun when anyone poked his head into the entrance. Meanwhile, I would shoot any rock wallabies, roos or top-knot pigeons we stumbled upon.

Like all treasure hunters, we started full of optimism. We took the Troopy out to the gold hole for Danny to peg it out and complete his sampling. The quartz samples he had had assayed had come up with only low mineralisation, but on the basis one rock had shown grains of physical gold, he was going to leave 'no stone unturned', so to speak, before giving up on the gold hole and its surrounds. Two months with no show of gold took its toll on Danny, as of course did the loss of his brother.

The passing weeks took their toll on me too. The cancer was firing up, and to keep the pain at bay, I had started smoking pot with Brufen chasers most days, with the Endone and morphine held in reserve for my last hurrah. I had also lost my appetite, even for a nice rock wallaby steak or roast topknot pigeon, and although I tried to eat as much as I could to keep my strength up, I was getting steadily weaker. As agreed, I had extended my search outside the bounds of the brothers' lease, looking for both George and any promising quartz outcrops. About fifty kilometres west of the lease, I pegged one green white quartz outcrop where the metal detector was making a decent noise all over the place and brought back some bags of samples with promising black veins of manganese, but no visible gold. Well worth assaying, though.

During this time, there were two other highlights worth mentioning.

The first was that Danny did finally bag his roo. They were few and far between, but one day, I looked down from on high and saw a pair of them, so I gave up on gold and flew back to take Danny roo stalking. It was bloody hot crawling through the low scrub on our bellies, and I was pretty weak, but all worth it when we got within range and Danny found himself with a big male roo in the cross hairs of his scope.

I whispered, "Don't pull, *squeeze*," which he must have done because he dropped the roo dead as a door nail with a head shot. This magnificent effort got us a week's supply of roo steaks, and Danny the camp nickname of 'Annie,' short for Annie Oakley.

The second was a big black chopper swooping low over our base camp. It didn't land, but it had to be 888.

They knew we were here.

Danny and I got on well. Although we had some great twilight chats, we were both essentially men of few words, comfortable in each other's silences and respectful of each other's moments of depression, when each preferred to be left alone.

Nonetheless, it got to Danny in the end. One night, he went to the Engel, pulled out two cold stubbies, flipped the tops with the back of his hunting knife, and handed me one. There were no new finds to celebrate, so I knew something was up.

"Jack, I can't handle this anymore. We are never going to find George or any gold either, and I can't stay here any longer watching you die. Let's both go home. I'll sell this worthless bloody lease to 888 and at least get some money for Brie out of it all. Will you come back with me while you can still travel? You don't have long to go and surely you would like to get back to your family while you can?"

I was sort of expecting something along these lines, as Danny had gone quiet for some days, and I had my reply ready:

"I won't be coming back with you. I couldn't bear my family having to watch my last weeks, either. I'll stay here; when it comes time to check out, I have the morphine, and in the meantime, I have plenty of pot and the serious pain killers.

Once I can no longer make it out prospecting, I intend to paint the cave and its rock art as a parting gift for my wife Ariel."

"As far as 888 is concerned, I have a better idea. I'll buy the Pioneer Mining lease from you for the same price they are offering, so that way, you and Brie will get your money, and 888 will get nothing."

"One other thing. I'm not religious, but I can't come to terms with ending up rotting away unburied. I'll add twenty grand more for you to come back out for my final day and take me out with the morphine. I'll ring in plenty of time for you to get here and will have a grave already dug alongside the big rock, so on the big day, all you need to do is play doctor. I get into my swag beside the hole, you do the deed with the morphine, make sure I'm dead, zip me up, tip me in, then fill in the hole."

"I'll even reserve a nice cold stubby so you can toast me when you've finished shovelling. A true desert funeral!"

There was a fair bit of argument over this somewhat macabre plan, but Danny eventually agreed. The arrangements were really pretty simple. I wrote Pioneer Mining a cheque for sixty thousand dollars and used my laptop and printer to produce the transfer of the lease to Mako Mining NL, which Danny signed as a Pioneer Mining NL Director to be posted to Tess. He would take the Troopy and trailer back to Alice Springs, leaving the dirt bike, and I would ring him every week on the sat phone, right up until I summoned him to return for my last day on earth.

Neither of us were into long farewells, so Danny departed two days later.

He made it back to Alice Springs in eight days, which was good going, considering he had two flats before he hit the Lasseter Highway and also had to stop and clean out the petrol filter at one stage. Our weekly sat phone call worked well, and I was pleased to hear how grateful Brie and Jo had been for me buying their worthless lease.

There are positives and negatives to being alone. The main negative is of course loneliness; I missed Danny's companionship. This was offset to an extent by a closer relationship with the desert: the endless landscape, the sunrises and sunsets, the awesome blaze of stars each night, and the all-pervading silence. It was amazing how much closer I came to the life around me: the zebra finches that had first given away the cave entrance to George and Danny had become completely tame, aided by feeds of broken up Malt-O-Milk biscuits and a biscuit tin of water that doubled as a bird bath. I was also visited by two plump topknot pigeons coming to have a daily drink at the pool. I looked forward to their gently cooing far too much to shoot them, so I fed them Malt-O-Milks instead. As I got weaker and consequently sat still for long periods, I was treated to constant entertainment watching the different insects around the cave pool and the spiny lizard that lay in wait for them under his rock.

Four weeks of our scheduled Friday sat phone calls went by, featuring AFL footy results, politics, and the life of Alice Springs from Danny's end, and details of air prospecting forays from mine.

Then, my sat phone went off on a Tuesday; out of schedule. Danny was both excited and worried.

"Jack, Jo just got another visit from 888. She told them we had sold the Pioneer Mining lease to you, as we agreed. For God's sake, watch yourself out there."

"No worries, Danny. Like we said, even if they do take me out, it will only cost me a couple of weeks, so don't worry about it. Don't forget, I'm the guy who taught you to shoot, and that I'm armed to the teeth with two long guns plus a shotgun and plenty of ammo."

It only took three weeks for 888 to make their play. A big black chopper with a gold 888 logo painted on the side flew low overhead. They obviously saw the Raven staked out down on the flat and also got a fix on the camp, as I had no time to bring in the gear; (in particular, the bright red Honda generator exposed way out in the open on its long lead). The 888-chopper landed right beside the Raven, and while that was going on, I loaded Dave's rifle and lay flat in the sniper position to check them out through the scope.

Just as well I did.

Two Chinese got out. Guy number one in the flying jacket was obviously the pilot, but guy number two was just as obviously a hit man. He was dressed in grey camouflage, carrying a military assault rifle (not your standard sporting gun), and if that was not enough, he had a sidearm in a holster on his belt. The only thing he was going to shoot out here with those particular firearms was me.

What to do?

I had ten seconds to make up my mind before the guy made cover on his way up to the cave.

On the count of three, I sighted six inches above his head to allow for the drop in trajectory, squeezed the trigger, and blew his head apart.

He dropped like a stone. The pilot dragged the body back into the chopper and took off.

I rang Danny as soon as the satellite was overhead.

"I reckon I just took out the guy who killed George," I said.

"Jesus! What happened?"

I explained, and then said: "They may come back with reinforcements, so if I look like being overrun, I'll buy you a signed note in a tobacco tin in the bottom of my fox hole, so at least you'll be able to explain George and my disappearances. I'll dig my fox hole under the overhang, so I'll be protected from the air."

A month went by with no further sign of 888, and Danny also confirmed that there were no announcements in the press about any outback shooting. We came to the conclusion that we were spot on with our theory that 888 were killing people for their leases; otherwise I would have had a visit from the Territory police by now.

My defensive action would have alerted 888 that we were on to them, and I calculated I was now protected to an extent, as they knew I had a radio and had no way of knowing what disclosures I had left in place were I to disappear like George.

I didn't expect another visit, but even so couldn't go back to the green quartz outcrop again, as I was getting too weak and drugged up to make it down to the flat, let alone fly the Raven, so I used my strongest moments painting the cave in oils. The pain was a daily visitor now, so I reckoned it was time to make important phone calls to Tess and then Danny while I still could.

The minutes dragged by as I waited for the satellite; I couldn't wait to speak to Tess again, even though it was going to be with bad news.

Connection.

Ringtone.

"Hello?"

It was her.

"Hi, kiddo, it's me."

"Dad? Where are you?"

"I'm sitting on a camp chair in the Peterman ranges, looking up at more stars than you've ever seen in your life," I said, to at least kick things off with normal conversation.

"Don't tell me you've found Lasseter's Reef?"

Time to come clean.

"Afraid not; if it's out here, it's still somewhere under the sand. I'm sorry to say I'm calling with bad news. I didn't know 'till after I left, but I have terminal pancreatic cancer and don't have much longer to go. Would love to see you to say goodbye, but you'll need to get here pretty quick."

A break in her voice.

"Oh no! Dad, we've got our pilots licences now, so we'll lease a helicopter in Alice Springs and fly you out to hospital. All we need is your GPS reference."

"No, I'm afraid I'm well past that. I'd love you to come, but don't bring your mother, as I don't want this to affect any new relationship she may have – now I can't come home and clear myself it's best she forgets me and finds someone else. You also need to realise I've wasted away a lot as I can't eat properly any more, so you will be faced with a pretty awful sight. You won't need a helicopter. Have you got a pen?"

She had one right there.

"Just fly commercial to The Alice, and Danny Cooper will drive you and Ben out here in his Toyota. He's a great guy who has been my partner in the desert, and he'll have quite a story to tell you." I gave her Danny's phone number and address in Alice Springs.

"Don't be too sad about the cancer. Everybody has to die sometime, and if I can see you once more before I go, I will die happy. There's also something I want you to do, but we'll talk about that when you get here."

A sob.

"I love you, Dad."

"No blubbing. You've got things to do," I said sternly.

Then signed off with a little dark humour:

"One of which is to buy an Esky, a bottle of Four Pillars gin, some Mediterranean Fever Tree tonic and a lemon. You're in charge of my last drink."

"See you soon."

I hung up before she realised I was crying too.

Next call was to tell Danny it was time for the end game, but that it had now changed slightly. Tess and Ben were coming to Alice Springs, and Danny was to bring them out to the camp instead of coming alone. He was much happier with that, as it shared the responsibility of my assisted dying. I told him to tell Tess everything about 888, including my sniper role.

It only took them two weeks to make it out, which was just enough time for me to finish the painting for Tess to give to Ariel as my parting gift. I couldn't work on it for long stretches, as I now needed morphine daily and had to concentrate when painting, so in the event managed the last brush stroke only three days before they arrived, just time enough for the paint to dry. Danny had rung on the sat phone each day on the way out, so on the big day I was ready to receive visitors, which basically meant charging up the electric razor, trimming my beard and not shooting up that morning.

Sound carries a long way in the desert, so I heard Danny before I saw him.

The big surprise was that not one but two Toyotas hove into sight. Using Dave's rifle scope from my perch on the ridge, I picked up their dust clouds long before they got to the flat where I had staked down the Raven. I recognised Danny's white Troopy and trailer in the lead, plus a new model Toyota Land Cruiser eating red dust a kilometre behind, towing its own trailer loaded with petrol cans.

Finally, they arrived at the flat below.

Danny, Tess, and Ben climbed out of the Troopy.

Dave, Jules, and Ariel emerged from the Land Cruiser.

I had thirty minutes to brush my beard before they trekked up to me. Tess was lugging a baby Esky. Aha, my Four Pillars gin and tonic. And I reckon it was going to be nice and cold.

They did a good job hiding their shock at my appearance but didn't look all that happy.

"Sorry you have to see me as thin as this," I said, turning on the outback adventurer's grin I had been practicing.

Ariel got in the first kiss, then Tess, then Jules.

Everyone managed not to cry.

After the greetings, we had a lot to talk about. Ariel's news was the best. "This is way beyond the call of duty for an ex-wife," I had opened with.

"I'm *not* an ex-wife," she replied. "In the end, I couldn't bring myself to file the papers. We're still married, although I have to say you're really testing the 'in sickness and in health' part of the deal," she said with the smile I knew so well.

"I've made you a present, but it'll cost you a kiss," was my response.

Got one.

A good one, too – thank goodness I'd cleaned my teeth!

"I painted our cave for you as a parting gift. It's on the easel just inside the entrance. You will see beautifully preserved aboriginal cave art on the walls that could also be of great interest to naturalists. This whole area must have originally had plenty of water. I'm sure one image shows a Tasmanian tiger eating a quoll; you can clearly see the thylacine stripes and teeth on the tiger and the spots on the quoll. If I'm right, either that Tassie tiger's a long way from home, or the artist was!"

Danny turned on the light sticks, and they all went in for a tour of the cave and pool.

Ariel emerged and gave me a gentle hug. I think she was worried I'd break.

"Darling, it's the best painting you've ever done. It's really, really wonderful. Arthur Streeton, eat your heart out!" she said.

"It's the drugs," I smiled back. "Should have tried them years ago!"

Time for the last requests.

"Before our little problem with 888, I wasn't going to tell any of you where I was, because I didn't want you to see me this way," I said. "But lying here, I have had plenty of time to think. Danny has been right all along; 888 is determined to extend their exploration lease and is prepared to kill to do it. Thanks for the loan of the Browning, Dave; without it, I would be dead somewhere out there myself. You sighted it in perfectly; I made perfect head shots on twelve rock wallabies, two roos, one rabbit and one 888 assassin without a single miss, so don't forget to remind the guys back at the pub I could've made the Olympic team! The Browning's back in the cave, all cleaned and oiled, and so is my Greener, which I want you to have."

"Remember the old saying, 'set a thief to catch a thief?' I think we can use 888 to get to Anna Cheng and force a confession out of her. Danny and I are convinced this lease is worthless, so we can offer 888 that as bait."

I had a sudden wave of nausea and had to stop for a rest, so Danny continued for me.

"Mako Mining owns this lease now, so you guys are free to bargain with 888. Jack showed me the S&J Agreement and explained how Silas Silver stole Jack's share of the Agency using the criminal clause. If you get a confession out of Anna Cheng, you can get Silas charged with fraud and use the same clause to get the Agency back, which must be worth a hell of a lot more than this useless piece of dirt," he said.

The wave of pain eased, so I got going again:

"The mining lease and the Agency Agreement are in my briefcase back there, so that is all you will need."

More pain. Another rest.

"How will we do it?" asked Tess. Bless her, she used the plural.

"Just find where Anna Cheng is, then seek a one-on-one meeting with the CEO of 888 Group in Sydney and put a deal to him. We agree to sell the Mako Mining lease to 888 at their asking price the day Anna Cheng records an official confession to the Agency fraud. Then leave the rest to them. My bet is that 888 will hit her a lot harder than we could with any legal action. If she folds, it'll break things wide open."

"Now I see. Set a thief to catch a thief," Tess responded.

More pain. Another rest.

Ariel put her hand gently over my mouth.

"No more talking, darling."

"Let's all have a drink. Danny said you promised to have ice and cold stubbies in the Engel fridge, and Tess has your Four Pillars gin and tonic in the Esky, together with a nice fresh lemon."

Bloody good idea! Everybody ran around fixing drinks; there were four cold stubbies left in the Engel, so Dave and Danny had those, while the rest of us experienced the world's best G&T, with two precious ice cubes and a lemon slice in each glass. I couldn't really taste mine, but didn't tell them and spoil their treat.

Another rest.

By now, the sun was going down, and it was nearly time to check out. At least I knew for sure I wasn't going to hell – hell is not the place they scare you with in church. Hell is wasting away in a care home or a hospital.

Although only Danny knew it, the next conversation with each of them would be my goodbye.

"It's a bit hard for me to concentrate talking to everyone at once. Can I have a chat to each of you in turn?"

Danny knew why, so he went first.

"I'll never forget you avenged George, mate. You want me to do it now, don't you? I'll do what you want, but I'm giving back the twenty grand. You getting the bastard who killed my brother is payment enough."

"No, you must keep the money as I still need you to do the deed," I said. "I could inject myself, but I don't want them to witness that, and I can't have any of them carrying any guilt. This way, they can pretend you're a doctor, and they are just my family and friends saying goodbye. No-one here would ever tell, but you are seriously breaking the law, so you are more than earning your money. I've dug the grave beside the big rock like we said, so all you need do is hit me with a full syringe of morphine once I've said goodbye to everyone, and then bury me in my swag. The morphine and syringe are in the other Engel. It's been great knowing you, and I can't thank you enough for this last favour. I just wish we'd found Lasseter's gold."

The big, tough back line enforcer of the Pioneer Footy Club back line teared up, the pussy. He nodded without speaking, patted my shoulder, and went back to get Dave, the next in line.

Our talk was longer, as one would expect of best mates with a long history. I came clean with him, as I would with each of them.

"You won't have guessed it looking at me, but the pain from the cancer has become unbearable, and I can't go on. I've only held out this long to say goodbye, but as soon as the stars come out, Danny is going to hit me with a massive dose of morphine and end it all. I'll die happy, having seen each of you today."

"One more thing. Once you get back to civilisation, you should register an exploration lease around the last quartz outcrop I logged 50k away. The GPS coordinates are in my briefcase. The metal detector signal was going off the scale, and the samples I chipped off the outcrop had manganese running through them, which can be a precursor to gold. I reckon the assay results will have to be good, so I'm sure you could sell the lease on to one of the big miners, if you guys don't want to keep going yourselves."

"Just don't sell it to 888!"

"As for Ariel and Tess..." I choked up.

Dave was more of a mystic than Danny. He understood straight away, and also knew exactly what I wanted to hear.

"I'll look after them. Tess and Ben have each other, but Ariel will be lost. For starters, we'll kidnap her and drag her up to the Whitsundays."

"Oh yeah, and if you ever get to meet Huey up there, get him to send Lorne a couple of decent waves, will you? And if it's not too much trouble, you might also ask the boss to send a kingfish or two past Doc and I while he's at it."

With those parting words, two best mates said goodbye laughing.

Next was Jules.

I didn't have to struggle through explaining what was about to happen. She already knew.

Two first loves said their goodbyes with laughter, not tears.

A big wave of pain, so I had to call time out, which involved my second and last Four Pillars gin and tonic.

I shooed the crowd back into the cave with the words: "You stay, Tess; you're next up."

She grabbed both my shoulders and looked me in the eyes.

"Dad, what are you *doing*?"

Women are more perceptive than men. She knew only too well.

"I'm doing what I have to do, kiddo. This is my last day, and seeing you all is more than I could ever have asked for. Danny's going to give me a big dose of morphine as soon as I'm finished saying goodbye, then I'll just drift away. Won't hurt a bit."

This was the only time in her life I had ever seen her beaten. She cried without a sound, kissed my forehead, raised her hand in a wave, and walked slowly back to the others without looking back.

Women are more perceptive than men. Ariel came straight out of the cave, kneeled down in front of me, and took both my hands.

"When?" was all she said.

"As soon as I've finished saying goodbye to everyone. You were always going to be the hardest."

We talked of our life together until the next wave of pain hit, and I told her to marry again if the right guy came along. That just made her mad.

"Why d'you think I couldn't go through with the bloody divorce? You are the love of my life, and that's it. I couldn't leave you, and here you are leaving me. It's not fucking fair!"

We ended up laughing through our tears.

Ben was last, and in one way the most important.

"Look after Tess, mate. She's going to be pretty sad."

"Of course I will. You're a hard act to follow, Jack, but I'll do my best."

Ben chose to be practical rather than emotional. Thank God for that, I was starting to fade, and all the crying was getting to me.

"Mako clothing and boards are going gangbusters, so we have plenty of money. We're going to start a national shark patrol using Jet Rangers. We'll paint them Mako blue with your Mustang jaws and sling a bloody great siren underneath them. I reckon the sharks will be more scared than the surfers! I'll get Tess up flying as soon as the first one is delivered, to keep her busy."

"That's great. I want to look down from my cloud and see Mako shark patrols all over the place. See if Tess can get the Agency back, to help pay for them."

I took off my faithful Rolex and handed it up to him.

"This is for you. It has kept perfect time for thirty years, surviving the Vietnam War and my helicopter crash at Long Tan, but is long overdue for a service. You'll need to adjust the band to your size, because my wrist has got very thin. Now can you go and get Danny? It's time for Elvis to leave the building."

He gently shook my thin, thin hand.

I think he thought it would break.

Perfect timing. The sun had gone down, and the stars were coming out. Danny came out of the cave, holding a syringe and two phials of morphine, with everyone alongside.

"Let's do the deed on my favourite camp bed," I said by way of lightening the mood. "That way, I can look up and see the stars."

Dave and Danny helped me into my swag, then carried the bed with me on it out into the open. I lay back on the pillow, and at last felt at peace.

Ariel held one hand and Tess the other, just like the day we walked into court. I smiled up at them and above them, the blaze of the desert heavens. Breaking the silence, a farewell call from Milly, the mopoke that lived on the ridge above the camp.

I looked up at Ariel and gave her my best smile.

"Darling, you're still young. Remember me, but marry again."

Then turned to Tess. "Kiddo, follow your dreams. I'll be watching."

I can't bear their tears anymore.

"Okay, Danny, count of three."

"One."

Goodbye, you two.

"Two."

I squeeze their hands.

"Three."

I'm lying on my Gordon Woods. I smell its fibreglass resin. Getting cold, this winter.

Jack paddled out smiling.

Chapter 23
Tess

We buried Dad in his swag beside the big rock, in the grave he had dug himself.

Once we covered him over, there was only the inscription he had chiselled on the rock to show he had ever lived:

Jack Johnson
1947-1995

Not good enough. I found Dad's cold chisel and hammer in the toolbox, marked out the three extra letters I needed with a Sharpie, and got to work:

Jack Johnson DSO
1947-1995

I took a photo of the grave and rock, as I intended to do a painting of my own once we got back home, plus some extra flash shots of the cave, its rock art, and pool.

While I was chipping away the extra three letters, the others broke camp and loaded everything into the Toyotas and trailers. By the time we left, there was nothing remaining but the cave in its original condition, and Dad's inscription carved on the big rock. Danny and Dave drove the Toyotas, with Mother and Jules, whilst Ben and I flew out in Dad's Raven.

Ben hovered over Dad's final resting place for me to take one last shot and then zoomed low over the Toyotas heading for the fuel rendezvous, trailing their plumes of red dust.

I thought I'd be useless for a long time, but a cold determination took over as soon as we were in the air.

I looked across at Ben and said: "Silas Silver drove Dad into the desert to die alone, just for money."

"He's going down."

"Your dad worked out just the way to do it, too," said Ben. "We need to get our ducks in a row. Someone in the Agency will know where Anna Cheng is, and your mother has the contacts to get all the info we need on 888 before you confront them."

I told him my thoughts: "If we do get a confession out of Anna Cheng, I intend to go straight to the media, followed by the police. Silas Silver won't know what hit him."

"Mother will have some ideas of her own. She has gone quiet ever since Dad died. I know her; she's not quiet just because she's sad. She's thinking."

"One last thing," Ben said awkwardly. "I promised your Dad I'd look after you."

"And I will. All your life."

I squeezed his joystick hand, and we flew on in silence.

Back at the Alice, we all congregated at Danny's place. What with recent events, Jo was relieved to get Danny back in one piece and turned on one of their famous Alice barbeques with plenty of chops, massive steaks, and cold drinks. An Alice Springs wake put on by Jack's Alice Springs mates. Danny confirmed he would send in Dad's last samples in for assay, and we agreed we would keep him in the loop as our attack on Silas Silver unfolded.

Mother had been thinking. And she was focussed. Gone was the socialite, and in her place was a woman who had lost not only her place in society (which she now seemed to not care about) but the only man she had ever loved (which she very much did). She was out for revenge, and Silas Silver was going to pay. By the time we arrived back in Melbourne, she had a strategy in place to start our grand plan.

Chapter 24
Ariel

I had spent all those months waiting to tell Jack I was still his wife, and now he was gone. My world was diminished without him, but I could not afford to get morose and start drinking, or whatever. Tess and I were going to set things right, not only for our family's reputation but for Jack's legacy.

As soon as we hit Melbourne, I rang Fred Swain, an old boyfriend who now happened to be deputy chairman of the Australian Securities and Investments Commission.

"Freddie, I need a favour," I began. "I need everything you can get on the 888 Group, registered in Sydney; particularly their mining division, 888 Mining. I need to contact their CEO for a very difficult negotiation, and the more I know about them in advance, the better."

"Okay, I'll get the team to run a full report. I hope you're not intending to invest in the 888 Mining float in Hong Kong. They are a bit on the nose as far as their casinos are concerned."

Ah Freddie, obtuse as always. ASIC were after 888 for money laundering, and this was Freddie's way of letting me know, without compromising his position. I resolved to push him further once I had the report in hand.

The report only took ten days, which meant ASIC had given us a priority (it's not who you are; it's who you know). It showed that the 888 Group was listed in Hong Kong, with interests in three Macau casinos and, even more interestingly, ownership of a working gold mine in Brazil. In the same letter as the report was the prospectus for the 888 Mining float, which was to be launched on the Hong Kong stock exchange two months hence. The prospectus included a section on 'Australian Gold', headed somewhat ambiguously with a colour plate of the 'Welcome Stranger,' the largest gold nugget ever found anywhere in the world (albeit in 1869, in Victoria, thousands of kilometres away from the 888 desert leases). Within the prospectus was a map of 888's Peterman Ranges leases, claimed to cover 'Lasseter Country', the probable location of Lasseter's legendary five-mile gold reef, worth billions if found. Detail on the leases included the new one acquired from Ida Postle, noted as "1996 expansion of our holdings across Lasseter Country." We rang Danny about it, and he had yet another conspiracy theory to contribute:

"I reckon I know what they're up to. It's a stock market scam; they're going to salt their Peterman's lease with gold-bearing rock from Brazil and make a killing on the 888 Hong Kong share float."

Sometimes it's useful to have a practical guy on the team, in addition to forensic accountants. We couldn't prove a thing, but Freddie was very interested in Danny's theory, and assured me that ASIC would query any claim of a gold find by 888 plus require them to produce verification of all assays by a government appointed geologist.

Meanwhile, we had done some salting of our own. Jack's last manganese-rich samples tested at eighty grams of gold to the tonne; well worth taking to the stage of drilling test cores. Instead of coming from Jack's last find fifty kilometres away, Danny had logged them as coming from the gold hole on the Mako Mining lease; ideal information for 888 to feed to its Hong Kong broker prior to their float. We still had Jack's GPS coordinates of where he had pegged the real find, and Dave, Tess, and Ben resolved that Mako Mining would apply for a fifty-hectare exploration lease of the surrounding area once the dust had settled, as Jack had advised.

Maybe one day we would mount a new expedition to go back and have a better look.

But right now, we were ready to send Tess to Sydney.

Chapter 25
Tess

As it turned out, we had no trouble locating Anna Cheng. She had opened an ARI branch in Hong Kong (no doubt using her ill-gotten gains from Silver Advertising) and was already trading there. Finding her would be as easy as walking into her office.

Organising a meeting with Mr Chu, the Australian CEO of 888 Group, was also a walk in the park. Mother acted as my PA, and as soon as she announced me as a Director of Mako Mining wishing to discuss the sale of our Peterman's lease, the door was opened wide and a meeting scheduled two days later.

Despite my protests I would only wear them once, Mother insisted on taking me shopping at Georges for a black pin striped power suit, white blouse, and black shoes, as befitted the director of a serious mining company.

I wore the new outfit home to show off my new image; which must have had some sort of impact on Ben, as he followed me up to the bedroom with a gleam in the eye. I just had time to get the new suit onto its big plastic hanger before he threw me on the bed.

"I hope my wife never finds out. I've always wanted to root an ice queen executive!" was his comment as we lay spent.

Men are such visual animals.

On the other hand, we women are the perceptive ones, although it didn't need rocket science to work out that it doesn't take even the most fastidious of us an hour to change into jeans.

Mother looked stern.

"I hope you didn't crease the suit," she couldn't help commenting. Even though we were now married, Ben went bright red and retreated to the kitchen. I didn't turn a hair.

"I'm afraid Ben tore the zip, but we can always use a safety pin," I replied.

At least we were laughing again.

As was fitting, I completed my equipment for the meeting with Dad's own black leather briefcase. In it was the Mako Mining lease, together with the salted assay reports on the gold hole, photocopies of selected press articles on Dad's case, featuring photographs of Anna Cheng, and most important of all, a Lease transfer form, filled out but unsigned.

Two days later found me deposited by taxi at Australia Square Tower, once the tallest building in Sydney and still one of the city's most impressive. 888 Group occupied the entire fortieth floor, and Mr Chu's palatial office a large chunk of that. The office was huge, decorated entirely in black and red, with a big '888' in gold bass-relief standing out on the wall behind Mr Chu's massive black-lacquered desk.

Mr Chu himself matched the decor, resplendent in a black silk suit with a gold tie fixed with a large gold nugget tie pin. He was short and stocky, and for some reason, I saw him in my mind's eye climbing into the ring to take on Meishai: Thailand versus China, for the World Middleweight Title. I must have smiled at the thought, as it immediately broke the ice.

Mr Chu smiled back, gestured to the strategically low chair in front of his desk, and offered tea, which I politely declined.

Then we started in on the meeting itself. Mr Chu fired the opening shot:

"I was told you were beautiful, but not this beautiful."

Quite the charmer.

"It's all in the makeup," I replied.

"May I call you Tess?"

Time to cut the crap and get down to business.

"Certainly. Thank you for seeing me at such short notice. I have come to sell 888 the Mako Mining Lease in the Peterman's."

"But there is one special condition that requires some explanation, and that is why we insisted on a one-on-one meeting."

"Are you familiar with my father's conviction last year in Melbourne?"

He was. He had been well briefed.

"He didn't do it, and with your help we can prove it."

I summarised the case, explaining Anna Cheng's key role in the conviction and the perjury by Silas Silver to steal Dad's half of S&J.

"We are convinced that Silas Silver found out about Anna's research fraud and held that over her to make her set up my father on the sexual assault charge.

"This is where our request to you comes in. We need you to use your Hong Kong connections to get a video confession out of Anna. Get us that, and we will sell you the Peterman's lease owned by Mako Mining at your asking price."

Mr Chu nodded and smiled.

Good sign.

I clicked open Dad's briefcase and laid copies of the Mako Mining lease, the GPS location of the gold hole salted in documentary form with the assay of Dad's green quartz outcrop, and the lease transfer form on the desk in front of Mr Chu.

"We have found shows of gold-bearing quartz already; plus a number of samples assaying high enough to warrant extensive diamond drilling. If we can resolve the sale quickly, you may be able to announce the 888 acquisition of the Mako Mining lease in time for your Hong Kong float."

"Anna Cheng will be easy to find. She has opened an Advertising Research International office in Hong Kong. Here is the address, and here are some press articles with her picture."

"That's it."

Mr Chu looked at me and smiled again.

"I'm glad I never met your father," he said. "He was a very good shot."

"And he would be very proud of his daughter. Your father and I may have started as enemies in the desert, but you should know that we Chinese value family honour above all things. Will you join me for lunch?"

After my US experience I was a bit wary of lunches, but even though he was almost certainly a serious white-collar criminal, this was where the deal was to be made, and that was what I was here for.

"I would like that," I said, smiling right back.

So up we went to the Summit, the revolving restaurant on the forty seventh floor of the same building.

Apart from the amazing view, The Summit offered some of the best food in Sydney.

Being a girl of simple tastes, I went for the Sydney rock oysters and John Dory, teamed with a Vasse Felix chardonnay, whilst Mr Chu stuck to traditional Chinese: steamed eel followed by Peking duck, washed down with half my bottle of chardonnay and followed by a bottle of 2010 Penfolds Grange and topped off with a snifter of Lois Tres cognac. At $950 for the bottle, I had to at least try the Grange, if only to make Dave jealous when I returned to Lorne. I am no wine connoisseur so couldn't describe the wine to Dave except to say, "It tasted really nice."

Mr Chu may have known his wine, but he couldn't hold his grog. He went progressively red in the face and had lowered his guard somewhat by the time the creme brulé and the Lois Tres cognac arrived.

"You can be confident we will get what you need from Anna Cheng," he said, shooting his left shirt cuff to free its gold nugget cuff link and reveal his wrist. "Do you know what this is?"

At first, I thought he was boasting about his wafer-thin gold Patek Philippe watch, but then he turned his hand over to reveal a little dragon tattooed above the watch band.

"It's a dragon. Isn't it beautifully done?" was my response.

"Yes, it is a dragon. A *black* dragon. You are now one of only six people in the world who know that I am a member of Black Dragon, one of the oldest and most feared triads in Hong Kong. You may be assured Ms Cheng will give us everything we want."

Scary.

Set a thief to catch a thief.

Loose lips sink ships: Freddie Swain's team was going to be highly interested to know of the Black Dragon connection, as ASIC continued to build their case against 888.

Lunch over, Mr Chu summoned his black Bentley and driver to whisk me to the airport, mission accomplished.

Anna Cheng was about to get the fright of her life.

Chapter 26
Anna

I left Australia for Hong Kong two months after the trial, with Silas Silver's thirty pieces of silver (or to be precise, the S&J cheque for fifty thousand dollars) in my briefcase. I had earned every dollar, not only for my part in convicting Jack Johnson and the subsequent media appearances, but for enduring the degrading sex visits by Silas.

Silas was not an attractive man. He looked like the accountant he was and also like the ambitious accountant he was; had married for money in the person of his wife Zelda, a large domineering woman who happened to be heiress to the Goldstein printing empire. Millions in waiting, but in the meantime, Silas had to put up with Zelda holding the purse strings and ruling the roost. He hated that and it also transpired, hated Zelda.

Sex on the night of the party was only the start. Commencing the week after the trial, he wanted more.

After the first week had gone by, the doorbell went, and there he was. I hoped he'd come to make the $50,000 payment he had not only promised me but had informed the media was to be the Agency compensation for my 'ordeal'. Maybe he had his chequebook in his coat.

He didn't.

He hadn't come to pay up; he'd come for sex.

"Now it's all over, may I have the money you promised?" was my opening remark.

"It's not *quite* all over. You still have the appearance on The Morning Show to go; then you get paid."

"In the meantime, I will have you whenever I want."

"Take off your clothes."

I did.

"Let's start with your mouth."

We did.

Finished on the rug.

Then he insisted we share a glass of wine. I felt more like throwing up, but obediently started to put on my clothes before getting the wine.

"I didn't say get dressed."

"I like you naked."

"I get dressed. You don't."

I was caught in a horrible power trip. I folded my clothes over the back of the sofa and produced a cold bottle of Sav Blanc and two glasses from the fridge.

"I don't go for Sav Blanc. Don't you have bubbles?"

I didn't.

"Buy some Verve before my next visit. You can put it on expenses."

He also insisted I break up with my boyfriend so I would be 'available' at all times.

It didn't stop.

Two days later: doorbell.

Silas.

"Hi honey, I'm home!"

Oh shit.

"Strip."

I strip.

"Down on your hands and knees."

I obey.

He seemed obsessed with taking me from behind, his hands on my hips to control the rhythm. Probably couldn't get that at home.

And so it went. I was trapped in a nightmare of my own making; despite the Melbourne University Psych Degree claimed in my resume I'm not really a qualified psychologist, but you didn't need to be one to know I was the victim of a very sick puppy. I was paying the price for Silas's domineering wife, added to a lifetime of being the fat guy who never got the girl, added to a serious case of sexual frustration, almost certainly stimulated by evenings watching porn, no doubt after Zelda had retired to bed with a good book.

In the end it was The Morning Show interview that saved me. I handled the expected sympathetic questions from the female host according to script, but the male host came out of left field with a worrying question:

"What do you have to say to the Truth reporter who claims it didn't happen at all, and you did it for the money?"

I went for the tears and left the female host to bail me out, ending the interview somewhat shaken. Fortunately, it also shook Silas enough to get me out of the country without further delay. He turned up that night with the promised cheque plus a one-way ticket to Hong Kong.

Sex was different that night. Silas said he wanted me to 'enjoy our last night together' and was quite gentle. I think the bastard was starting to believe his own fantasy and fall for me.

He even drove me to the airport the next day.

I achieved a small measure of revenge with our farewells.

"Once you are settled in Hong Kong, I could fly over and see you from time to time," was his parting remark as they started boarding.

He wasn't about to get me back to Australia for any fraud charge now, so at last I was free to treat him the way I felt.

"I don't ever want to set eyes on you again. You are the filthiest, most evil prick I have ever met, and I hope you get what you deserve."

Then turned on my heel and joined the queue without so much as a backward glance.

I had already sold my car, arranged for Melanie to sell my furniture, and transferred my bank account to Hong Kong, so all I had to do when I arrived was to deposit the S&J cheque and rent a flat. I had plenty of money, so went upmarket on that, as I intended to 'follow the money' right from the word go.

I signed up for an eleventh-floor furnished gem overlooking Victoria Harbour and prepared to launch myself onto Hong Kong society.

The first step was to reconnect with old school friend, Yu Yan, now married to a Director of Jardines, who as well as being filthy rich was a well-respected member of the Royal Hong Kong Jockey Club.

I shouted Yu Yan and husband Jian to dinner at the new Ozone Sky Bar to celebrate my arrival, and they reciprocated by inviting me to the Hong Kong Cup as their guest. First base had been reached.

It was there I met the man of my dreams.

At a betting window, of all places.

A fat, sweating, punter pushed in front of me to place his bet on the big race when a voice behind cut in.

"I think the lady was first. Get back and wait your turn!"

The punter took one look at the tall, athletic man in black, mumbled an apology, and did what he was told.

My God, my knight in shining armour was handsome. Lancelot, eat your heart out! Or was Sir Galahad the good-looking one?

"Thank you so much," I found myself stammering. "Now you've got me to the betting window, have you got any tips? I've just arrived from Australia and have no idea of the form."

"Well, I'm putting my money on State Taj. He's Australian trained and the hoop is Damien Oliver, who they reckon can ride a bit. Try him."

We both did exactly that and nearly spilt champagne over each other when State Taj bolted it in, the first Australian trained winner of the Hong Kong Cup. What a way to start a relationship; for start one it certainly did.

Two happy winners.

Two glasses of Dom.

Conversation.

This started with an exchange of names, as such conversations usually do. His was Liu Wei.

I went for the standard opener:

"What do you do for a living?"

Liu Wei smiled. Nice teeth.

"At the moment, I'm a taxi driver. But I'm *going* to be a film star."

"Really?" was about all you could say to that.

"Really. A scout from Golden Harvest came to our Kung Fu school last Thursday, and they want to interview me for a part in their latest action movie."

"The guy in the queue was lucky he didn't take you on then," I said laughing. "When a superhero says back off, you'd better back off."

"Okay, Lois Lane, how about dinner before I have to go save the world?"

"Only if there are no phone boxes around. I don't want you disappearing on me!"

Dinner was set for the next night.

I tidied the bedroom.

Just as well; we could hardly keep our hands off each other long enough to get back there.

166

For the first time in my life, I was in love, and it was clear Lieu Wei felt the same way. It changed everything. Money was no longer my sole purpose in life, I just wanted to wake up each day beside Lieu Wei and be worthy of him.

Things fell into place as if by magic. We decided living apart was a waste of time, so Lieu Wei left the dockside pad he shared with his brother and moved in. He brought with him the most wonderful art collection accumulated over many years, all unknown artists, but every picture a brilliant piece of work.

There are many ways to make money. You can win it, steal it, marry it, or (shock, horror) even work for it. I once read 'The Pursuit of Excellence', an American self-help book dedicated to success. One of its most impactful passages said something like 'achieve excellence and the money will follow'. This had not registered, as my focus had been on only chasing the money itself (a not unreasonable goal for a girl whose parents had laboured seven-day weeks in a sweat factory to send their daughter to Hong Kong to be educated, then Australia) but for the first time, the new, honest way took hold.

Lieu Wei literally fell on his feet at Golden Harvest, becoming one of their leading stunt men in the space of only three months. He still had a way to go before becoming the next Bruce Lee, but he had fun, made good money, and, with his friendly disposition, built connections with all manner of people in and around the studio, from the guy who cleaned up the spatters of fake blood to the executive observers who were just as star struck as the rest of us and were always hanging around the studio cast parties.

I also came to know the right people and one evening found myself sharing a Mai Tai with a guy called Ji Ho, one of the Executive Producers. We started talking about US film stars and Australian TV commercials, and that's when I got my big break.

"How do they select the best talent in Australia?" Ji Ho asked.

"Well, with known talent, they usually go by their Q Rating," I said. "Don't you use that here?"

He didn't.

Hadn't even heard of it.

As it turned out, neither had his boss. I gave both of them one of my new ARI Hong Kong business cards and received a call the very next day, asking me to come in and explain it all.

It was only a week's work after that to get ARI appointed Hong Kong Agent for Q Rating Research by its US principal, and I started implementing Q Ratings for Golden Harvest straight away.

No falsified results anymore; I had gone legit, and it felt good.

Over the next six months, things took off. ARI Hong Kong now boasted an office with six staff, and things were going amazingly well. I felt only excitement when I was asked to come into an executive suite at the Mandarin to help make a film to promote the studio.

I wore my black Jimmy Choo dress with the gold Tiffany necklace and bracelet which I had brought all the way from Australia, cabbed it to the Mandarin, and went up to the twelfth-floor suite booked by Golden Harvest.

I was greeted by Golden Harvest Production Manager Li Chang no less, a cameraman, and two others. One, dressed in a Brooks Bros suit with gold tie, was obviously some sort of Executive, and the other was either his bodyguard or a well-cast villain from a new action movie. He was huge and seemed to have no neck; he must have come from northern China.

Li Chang made the introductions:

"Anna, we have invited you here to make a very important video."

He took my hand, to confront the man in the Brooks Bros suit:

"This is Mr Kun. You must do exactly as he says."

Something was wrong. Li Chang didn't look like a man happy to be making a promotional video. He looked terrified.

Mr Kun spoke for the first time.

"You may go," he said to Li Chang, who practically ran out the door.

Then Mr Kun turned to me. His black eyes were cold.

"Do you know what Black Dragon is?" he asked.

I did.

"We've made movies about them," I said.

"They were Hong Kong's most feared triad in history."

"Not were. Are."

"I am Black Dragon."

"We require you to make a video for us. It concerns what you did in Australia before coming here."

"Here is the script," he added, handing me two sheets of paper. "You may like to expand on the written script or use your own words, but all essentials must be covered."

I looked at the two-page script. Essentially, it was my confession to setting up the sexual assault charge against Jack Johnson under the instructions of Silas Silver, then lying to the police and perjuring myself in court. The details were precisely correct.

"I'm not doing this," I said. "If it got out, I could be extradited to Australia and thrown in jail."

"Let me explain further," Mr Kun said. "If you refuse to make the video, we already have your confession in the suicide note we will leave here after Feng here throws you off the balcony."

"Your choice."

I chose life.

We made the video in only three takes. If I was going down, so was Silas, so I added an unscripted accusation of his subsequent regular sexual assaults of me, for good measure. The tears they filmed were real.

Mr Kun was pleased with that bit, and even offered the encouragement that it may help keep me out of jail if I was ever extradited to Australia.

The cameraman packed up his gear, and Mr Kun bade farewell:

"You have done well and need not fear Black Dragon, so long as you keep to the confession in any media interviews, or if you end up in court back in Australia. If you do not, you will be killed. Black Dragon can reach you anywhere in the world."

Feng had not said a word during the entire proceeding but now added a farewell of his own. He turned at the door and said, "I'm glad I didn't have to kill you. Please congratulate your boyfriend on the big fight in Fallen Angels."

Even hit men have heroes.

Chapter 27
Tess

I was in a Mako Girl production meeting at Surf Concepts when my mobile rang: "Tess Johnson? This is Mr Chu. We have the confession you asked for." "When can you come to Sydney?"

I flew up next day.

Taxied to Australia Square.

Pressed the button for the fortieth floor.

Was once again ushered into Mr Chu's office.

We bowed and shook hands.

"Please sit down, Tess," he said warmly. "I think you're going to like this." I sat in my chair and swivelled it around to face the flat screen monitor on the wall.

Mr Chu pressed a button on his desk array.

Video controls rose silently up from a hidden module on the black lacquered desk-top, and Mr Chu loaded a DVD into its cradle.

"You were absolutely correct about what happened to your father. Watch this."

I did.

There on screen was all the evidence we needed to vindicate Dad and nail Silas Silver for perjury, fraud and even 'real' sexual assaults of his own. We had him dead to rights.

"Will Anna Cheng confirm this to the police and the media?"

"Yes, she will."

"Now I think you have a mining lease to sign over."

I swivelled the chair around to face Mr Chu, who was grinning as if he'd just won the lottery. He passed over his gold Mont Blanc pen, and I signed the transfer as promised.

It was only eleven o'clock in the morning, so no Summit lunch this time around. Instead, Mr Chu pressed another button, and in came his PA to serve a full-blown tea ceremony, which Mr Chu explained was a Chinese tradition often enacted to consummate important deals. He also explained that premium Chinese teas were as highly regarded as fine wines and can sell for up to a thousand dollars a packet, as was the one we were having. I would have preferred a five-dollar iced coffee at the Arab with Ben, but that's just me.

"I hope this video will work for you, Tess. Black Dragon often operates outside the law, but we pride ourselves that we always do so with honour. There is no honour in what Silas Silver did to your father. He is beneath contempt."

Couldn't have put it better, myself.

I also couldn't wait to get down in the lift and ring Mother and Ben that we were about to clear Dad's name and nail Silas for what he had done.

Ben picked me up at the airport, and we headed straight to Mother's place in Toorak for a council of war.

Mother had it all thought out.

Ever since she had put Dad's death notices in the papers, she was a widow on a mission, her grief still raw and her anger unsatiated.

"Merely getting your father's conviction quashed is not enough. I want to make sure the police charge Silas Silver with fraud. I want him jailed for what he did and the harm he has caused our family."

"The way to push a police priority is media pressure, just the way Silas did to your father. You have had more to do with the media than I have Tess, what do you think is the best way to go there?"

I knew exactly what to do.

"My first thought was to go to the papers, but on thinking it through on the plane, I believe we should take it straight to 60 Minutes. The video footage is compelling, and a TV expose' will make such a large impact, the press will follow."

The die was cast.

I rang Channel 9 in Sydney for an appointment with Ted Hanley, Executive Producer of *60 Minutes.* Ted already knew me from my one minute of fame on Wide World of Sports, and of course was very familiar with the details of Dad's case and conviction.

I didn't need to say much.

"I have an exclusive for 60 Minutes, which the family is willing to give nine network for no fee. You will recall my late father's conviction for sexual harassment last year. I now have a video confession from the girl in question that it was all a setup, proving conclusively he didn't do it."

He nearly came down the phone.

"When can we meet?" was the immediate response.

The meeting was set for three days later, so it was back into the power suit and onto another plane, this time with Mother beside me.

We were treated like royalty; first, a meeting at headquarters to be followed with lunch at prestigious Sails Lavender Bay restaurant with executives of both Channel 9 and 60 Minutes.

Anna's video blew them away.

"This is going to be huge. Legal will of course require us to do things properly, and verify the story with Anna Cheng in person before we go into production. Do you have any objection to us following up directly with her?"

We didn't. I handed over the contact details of Anna's office in Hong Kong so they could commence the verification process.

They had obviously thought things through, as they had already mapped out the bare bones of the show. They wanted more from us than just Anna's video; hence the follow-up lunch. Ted put it to us with an air of unbridled enthusiasm:

"This could be one of the best Australian 60 Minutes ever. It will not only mean a war hero is vindicated and justice is done; it is a chance to tell your family story."

"And it's quite a story, isn't it? We have the press articles and TV footage going back years. Jack's war record, his advertising awards, plus the amazing work he did on the Mako sports car, your Fashions on the Field wins, Ariel; your billy cart crash, Tess; then your famous shower and equally famous tilt at the Million Dollar Wave; and finally, this video from Anna Cheng. It will make brilliant television, but more than that, it will show the world your amazing family as it really is. We will need to work with you both to put those segments together."

He had a point. My expulsion over the shower picture had always rankled, and this would give me a platform to put Boss Hog in his place, in front of the whole country. I was also able to reveal a clincher to add to the show. Up to now, our story of Dad's quest for Lasseter's Reef had not been publicised. To date, we hand only published his death notice and refused all interviews, but now was the time to tell the end of his story.

"You may have wondered where Dad disappeared to after his conviction. He was always fascinated by gold and took his helicopter into the Great Sandy Desert to look for Lasseter's Reef. He didn't really believe he would actually find it; he disappeared to protect his family from any more grief from you people in the media, and it cost us having him with us for the last year of his life."

A tear. Mother squeezed my hand under the table.

I asked their tech guy to connect my laptop to their wall monitor and then clicked on the first picture:

"Here is a photo of aboriginal paintings in the cave where Dad died of pancreatic cancer. We think it shows an image of a Tasmanian tiger that must have migrated north at the time Tassie was joined to the mainland and there was water in the centre."

Next slide:

"Dad painted the cave wall in oils, and you may also like to show that."

Next slide:

"Like many who tried before him, he never found Lasseter's Reef, but he did find peace. Here is a photo of his grave, which I am in the middle of painting as a companion piece to his last work."

The Executive Producer nearly fell off his chair.

"Holy shit; we've gotta get a camera crew up there," was his excited response.

"I'm afraid that will not be not possible. We will only reveal the site of the cave to the elders of the Walpiri Tribe. It is sacred ground to them, and with my father buried there it is also sacred to us, so neither they nor we want adventure tours or gold prospectors going there. The photos and paintings should be enough for both the show and the naturalists."

In the end, it took two months to produce our 60 Minutes special. Not only did they need to interview Anna Cheng in Hong Kong, which involved legal clearances, but they really went to town on the other aspects we had discussed, which involved a number of takes with me and Mother.

The production time gave me the chance to finish my oil painting of Dad's grave, which I was determined would be done in his 'Arthur Streeton' style so the two paintings would display well side-by-side. I spent a whole weekend with Mr Collins being coached on Dad's technique. A perfectionist as always, Mr

Collins got the best out of me, although also honest as always, he rated the end result short of Dad's best and well short of Streeton's worst. It was wonderful to spend time with my old teacher again, and apart from giving him a kiss that made him blush, I resolved to give him due credit on 60 Minutes for his help with the painting. I hoped that would make the school appreciate the treasure they had in him.

As far as the show itself went, my favourite part was the sign off by Mother in full-screen close-up: "I hope you enjoyed the show, Silas. We'll be making a statement to the police as soon as possible. Expect a visit."

The next day, Channel 9 commenced the standard two weeks of promotion leading up to the show. Which must have been torture for Silas, as the promotional teasers gave a good hint of things to come:

"NOT GUILTY: The true story of Jack Johnson coming exclusively to 60 Minutes," was the theme.

The show was finally screened in 60 Minutes regular Sunday night time slot, and it hit Australia like a bomb.

At seven o'clock next morning, Mother's doorbell started ringing. This time we didn't slam the door on the procession of press and radio interviewers, who as predicted were all over it. Even the ABC Nightly News sent their crew, so Tuesday was going to be a big day in the media.

Which it was.

On Wednesday, between calls from a hysterical media pack, I took an interesting one from Bill Robinson of Silver Advertising:

"You don't know me, Tess, but I was a good friend of your father's, back when we were S&J Advertising. We just wanted to call and say how sorry we are for your loss. Jack meant a lot to us, and we will all miss him."

"You may also be interested to know that Silas Silver hasn't appeared at work since 60 Minutes was screened on Sunday. I hope he's on the way to jail."

But he wasn't.

He was in his garage with the doors closed. Dead in MAKO1, with the engine still running.

A suicide note was tucked under the windscreen wiper. It consisted of only three words:

I'm sorry Anna

Chapter 28
Tess

Six weeks after the revelations on 60 Minutes and in the press, Mother organised a memorial service for Dad at St John's Toorak, which was filled to overflowing with a large number of dignitaries, plus true and returning 'fair weather' friends. This was the start of a long string of 'redemption' events coming from a number of directions.

That same Sunday, the golf and tennis clubs that had enforced Dad's resignation flew their flags at half-mast. Both Club Captains wrote to Mother with their condolences and assurances that Dad would be reinstated in club records.

She tore up both letters.

Didn't stop there.

She commenced proceedings in the Magistrate's Court to posthumously quash Dad's conviction. This was heard by the same magistrate who had found against him the year before.

This time she ruled in Dad's favour.

Following that, Mother commenced a civil action against the estate of Silas Silver, claiming full ownership of Silver Advertising under the same 'criminal' clause Silas had hit Dad with. It never made it to court, as Zelda Silver agreed to a deal transferring everything to Dad's estate, on the assurance that there would be no more actions or publicity by us involving Silas or her family.

It appeared that Mother's family was not the only one who valued their social standing. Mother both sympathised and agreed. After all, none of what had happened was Zelda's fault, at least not directly.

Dad's will left me sole owner of Silver Advertising, with no experience or desire to run it. I recalled Dad's admiration for Fletcher Jones men's clothing manufacturers; they had always made his suits and had implemented one of

Australia's first staff shareholding schemes. We decided to set up a similar structure at the Agency, which was to be renamed Jack Johnson Advertising in Dad's honour.

It all worked fine.

Bill Robinson was promoted to Managing Director, and a staff shareholding scheme covering 49 percent of the Agency was put in place, with shares issued to everyone from the tea lady to Robbo himself. I retained a fifty-one percent shareholding and remained a director, to keep an eye on them.

The staff loved it.

Everyone worked their guts out, and everyone made good money from the successes that flowed from it.

Ben was determined we were going to set up our shark patrol helicopters right around the country as he had promised Dad, and thus I did not have the time to become involved in the day-to-day running of the Agency. I did help somewhat, though, even if nobody but me knew how it really came about.

Following Dad's Conviction and the consequent change of Agency ownership, newly-appointed Mako Automotive President Mike McFarlane had served notice that their contract with Silver Advertising was to be terminated at the end of the current year's media contracts, removing millions from Silver Advertising billings. Silas had sat on it, and nobody else in the Agency knew a thing until after his death.

Following the restructure, we had notified all clients of the change of ownership and management of the Agency, and it had an immediately positive effect on Mako Automotive. My mobile rang at breakfast one morning.

"Hi, Tess, it's Mike McFarlane."

"How about lunch?"

"Ben and I would love to, you bastard. When are you going to fly us over?"

"Touché."

"Only joking," he added.

"I really rang about our Advertising Account. As you will know by now, we served Silver Advertising with a termination notice following your father's death, which was the least I could do after Silas Silver shafted your father. I understand you have taken the Agency back, and I'm ringing to say we are now happy to stay with Jack Johnson Advertising, as every campaign you have done has been successful. Not only that, but we want to talk about a new worldwide campaign. This is highly confidential, but we are going to re-enter Formula One

176

under the Mako Racing banner and will need a full submission on worldwide advertising and promotion."

I was responsible for fifty people now, so I couldn't let my own feelings influence my reply, especially with Ben eating his scrambled eggs just across the table.

"Thanks for that, Mike. You have a very dedicated Account Group in place here who were never told by Silas Silver they were going to be fired at the end of the current contract, so we'll continue business as usual and very much look forward to the new brief."

Ben did pick up on the 'bastard' reference however.

"Why did you call Mike a bastard? He's doing you an enormous favour!"
"Well, he is a bastard. Half our clients are. Just ask Robbo," I laughed.

"The Agency guys refer to those ones as 'pigs' behind their backs, so 'bastard' was actually letting him off lightly!"

Money. Money. Money.

We were making plenty, but we needed plenty. The cheapest Bell Jet Ranger helicopter cost upwards of a million dollars even before our modifications. Our plan was to buy the first one and patrol Victoria's Surf Coast beaches ourselves, then if the demonstration was successful, go for government assistance to subsidise other shark patrols right around the country.

Chapter 29
Tess

Each of us grieved for Dad in our own way.

Mother had nailed both Silas and 888; although she was still sad, and rarely laughed.

Revenge was not going to heal her; only time would do that.

Dave and Doc went fishing in *Lucy*. The first day they went out after Dave had returned from the desert, Dave went a little weird, in Doc's opinion. They were outside the Heads trolling for kingfish, when suddenly they came on the bite in a big way, despite none having been previously sighted that season. Doc had just gaffed their sixth one, when an albatross soared over the boat. His magnificent three metre wingspan was not the only thing that stood out about him.

"Look, he's trailing an injured leg," said Doc.

"Did it in 'Nam," said Dave.

"The last thing I asked him was to get God to send past some kingfish."

Jack?

No, impossible.

Whatever.

Dad's two old friends retrieved two cold long necks from the Esky, flicked off the tops and toasted their old mate, as one does.

Early next morning, I had my own paranormal experience.

Ben and I were sitting alone in the rain at Lorne Point, enjoying a nice little three-foot swell before the crowd arrived or the wind got up, when two freak waves came out of nowhere. Both glassy, and both twice the size of any wave we'd ever seen in all our years surfing our favourite spot. Ben and I experienced the best rides we'd ever had at Lorne Point.

Big sets don't come in twos, they come in sevens. And at "Lake Lorne," they don't come at all.

"Dad?"
"Have you really met Huey up there?"

No answer.
No albatross.
But the show wasn't over. Immediately after the two mysterious waves, the rain stopped and we were treated to a perfect rainbow arcing across the sky, with one end seemingly hitting the water just out to sea from us.

This one really did have a pot of gold at the end of it.
In the guise of a thought.

A thought from an art director in heaven?

Who knows?
"Hey Ben; imagine if that rainbow kept going right down into the depths. I was awake long enough in science class to know it doesn't really, but if it did, just think how it would light up all the fish!"

"I've just thought up a new *Mako Girl* line, which I'm going to call 'Under the Rainbow."

"Dad?"
"Are you there?"

No answer.
No albatross.

I'm imagining things.
Whatever.

Following this epiphany away I went, painting a new impressionist series of eight ocean creatures, each one lit with all colours of the rainbow, as if from a prism.

We launched it for Christmas in every Surf Concepts outlet, and like each range before, it was a sell-out.

This time, sales didn't stop with Surf Concepts.

Out of the blue came a phone call from Greenpeace, asking if our licence would allow them to include the Under the Rainbow range in their catalogues and retailers under the Greenpeace banner, using the caption:

'It's Their Ocean Too.'

Our *Mako Girl* Exclusive Licence with Surf Concepts did not extend to fish, so we were able to answer 'yes' to the Greenpeace deal.

The tee shirt with my rainbow sunfish ended up a Greenpeace icon; the largest selling tee shirt in the world.

Money. Money. Money.

Enough to buy and customise our first Bell Jet Ranger shark patrol helicopter.

That summer, the fishing along the Surf Coast was the best in years. The fish had come in close, so even the smallest tinny had good catches to boast of. The sharks had always been there out deep, but this year, they followed the fish in, so there were sightings virtually every weekend.

Just as well our Mako Shark Patrol was up and flying.

Boxing Day always heralded the influx of the big crowds at every beach along the Surf Coast, as families from Melbourne and Geelong arrived for their Christmas holidays, and thousands hit the water.

The crowded line-up at Fairhaven was the first to get a fright.

A Mako blue Jet Ranger with gaping shark's jaws painted on its nose swooped low over the surfers, let go a siren blast that would have done the MCG proud, and then dropped a red ribbon marker, only a hundred metres out to sea from the line-up.

It almost hit the great white on the nose.

Then the 'flying shark' hovered over the Fairhaven Surf Club, giving another healthy blast on its siren. The surf patrol must have actually been awake, as they launched both their rubber duckies in under three minutes.

We dropped another red ribbon marker to show where the shark was.

The rubber duckies chased it out to sea.

We blew the all clear, and the surfers paddled back out.

Mission accomplished.

The flying shark then headed off to Aireys, then Sunnymeade, then Urquhart's, then Guvvos, then O'Donoghue's, then Point Roadknight, then Middles, then Anglesea Surf Beach, then Grinders, then Addis, then Bells, then Winky, then Jan Juc, then Torquay's main surf beach, where it scared the crap out of about a hundred Boardies, ten surf skis, and a thousand or so bathers with its siren when we dropped our markers on a big bronze whaler even closer in than Fairhaven's great white. The shark was also chased out to sea by the Torquay surf club's rubber duckies. It took them ten minutes to launch their chase boats, a pathetic effort we happily radioed to a euphoric Fairhaven surf patrol.

Then it was off to Possos, then Point Lonsdale, and finally Poo Point at 13th Beach before we turned around and flew back to Lorne.

Our patrols continued right through the summer holidays, with a total of eighteen sharks spotted and chased out to sea.

We all have our talents. While I had the edge on Ben on a surfboard, it turned out he was a natural chopper pilot, far better than me, so he did the flying while I dropped the markers as bombardier. He could make the Jet Ranger do just about anything, so I often referred to him as 'Maverick', joking he should join the RAAF Roulettes stunt squadron, a suggestion he declined with a laugh: "No way, Goose, don't want to show them up!"

The Mako Shark Patrol gained plenty of publicity, not the least from the surf clubs we were working with. Our grand plan was to eventually tie the shark patrol choppers to the clubs themselves, piloted by qualified club members. Sharks are always newsworthy, so the media got into the act, with Channel 7 sending their news helicopter to film us dropping a marker close to the line-up at Bells; there wasn't really a shark there, so no siren. This was great promotional footage, and come March, I found myself once again in my power suit up in Canberra, meeting the Minister for Sport alongside Ron Sutherland, President of Life Saving Australia, with the objective of gaining funding for a National Shark Patrol Program.

Many of those who have meetings with our politicians like to come away with selfies; and a photographer is invariably present for the purpose of those photo opportunities.

Ron was photographed shaking the Minister's hand in the traditional way, but my selfie was a little different. When I put out my hand to be shaken, the Minister grabbed me in a hammer lock. We ended up side by side, with his arm firmly around my waist, me looking like a rabbit caught in the headlights, and him grinning at the camera like a date on prom night.

In that capacity, he even went for the farewell kiss at the door.

I strongly suspect he had my shower poster up in his pool room, and that our selfie was going to be passed around his golf mates, but in any event, we secured his promise of national funding.

"I hope your Clubbies will appreciate the supreme sacrifice I just made for them," I remarked to Ron as we descended in the lift.

"D'you get much of that?" laughed Ron.

"Not a whole lot. My husband's a champion boxer," I replied.

Back at Lorne, said husband laughed just as loudly as Ron. He's not always as sympathetic as he could be and stated a 'harmless little kiss' was small payment indeed for a twenty-million-dollar fleet of 'flying sharks.'

While we waited on government funding, Mako Clothing had to continue paying for the running costs of the local shark patrol, and the surf clubs wanted us to instal a rescue winch and larger side door in our choppers, so we needed to keep on with our fund-raising.

I had kept the original paintings from each *Mako Girl* series, and also had Dad's and my paintings from the desert, plus Mother had framed the best of his original sketches from Vietnam, as well as having six of his oil paintings hanging at home. Together, they would make an impressive exhibition.

Back in my power dress, I went to see Charles Morgan, President of the Geelong Gallery and a long-time friend of Dad's, who had already introduced himself at the Toorak memorial service. I took along my laptop, with image files of some of the pictures.

My idea was to exhibit all the paintings under the title 'In the Name of the Father.'

Mr Morgan loved both the paintings and the idea.

He had followed our family drama as it unfolded and was convinced that the proposed exhibition would pack out the gallery, given the right publicity. Being very community minded, Mr Morgan also agreed that part of the entrance charges could be put towards our Shark Patrol Fund, which would guarantee local media support. He had to get the approval of the Gallery Board but ended our meeting with a wink and the assurance of a 'lay down misere'. He reckoned it would take about six months to put everything together.

I excitedly drove straight to Mr Collins's house to tell him what we were up to with the gallery, and he had a surprise for me. He took me into his study, which had some incredible portraits on the wall, all done in oils. Two I recognised immediately. There was our House Matron, holding a distinctive blue tin of Saunders Malt Extract in one hand and a tablespoon of gleaming malt in the other, and there was Burt, our groundsman, leaning on his ancient cast iron roller, smoking his ever-present roll-your-own.

"I have never shown these paintings at art class or in public, but I did them myself," he explained. "If you like, I will paint your portrait to help with the exhibition."

Would I ever!

"Forget *my* exhibition. These portraits are absolutely fantastic! Any of them would win an Archibald in a canter," I said. "How is it that the student has to coax her teacher to realise his full potential?"

"Why have you wasted all this time teaching?"

Mr Collins gave his gentle smile.

"Teaching is not a waste of time. You are the best I have taught, but there have been others, and if I have managed to introduce an appreciation of art even to those with no talent at all, that is enough."

"You have all made me happy beyond words, and those students to come will continue to do so."

"Now dry your eyes and have a cup of tea."

We arranged that I sit for Mr Collins each Sunday, so Ben had to use a Clubbie as bombardier on those days, a job which immediately became oversubscribed. Mr Collins had told me to wear whatever I thought best showed my character, so I lost the power suit and turned up for the first sitting in the faded denim shorts, torn white tee shirt, and bare feet, which Ben liked best. Mr Collins agreed they were perfect and took a photograph to use when I wasn't sitting there in front of him.

He refused to show me anything during the weeks he painted me, but finally my portrait was finished. He made the last brushstroke with a flourish, looked up, and pointed the brush at me like Harry Potter's wand.

"I think I've captured you well," he said.

Then turned the painting round.

I was looking at an angel.

"Stop crying and have a cup of tea," said Mr Collins.

Geelong Gallery did a marvellous job setting up the exhibition, although it was somewhat embarrassing to find the gallery had named my portrait 'Goldengirl', which I reckoned was a bit over the top.

Apart from that my bio was fine, with a photo of myself and Ben about to board our 'flying shark' featured prominently.

Constant shark sightings along the Surf Coast helped fuel publicity, with plenty of local media coverage. I even found myself a guest in the K Rock radio broadcast box at the footy, (unfortunately, a year too late to meet the legendary Ted Whitten, one of Dad's all-time heroes, despite Ted once nearly breaking Dad's unsuspecting hand at an Anglesea Footy Club presentation night with his infamous, vise-like handshake). The Cats won, and the exhibition was inundated next day.

After the close of the exhibition, I went in to collect the Shark Patrol cheque, intent on another important mission.

My portrait had the standard bio of the artist beside it; and consequentially a number of prominent people had rung the school congratulating Mr Collins and offering big bucks to paint themselves, their wives, their children, their pets or all of the above. He had politely thanked them, but refused to take on any portrait commissions as he was 'only an art teacher'. It would have stopped there, but I was determined it wasn't going to.

I had an idea to put to Mr Morgan:

"I hear my portrait was the most popular in the exhibition," I said.

"And I have a suggestion."

"How about Geelong Gallery entering it for this year's Archibald National Portrait Prize? Mr Collins would never enter himself, but I reckon I could talk him into letting you do it on his behalf, provided the prize money would be used to set up an Art Scholarship at the school."

Mr Morgan went for it.

Mr Collins was harder to convince, as he was a shy man who hated publicity, and seemed to have no idea how talented he really was. However, the art scholarship carrot won him over. Geelong Gallery filled in the entry forms, packed up the portrait, and sent it off to Sydney for the annual judging of the Archibald.

First, it won the Packing Room Prize; an achievement in itself.

Four months later, it won the Archibald Prize; the first portrait in history ever to win both.

Boss Hog turned on a champagne dinner for the entire school staff, made a nice speech, and gave Mr Collins a raise.

Mr Collins and I had another cup of tea.

With the federal election timed for the coming November, the government fast-tracked its promise of national funding, with immediate five-million-dollar grants to the Surf Life Saving Associations in each State, to set up Shark Patrols on major beaches, with both sides of politics promising there would be 'more to follow once they had won the election'.

We set up our own Mako Surf Co Trust to help train surf club helicopter pilots, and by Christmas, there were four more Mako blue Jet Rangers complete with shark jaws, sirens, big doors and winches, up and flying (three of them in marginal seats), making five in total when you included ours.

I hope Dad was looking down from his cloud, as sirens blared and marker after marker was dropped on sharks of varying size and threat. The only failure was the day the Coogee bombardier dropped his marker on a seal and cleared the beach for an hour, but hey, every big program has its teething problems!

A year later, I had a most unexpected reason to trundle out the power suit, which it turned out was getting plenty of use after all. I was invited to Government House, Canberra to receive a Companion of the Order of Australia medal in the Queen's Birthday Honours. Replacing knighthoods in an increasingly nationalistic Australia, only thirty-five of them are given out each year. Mine was for 'Services to Life Saving', nominated by Ron Sutherland, and endorsed by every Surf Club Captain on the Surf Coast. It even transpired that peace had finally broken out between Lorne's Boardies and Clubbies; upon my return from Canberra with my CA, I was the first Boardie ever to be made an honorary member of the Lorne Surf Life Saving Club. I became sufficiently drunk at that little celebration to agree to do my surf bronze, which the Clubbies held me to.

Then I got a letter from Boss Hog. My redemption at last.

Dear Tess,

I know we parted in less-than-ideal circumstances eight years ago, but I hope you can receive this letter in the spirit in which it is written.

I do not shrink from the action I had to take when I expelled you. For what it is worth, although I did not believe you then, I now accept you did not send that unfortunate shower photograph to Playboy, but even so, I had the reputation of the school to consider and at the time felt strongly there was no other course open to me.

You have achieved much since you left, and may I extend the sincere congratulations of both the school and myself on your Order of Australia, which is richly deserved.

Apart from that, the purpose of this letter is to invite you to open the School's new Art Centre which has now been built, due to the tripling of demand for this course. Mr Collins asked me to be sure to invite you, but as stated, I wish to also ask you if you would consider opening it.

You are something of a hero to both students and teachers alike and we would all count it a privilege if you would do the honours.

I look forward to your reply.

Yours sincerely,

Dr H St John Hogget, PhD MA
HEADMASTER

Fuck me!

I had promised never to darken the doors of the school again, but Boss Hog had me. I could never let Mr Collins down, so I was going to have to do it.

But I was going to get my pound of flesh.

I rang Boss Hog direct.

"Hello, Doctor Hogget; this is Tess Johnson. I received your letter about opening the new Art Centre."

"Thank you for calling, Tess. What do you think?"

"I would be happy to do it, on one condition."

"As you know, I left the school quietly and under a cloud. If I do come back, I want it to be with a bang. We are still promoting our National Shark Patrols, and I would like permission to arrive in our shark patrol helicopter, and land on the oval in front of the new Art Centre."

"It's not just to big note myself. My husband Ben and I want to start a Scholarship for one school leaver per year to qualify as a Shark Patrol helicopter pilot. We would offer it only to those who fail their HSC and cannot get to university. The selection would be up to the school."

"What do you think?"

He liked it.

He agreed.

Best of all, Mother was invited. She and Dad would never see me graduate, but at least she was getting the chance to be proud of her daughter in public.

Ben timed it to perfection. The opening was scheduled for two in the afternoon. By 1.45, parents and students were assembled on the lawn in front of the new Art Centre, with the Senior School teachers all resplendent in their robes, facing them on a raised platform, just like on speech day.

At 1.55, Ben roared in at tree-top level, breaking God knows how many civil aviation regulations and only missing the flagpole on top of the school tower by about a foot. Then he hovered low over the crowd and I hit the siren (hadn't told Boss Hog about that, so everyone got a most satisfying fright).

I was back!

This time, all tarted up as Tess Johnson, CA, with the fabulous gold and enamel Order of Australia medal hanging round my neck on its beautiful blue sash.

I'm not much of a speaker, but the kids didn't care. They clapped me to the podium; they clapped even louder when I announced the Mako Shark Patrol pilot's scholarship, and then stood and cheered as one when I told them they had the only art teacher in the world to win an Archibald and they'd better bloody well appreciate him.

All good, but the look of pride on Mother's face was the best thing of all.

Whatever I thought of Boss Hog, I had to hand it to him; he had a sense of occasion. He rose and made an unexpected and unusual presentation. The girls first eight from my year appeared from round the back of the building, carrying an oar on their shoulders. It is our tradition when a school crew wins the Head of the River, everyone gets to keep their oar with the names of the winning crew painted on the blade. This one had ten names on it instead of nine. Two bows were painted in; G Bingley (the actual bow), and me. Best of all, Claire de Coursey had to stand there with the others and clap.

Serve her bloody well right, the bitch.

Apparently, the presentation oar had been Willy Willy's idea. He gave me an exploratory hug, then offered congratulations I had not gone to fat, "like some ex-rowers I could mention," a comment which not only clearly applied to Willy Willy himself, but to Claire, who had seriously porked up. Can't help your genes, but I reckon she had given the cream sponges a nudge to help them along. Not only that, she was now married to Jonathan Onslow; whose family owned half the Western District, but who was undoubtedly the most snobbish and useless human being I had ever met. Not only that, he was notorious for being cruel to his dogs.

I cast my mind back to Bug's divinity class.

"*Vengeance is mine*," sayeth the Lord. "*I will repay.*"

What a day! The Art Centre building may have changed, but Mr Collins was just the same as always. Mother and I joined the senior art class for tea and Tim Tams, and I even managed to squeeze Mr Collins's hand when no one was looking. It took him four cups of tea to survive all the attention, but I know he appreciated it underneath.

Back at Lorne, the power suit had its usual effect on Ben, who threw me over his shoulder and headed straight for the bedroom, so it was a couple of hours before I got to raise something that had been on my mind:

"What say come winter, we talk your Dad and Danny into going back to check out Jack's last find?"

"No, it would only depress you going back there so soon, and I promised your father I'd keep you happy. We've registered the new exploration lease just like Jack wanted and maybe go back one day, but right now I've got a better idea. We've got the sharks on the run now, so how about we go after bush fires next? Let's hit the States and qualify as pilots on Elvis Sky Crane water bombers. We can even stopover in Hawaii and go surfing with Lance."

Wives should obey their husbands (whenever possible), so that's exactly what we did.

But unless we go back to the desert, I will always wonder. Maybe Lasseter's Reef is nothing but a dream, but you always told me to follow my dreams.

"Right, Dad?"

Chapter 30
Ariel

I settled down to a world without Jack.

Following the excitement of her Order of Australia, Michael Collins's winning the Archibald plus the final acceptance by the school that had expelled her, Tess was off with Ben chasing sharks away from Surf Coast beaches in their new mako shark helicopter, plus coordinating the National Shark Patrol training program. It was good to see her busy, although there was grief there that was perfectly understandable but still sad to witness. At least Jack had had a good death, and we were all able to say our goodbyes.

As for myself, I was coping with the support of friends, although I was still pretty lost. But things were about to change.

Once the Silas drama was over, Dave and Jules dragged me up to the Sheraton Mirage Port Douglas for a two-week holiday, as Dave had promised Jack.

Being essentially of a lazy disposition, I envisaged two weeks poolside, reading, working on my tan and drinking plenty of cocktails with silly umbrellas in them.

This was not to be.

On the very first night I was frog-marched down to Palm Cove for dinner with Alistair Darnley.

As an old diving mate, Alistair had avidly followed the story of Jack's court case and time in the desert. He had read and seen most of it in the media, but we filled in the gaps, including Jack's battle with the 888 assassin and his choice of the right to die at the hands of a friend. Alistair was highly supportive of both, and then lightened the mood with some great stories of diving Truk Lagoon with Jack and Dave, plus the apparent impossibility of teaching Japanese tourists to scuba dive.

But this was a dinner with a purpose.

Jules and Dave had decided that reading romance novels beside the Mirage pool wasn't strong enough grief therapy and had lined up Alistair to take me through a full PADI open water scuba diving course, starting next day.

Alistair gave my shoulder a squeeze as we all headed up to our guest rooms. "We'll have fun Ariel. And I even have a graduation incentive for you. As soon as you qualify with your open water ticket, we're all sailing to the outer reef. Dave and I want to show you Jack's favourite dive spots and even get you to feed Monty, Jack's moray eel who still lives at Agincourt Reef."

Once we got underway, Alistair was the complete professional with the PADI briefing and first pool session. Gone was the gracious dinner host and in his place was a bloody slave driver who insisted I got every fact and every drill exactly right. At the end of the first pool session, he stipulated the same rules he had set for Tess for the duration of the course. Exactly the same rules:

"Rule number one is you do everything I say."

"Rule number two is these are FINS, not flippers. Every time I catch you using the word 'flippers' you owe me a bottle of wine – I prefer red!"

"Rule number three is you wear one-piece bathers for our next pool session. Your string bikini is putting me off even more than Tess's little blue number did last year!"

Instead of dropping out first day I found myself loving every minute of it.

In particular, every minute of Alistair.

WTF?

Starting the trip back to the Mirage, Jules and Dave were nervous about my reaction to their scuba course ambush but needn't have worried; they had a happy passenger on board.

The happy passenger was doing a bit of thinking. Alistair was a very attractive man who didn't look anything like his forty-seven years. As Portsea's most popular widow (except with the wives) I had refused a number of requests for dates or other assignations as I had no interest in a new relationship despite Jack's last wish. Quite the contrary, I had been appalled by the advances of a number of married members of Portsea society; some merely suggestive and some completely blatant, including a try by none other than Culverton Thompson himself, who I had to send packing after he turned up at the front door one Friday evening with a cold bottle of Verve under his arm and the information: "Jenny is in Sydney for the weekend."

But for some reason the wheel had turned. I found myself flattered by Alistair's attention, and couldn't wait for next day's lesson. Attraction cannot be scripted – it can happen at any time, sometimes completely out of the blue and sometimes even if you have lost the love of your life and think it could never happen again.

Like Tess before me, I did what I was told. Lost the string bikini, bought a one piece from the Port Douglas swim centre plus a very expensive bottle of Hill of Grace shiraz from the Sheraton Mirage cellar, and commandeered the hire car to return alone for the second pool session.

"Promise you won't renege," said Jules as I climbed into the car.

"I'll be a model student," I replied.

I think I must have had a giveaway glow, because Jules replied, "Hmmm," with just the hint of a smile.

Back at Palm Cove it only needed one look between us to know I was more than just a friend Alistair was teaching to dive. The pool lesson was fun, but there was more connection than that.

Much more.

From there on things just happened; as these things do.

At the end of our session, I climbed out of the pool, took off my FINS, looked Alistair in the eye and said, "Flippers!"

"Right! That's it! You owe me a bottle of wine!"

"I happen to have one in the car. Hill of Grace Shiraz '69, in fact."

"Seeing you're supplying top shelf red I suppose I should cook us a decent dinner to go with it. I happen to have a freshly speared coral trout in the fridge."

Great dinner.

Good, Good, Good Vibrations.

Alistair and I were not teenagers on our first date, but there was an elephant in the room that made us both every bit as nervous as if we were.

Jack.

Alistair took on the elephant head on as we finished washing the dishes.

"Ariel, I know Jack is gone, and I know very well what I am feeling for you, but I could never take advantage of your loneliness."

"What do you want me to do?"

I knew exactly what I wanted him to do, and I also knew what my answer would be. Had known all day.

I didn't say a thing. Just dropped the dish towel, slid my left hand behind his neck, my right hand into his hair and kissed him.

Really kissed him.

My eyes were open and so was my mouth. We knew our first kiss would happen only once, and we both wanted to remember it.

I had been training in the Palm Cove pool taking off my mask and tanks, and holding my breath for minutes on end, so it was a long kiss. Eventually we came up for air, but being fully trained divers only needed a quick breath before moving right along to the second. It was even better than the first. I moved against him with a hunger born not of loneliness, but of good old-fashioned lust. This was new and it was real. I couldn't believe what I was feeling.

With our second kiss still going, his hands moved up under my tank top. There wasn't a bra to impede progress, as I wasn't wearing one.

Wonder why?

One hand made its way under the waistband of my pants, then lower. Just like that teenager I wasn't, I couldn't do much more than tremble, so it was up to Alistair to carry me through to the bedroom; no trouble at all for a guy used to heaving heavy scuba tanks around for a living.

What a night!

Sex with Jack had always been good, but this was different because Alistair was different. He started with his tongue, making me wait until I went crazy wanting it. Jack had never done that. Then he did everything it was possible to do, and I loved every minute of it – I owed a lot to those snow bunnies who'd gone before me!

I remember the sound of the breeze in the palms, and I remember moans in the night. I think they came from me.

We had to have fallen asleep at some stage, because I woke to the call of seagulls, shafts of sun streaming in the window slats, and the wonderful smell of fresh ground coffee wafting out of the kitchen, from whence the new man in my life was cheerfully whistling, "Land of Hope and Glory."

I hoped that didn't mean he missed England!

Even breakfast was Five Star. Time to call Jules and come clean.

The phone call was short.

"See you tomorrow."

A snort of laughter from the other end of the line.

"Go for it, you little slut."

"Why d'you think we booked the lessons?"

I stayed with Alistair until my PADI open water graduation four days later. This meant three more days of lessons and three more nights of love making, by which time we had worked out exactly what the other liked best (which in my case was pretty much everything). Even more important, we discovered laughter in each other.

On the fifth day we headed up to Port Douglas to sail to the outer reef with Dave and Jules in Alistair's seagoing cat *Reef Rover*, for my graduation prize. And yes, Monty was still there in his hole in Agincourt Reef. I trusted both Alistair and the diving glove he gave me and waved a strip of bonito at the hole entrance as instructed. Whack! A huge head lunged out of the darkness and snapped the feed out of my glove, clean as a whistle. I nearly had a bloody heart attack – if I'd known how big Monty was there was no way I'd have left shore! I'd been set up again and shook my fist at my three dive buddies as they hung in space festooned in laughter bubbles.

Back on board, Alistair made the whole thing special.

"Monty was Jack's very own pet moray eel," he said.

"He was the last person to have fed him, until you."

Tears.

Then Alistair kissed me, right in front of Dave and Jules.

They clapped.

We stayed on Alistair's big cat at the outer reef for three magic nights, dining on newly speared fish cooked on the little stainless-steel barbeque hanging off the back rail. Seagoing cats are perfect for couples – there are double bunks in each hull, and you can't hear a thing!

It was fantastic.

Alistair was fantastic.

I was fantastic.

So fantastic I stayed on for two more weeks after Dave and Jules flew home. Then I had to go too, as there was one final thing I had sworn to do for Jack and Danny.

I was going to expose 888.

Then I was coming back.

A lot.

Mother's latest 'suitable partner' plan was already doomed to failure, just like the first. Despite her ambition for me to finally land a Western District husband with plenty of acres, a cliff top house at Portsea and all the right connections, I'd gone and done it again. Instead of a larrikin surfer, this time I'd managed to fall for a diving instructor!

Go figure.

As it turned out, I need not have worried about what would happen if I ever talked Alistair into coming down south 'to meet the parents,' although I was not sure he was quite ready for me to hit him with that one just yet.

On our last night I did want him to know I was serious though, so instead of talking that day's diving and Alistair's friends I broached the subject of family.

"If you can juggle the dive school bookings, how about flying down south in January for the Sorrento Cup? It's sailed in couta boats and I can guarantee a great time – as a sailor you would love couta boat racing, and I'd love you to meet my friends. Dave is joint owner of a fifty-year-old couta boat called *Lucy*; named after the original couta fisherman's wife. *Lucy* was raised after sinking in a race and spending three months on the bottom of The Rip before they found her. Jack, Dave and their mate Doc Russell bought the wreck for a song and lovingly restored her. They only use her for fishing and have never raced her again; but the Queenscliff yachties tell us that before she sank *Lucy* had been one of the fastest Division One boats in the Portsea fleet. I'm sure I could talk Dave into joining the Queenscliff Yacht Club and entering us in the cup. Ben and Tess will make perfect foredeck hands, so once we introduce you to Doc, you'll know the whole crew!"

"We can also offer you a very interesting wreck dive. There are four World War One submarines sunk just outside the Heads. They lie at 90 feet, so Jules and I won't be able to dive with you as we don't have Masters tickets, but we'll be waiting up there on the tender to warm up the intrepid divers with a thermos of piping hot cream of tomato soup."

"Dave has also promised me he'll teach you to ride a surfboard. As a professional skier, you'll pick it up in no time. To turn you just lean the opposite way to wedeln – same as the old Arlberg style. Who knows, we may yet turn you into a big wave surfer like Tess! The only downside is my parents. They are very 'A list.' They own both a Western District sheep station and a million-dollar cliff top house at Portsea. You can imagine what they're like."

"What you're saying is, you're worried they won't approve," Alistair replied with a smile. "You need have no concern about my social status. Your parents may own a sheep station and a nice beach house but my father happens to be Lord Darnley. He owns half Gloucestershire and lives in a bloody great castle!"

195

"I'll be there. You can tell your parents I shall break it to Pater and Mater that I have fallen for a colonial farmer's daughter. They won't be happy, but stuff it."

"Bloody hell! You never even mentioned a thing! Did Jack and Dave know there's blue blood flowing under that wet suit?"

"No. I never talk about it. As far as I'm concerned, I'm an Aussie now and if any of my mates including Jack and Dave knew I was a Pommy aristocrat in hiding they would make me shout every round; that's if they deigned to drink with me at all. Bugger that!"

"The only concession I make to my heritage is I insist on everyone calling me Alistair, not Al. I shall be Lord Darnley one day and Lord Al Darnley sounds ridiculous. The Queen would probably strip me of the title!"

"Good God, if this gets out, Father's polo set will be all over you like a rash! Can you ride a horse?"

"I can ride a horse quite well. I am a two-goal polo player and have attended the Beaufort hunt at Badminton many times. Actually, that was the cause of me running away to Australia in the first place. After graduating from Cambridge, I managed to make it onto England's Winter Olympics Team as a downhiller and knew quite a few members of our Summer Olympics equestrian team. I attended a hunt ball at the Badminton horse trials and there the parents got going on some serious match making.

"Number one rider in the British equestrian team was Philomena Rowntree. Phily's Dad doesn't have a title, but he does have millions of pounds in the bank and in today's England that is just as good, if not better. Our respective parents decided that a marriage between their two Olympian offspring would be a match made in heaven, not to mention both the social pages and the bank, so push came to shove."

"Weekend stay overs were arranged, which didn't go at all according to plan. Phily and I get on fine, but despite adjacent bedrooms being dangled before us, love was not in the air. One reason was Phily was sleeping with the British equestrian coach and another was I was sleeping with my first love Mary Seymour, who skied moguls."

"I couldn't stand the parental pressure. After our team experienced its customary failure to win a single medal at the Winter Games, I bailed and headed to Australia with Mary, signing on for a season as ski instructors at Mt Buller."

"She ended up homesick and went back."

"I didn't."

"So here I am! I've had a great time. I love the life and have to admit that the love life of a scuba instructor is every bit as good as that of the ski instructor I started out as. The only difference is the snow bunnies up here have all-over tans!"

"But nobody has ever got to me like Mary."

"Until you."

This was not going to be hard. This was going to be easy.

"He's a great guy. He can cook. He can ride a horse. He's skied at the Olympics. He has a beach house at Palm Cove, right on the sand. He has a bloody great yacht. He's going to end up an English Lord. What's not to like; Mummy?"

"Why are you smiling?" asked Alistair quizzically.

"I'm imagining telling Mother about the castle, that's all."

"I'm flattered you want to," was his rejoinder.

A deep kiss was my rejoinder.

And so, to bed!

Our goodbye at the airport was definitely just au revoir. And not for long either.

Back in Melbourne I contacted Freddie Swain again, in his capacity as Deputy Chairman of ASIC.

"Freddie, it's Ariel. I promised you I'd fill you in on any dirt we found on 888 Mining. I've got quite a lot to tell, but not over the telephone."

He flew down from Sydney, and instead of arranging a meeting at ASIC's Melbourne offices booked us for dinner upstairs at Florentino. I would rather be eating fresh oysters on Alistair's veranda than having a wildly expensive dinner with Freddie, even at one of Melbourne's best restaurants, but what a gal's gotta do a gal's gotta do! Given my widowhood and ancient history with Freddie, I was wary I could be looking down the barrel of yet another 'my wife doesn't understand me' play followed by the inevitable proposition.

This became apparent when I was ushered to our table and beheld Freddie done up to the nines, looking very much the suitor in his tailored pin-stripe, with matching scarlet 'kerchief and tie. He went straight for the kiss on the lips, with attempted lingering.

I killed that nonsense straight up by backing out of the embrace, and then telling Freddie all about my 'new partner' at Palm Cove immediately we sat down.

That didn't mean two old friends couldn't enjoy themselves, which we did. Freddie had always been easy to please – all you had to do was listen, as he talked about himself and his latest triumphs prosecuting a disturbingly large number of dodgy Australian companies and corporate crooks; the latter including some well-known Sydney and Melbourne identities.

Which led us to 888.

I told him everything that had happened out in the desert. The Black Dragon connection with 888, Danny's suspicions regarding the two murders sanctioned by 888 Mining, Jack's taking out their assassin before he was also murdered, topped off for good measure with Danny's suspicions of 888 salting their Peterman Lease with Brazilian gold, as part of a planned Hong Kong stock market scam. Left out the details of our own little fraud, giving 888 test results from fifty kilometres away when we baited them with Danny's old lease, or how we had used the sale of it to coerce the confession we needed from Anna Cheng. No need for ASIC or the police to know about those minor details, or Tess and I could have ended up behind bars ourselves!

Freddie was mortified.

"Ariel, I am an officer of the Court and of the Commonwealth."

"And you have just admitted to me Jack *killed* someone," he whispered across the table.

"Maybe so, but you lot can't very well dig him up and drag him into court again, can you?" I whispered back.

"If he were alive to be tried, any decent lawyer would win a ruling of self-defence anyway."

The whispering was interrupted by the arrival of the creme Brule and the sticky dessert wine, which was just as well, as we were starting to look very like a married couple having a fight. Not the first to occur at Florentino, but not a good look.

Freddie mellowed after his second glass of sauterne, and cautious as ever, ended up volunteering some information of his own:

"You'll have read nothing in the papers, but we have already started proceedings against the 888 Group at the highest level," he said.

"I can't get into details as national security is involved, but I can certainly tell you your information will help considerably. You needn't worry there will be any recriminations regarding Jack's action, or your knowledge of it."

We parted at my taxi outside Florentino. This time Freddie gave me the hug of a friend.

His parting words were: "That husband of yours was quite a guy, wasn't he?" 888 was out of my hands now, and from what Freddie had said I wouldn't be hearing from ASIC again.

But two weeks later, I did.

A phone call was put through to Toorak, by a PA insisting I make an urgent appointment at ASIC's city office.

I went in next day, expecting Freddie.

But it was not Freddie. I was ushered into the board room, and two men I had never met rose to greet me.

One was Wes Picket-Heaps, Chairman of ASIC. The other was Tom Donovan, Attorney General of Australia. This was starting to look ominous.

After introductions, tea was offered in white bone china, with a nice plate of biscuits on the side.

Tea was not all that was offered.

In the middle of the table was an official-looking document and a pen.

"Thank you for coming in, Ariel," said the AG.

"I have to inform you that you have landed in the middle of an international incident that affects national security. Before I go further, we require you to sign the Official Secrets Act."

"Why on earth do I need to do that?" I asked.

"I know I gave Fred Swain some incriminating details about 888 Group which this is no doubt about, but as far as I'm concerned the matter should stop there. And why is Fred not present?"

The two men looked at each other; then Wes responded.

"We will explain, but first we need you to sign."

He pushed over the document and the pen.

"Please take as much time as you need to read it. Bottom line is The Act requires your complete confidentiality and silence on all matters we are about to discuss. Any subsequent disclosure by you would be a matter of treason and subject to prosecution. This thing is that serious."

I scanned the document while they finished their tea and crunched away on their Scotch Fingers.

Then picked up the pen, signed and dated the Official Secrets Act, and handed it back to Wes, who witnessed it before starting to speak:

"Thanks for that, Ariel. You will soon see why we needed you to sign it."

"Following your meeting two weeks ago, Fred briefed the 888 Task Force on your suspicions regarding 888 Mining, the likely murders they sanctioned possibly including your husband, Jack, and the suspected gold scam they have put in place as part of their Hong Kong float."

"Fred confirmed that he verbally swore you to secrecy about what he disclosed at your dinner, and I need you to confirm that you have honoured your commitment on that."

"Sure, my word is my bond. I have told no-one anything about what Fred and I discussed," I replied emphatically.

"Good. This means we can proceed without further ado," replied an obviously relieved AG.

"We first wish to thank you for providing the information you already have, and secondly inform you there will be no official action taken that would tarnish your husband's memory, or in any way reflect upon you, your family, or the friends who went with you into the Peterman Ranges. Between ourselves, we agree with Jack's judgement in the field that he was about to be killed, and thus acted in self-defence, but this is not a James Bond novel; and although he is Statutory Head of ASIO, Tom here is not M, Jack did not have a licence to kill and we would normally be obliged to refer his admission to the homicide of a foreign national to the Federal Police. This will not happen in this case, as national security considerations outweigh normal protocol."

"ASIC has been building a case against 888 in Australia for some time. This whole thing has not really been about mining at all; it has been about money laundering and moving assets out of Hong Kong in advance of the British handover on July 1 next year. Our focus has been on stopping a massive increase in money laundered through Australian casinos, plus dodgy money transfers and property acquisitions via offshore bank accounts, shell companies, false nominees and sadly, the corruption of a number of Australian politicians plus the senior management of some financial institutions and brokers."

"888 Mining is clearly about to launch a share scam on the Hong Kong Stock Exchange, to steal from Hong Kongeans desperate to get their money off the

Island before the handover, and their Australian entity has been used as a vehicle to bring in nine men under the guise of 482 Temporary Skill Shortage Visas for mining exploration. In fact, their skills were not in mining, but in money laundering and stand over tactics.

"We subsequently confirmed that five of these individuals were enforcers of the Black Dragon triad, and four were acting directly for other criminal organisations, operating lines of credit linked to a number of Hong Kong banks and stockbrokers. None of them went anywhere near the 888 mining leases. They were sent straight to Sydney, Melbourne and Hobart to build their networks using Chinese students and others to launder money via capital city casinos, and amongst other things purchase Australian shares and real estate via nominee companies, all linked to tax havens. It became much worse than that.

"The Desert is not the only place bad things have gone down. We strongly suspect Yu Tong, the Chinese student who you will recall disappeared from International House at Melbourne University was recruited by Black Dragon, and then killed for attempting to skim her turnover from the new Crown Melbourne Casino. We are convinced she was killed as a warning to keep the others in line.

"We regret we have something else to tell you, which is why we needed you to come in today. A week ago, Fred Swain went to Hong Kong to present our file on the 888 Group to the Hong Kong police, including dossiers on the nine employees of 888 we had deported. He had arranged to meet the Hong Kong Police Chief at headquarters the morning after his arrival, but never showed. The embassy followed up the same day, and the police gained immediate access to his room at the Mandarin. His suitcase was there still unpacked, but there was no sign of Fred, his laptop, or his brief case containing the 888 files. Added to that, the Mandarin confirmed his bed had not been slept in. Our embassy confirms there has been no ransom request or any other demand regarding Fred, and we fear he has been abducted and almost certainly killed."

"We can expect no help from the Hong Kong Police with any investigation or prosecution of 888, or Black Dragon. The British High Commissioner has made it abundantly clear that all the colony's police resources are needed to facilitate a peaceful handover.

"Neither the British nor Hong Kong Governments can afford any excuse for CCP intervention from the mainland, and it is clear they intend supressing any evidence of the enormous flow of assets being funnelled off the island by 888, and others. The last thing the Hong Kong Government wants is to greet their new masters with a war between the Hong Kong police and the triads."

"This scenario extends to Australia. The Attorney General's Department has received instructions direct from the PM that we are to cooperate with Britain, in ensuring there are no leaks from our end regarding the Black Dragon triad, or any money laundering out of Hong Kong."

"That doesn't mean we do nothing. We are acting to rescind all 888 Mining's leases in the Petermann Ranges, cancel the visas issued for every foreign 888 Mining employee, and deport the lot of them. All five members of Black Dragon, including Mr Chu himself have already departed our shores."

"Fred's disappearance in Hong Kong will hit our media within days, so it was vital to establish you have not told anyone else about your meeting with him or anything that was discussed. Hence the Official Secrets Act."

"Welcome to the dark side of diplomacy! I am sorry you have had to hear about Fred like this, as I know he was your friend. He was my friend too. These are difficult times."

I let my tea go cold and went home numb.

Even though they were being kicked out of the country, 888 Mining had got away with their gold scam Scot free. My only consolation was that at least we had used them as leverage to vindicate Jack, plus we were all in the clear.

But the whole thing left a nasty taste in my mouth.

I resolved to say nothing to the others, and instead to focus on talking Dave and Doc into racing their couta boat in the Sorrento Cup.

It was time to get on with our lives.

"Right, Jack?"

Epilogue
Lasseter's Truth

On September 22, 2009, the biggest sandstorm in Australian recorded history blew out of the Great Sandy Desert. A wall of dust five hundred meters high and five hundred kilometres wide rolled east, plunging first Broken Hill and then Sydney into darkness, with over sixteen million tonnes of choking red dust.

Some of it came from the Peterman Ranges.

Sand moved, exposing some features and blanketing others.

It buried the old drill holes on the now defunct 888 Mining lease, as if they had never existed. 888 was long gone, following their float on the Hong Kong Exchange that had defrauded Hong Kongean investors of millions.

The entrance to Jack and Danny's cave was now almost completely covered. A sand drift filled the little flat outside it, reaching almost to the inscription on Jack's gravestone rock. Fortunately, finches are not large birds, and they could still make it into the cave for water, just as they had during Jack and Danny's time (and probably for centuries before), but humans couldn't get in anymore, unless they happened to have an excavator with them.

The secret cave of the Walpiri would remain a secret.

Fifty kilometres to the west, the raging wind had exposed a metre more of Jack's green and white quartz boulder, scouring away the sand almost to bedrock, where two of his yellow nylon pegs now lay flat on the ground alongside a much older red gum one, the latter almost weathered away.

Just above them, the newly exposed quartz had veins of pure gold running through it up to two inches wide.

So had the two other outcrops that had emerged from the sand along a strike to the west; the first two miles, and the second five miles distant. They were obviously joined under the sand.

Lasseter's Reef.